Number 5

Number 5

GLENN PATTERSON

For Robin

With very best wishes

Glenn Patterson

13. 08. 03

HAMISH HAMILTON
an imprint of
PENGUIN BOOKS

HAMISH HAMILTON

Published by the Penguin Group
Penguin Books Ltd, 80 Strand, London WC2R ORL, England
Penguin Putnam Inc., 375 Hudson Street, New York, New York 10014, USA
Penguin Books Australia Ltd, 250 Camberwell Road, Camberwell, Victoria 3124, Australia
Penguin Books Canada Ltd, 10 Alcorn Avenue, Toronto, Ontario, Canada M4V 3B2
Penguin Books India (P) Ltd, 11 Community Centre, Panchsheel Park, New Delhi – 110 017, India
Penguin Books (NZ) Ltd, Cnr Rosedale and Airborne Roads, Albany, Auckland, New Zealand
Penguin Books (South Africa) (Pty) Ltd, 24 Sturdee Avenue, Rosebank 2196, South Africa

Penguin Books Ltd, Registered Offices: 80 Strand, London WC2R ORL, England

www.penguin.com

First published 2003
1

Set in 12/14.75 pt Monotype Dante
Typeset by Rowland Phototypesetting Ltd,
Bury St Edmunds, Suffolk
Printed in Great Britain by Clays Ltd, St Ives plc

A CIP catalogue record for this book is available from the British Library

ISBN 0–241–14194–X

For Brian, Paul and Kevin
And Numbers 14 and 4

Falloon

NEW PLEASURE AND COMFORT IN SPACIOUS ROOMS

Modern intermediate terrace house. Just recently erected. Pleasantly situated in healthy rural surroundings, yet ideally convenient to shops and all four main churches.

ACCOMMODATION COMPRISES:

Entrance hall into:

Lounge: 11′4″ × 10′10″ Tiled fireplace. Contemporary 'convector' fire.

Kitchen: 11′2″ × 6′0″ Polished metal sink and drainer, attractive plastic cupboard tops. Access to understair storage. Open to:

Dinette: 11′2″ × 9′ 10″

FIRST FLOOR:

Landing: Hot press, copper cylinder. Access to roof space.

Bedroom 1: 11′2″ × 11′0″

Bedroom 2: 11′2″ × 9′10″ Range of built-in cupboards.

Bedroom 3: 7′10″ × 7′8″ Built-in cupboard.

Bathroom: Panelled bath, WC. etc.

OUTSIDE:

Gardens front and rear.

Inspection invited. Easy weekly repayment terms. No confusing extra charges. Small deposit secures.

'Twenty-five down,' the man who said we were to call him Artie stood at the strip of wall between the two front windows, playing with the keys in his trouser pocket, giving us his pitch, 'twenty-five to pay.'

Pounds and years. I took twenty-five from twelve hundred, divided it by twenty-five and then by fifty-two, but my mind clouded and the numbers darted away like fish under rocks.

It was only just gone ten and already I felt I had been up for more than half the day. We had had such a walk to get here from the bus terminus, far beyond anything Harry or I knew of the city. We passed big houses with apple trees in the gardens, fountains, passed bungalows knocked together out of tin for victims of the Blitz. At one point we passed within earshot of a donkey, and though neither of us said so I think we would have turned back long before we reached the street if turning back hadn't meant spending a day more than was necessary in rented rooms.

I say 'street', but maybe that is overdoing it. 'Clearing' would be closer.

My Sunday-best court shoes left a trail of mud and cement dust wherever I walked on the bare floorboards. Artie's shoes were clean, because Artie had arrived by motor car, twenty minutes after we did, ten minutes after the time arranged.

'Mr Eliot?' Harry said, stepping over a puddle to meet him.

'*Artie*,' said Artie, early middle-age, sandy hair, a rawness at the corner of his left eyelid. 'Always Artie.'

Artie now transferred his keys from the left pocket to the right, leaving his hand in there with them, dragging a brace button briefly into view. I felt uncomfortable standing opposite the man. I would have loved to have sat down, but there was nowhere to sit, or even to lean, and nowhere to look but straight at Artie or out one or other of the windows.

A petite woman in a white cloche hat was backing out the door of number – 2, 4, 6 – 8, an end-terrace across the way, dipping her arms as she eased the rear wheels of a two-tone pram off the doorstep, dipping again for the front wheels. Her coat was royal blue, flaring from two outsize buttons between and below the shoulder blades. A cement mixer blocked the driveway to her left. She looked over her right shoulder at the narrow gap between the end of her front wall and the start of number 6's. I was a little taken aback. The woman was maybe eighteen. Her lips, even from that distance, were a distinct crimson bow. She looked at the pram, then at the square of churned-up mud to the side of the path. She looked at the door as though unsure whether to go back inside and start all over again.

Judging from the clean, white blinds at the windows, she was not here to view, and I asked myself why else she should be so dressed up on a Tuesday morning in the middle of March.

Artie sneaked a look at his wristwatch. Crown, brow, tip of the nose, bottom lip plumped out. He drew the lip in again, glanced up. The skin was red and finely cracked where his hair and forehead met. He put both hands back in his pockets.

'Twenty-five, twenty-five,' he said to himself through a sigh.

'How many are left?' Harry asked from the dinette, where he had been counting plug sockets (Harry had as much notion of what to look for in a new house as I had), and Artie, brightening, told him only this one and the one next door, as he moved to where there would eventually be a door, to the left of the beige-tiled fireplace.

'The other two streets are sold out entirely.'

The other two streets ran parallel to this one and, so far as I had been able to see in passing, were laid out the same way: three opposing terraces of four, twenty-four houses in all, each end-terrace with a driveway, the two houses in between separated by a covered alley.

However she had solved the problem of the path, the woman in the white hat and blue coat was backing the pram off the kerb, there being as yet no footpath to speak of and no cars to watch out for but Artie's. The road was made up of ribbed concrete slabs. I saw two miniature pink hands and two turquoise sleeves reach from beneath the pram's maroon hood and wobble as the woman bent her full weight to the task of pushing the pram up the street.

A small brown spider descended, upended, the wall between the windows, drifting to one side, righting itself when it encountered sill. I had my thumb tensed ready to crush it, but its busyness reprieved it: for the first time since I walked through the front door the house seemed alive and possible. For a while after it had scurried off, I continued to stare at the spot where the spider had landed.

About 18s 8d. Twenty-five from twelve hundred, divided by twenty-five, then by fifty-two. Excluding interest.

My mother's training, never say can't until you've tried. If I'd had a pencil and a bit of paper I could have made a fair stab at the interest as well.

I calculated that by the time we had paid off the twelve hundred pounds I would be forty-nine and Harry would be forty-eight. The woman pushing her pram up the ridged concrete roadway would be . . . what? forty-three? . . . the baby in the pram in its twenty-sixth year. The century would be eighty-four, my mother thirty-three years dead.

I heard the sound of the back door opening and caught again the sewery scent of excavated clay.

'Twenty-two and a half by thirteen,' said Artie.

Two hundred and ninety-two and a half square feet, thirty-two and a half square yards.

'Stella?' Harry. 'Garden!'

'Coming.'

Ivy Moore was *seven*teen.

'Eighteen next birthday,' was how she said it. 'I'm getting ancient.'

She didn't sound like she was joking. It was mid afternoon, the Thursday after the weekend Harry and I moved in. Ivy was talking to me from her kitchen. I was on the red tweedy sofa in her living room, hands clasped round the handle of an ornate baby's rattle, contemplating the framed photo on the mantelpiece. Ivy in her wedding dress, sixteen years old, hair black like shellac, as petite and perfect as a porcelain doll.

Ivy brought me a cup and saucer.

'That's awful, that photo,' she said and went back out to the kitchen for the teapot. George was sick on the tea tray just now as Ivy was setting it on the hearth and she had had to wipe him down and then scald the tray and leave it on the back step to drain. George did not look like a baby who had been sick. He sat on a towel in the middle of the floor, pushing both his well-padded fists into his mouth, laughing at I didn't know what. I shook the rattle, one of the fists came away wetly from his face and George went cross-eyed as he reached towards the sound. I dropped the rattle. The baby fell forward. Ivy came into the living room.

'Georgie, Georgie,' she sang and sat. George, unable to pick up self and rattle, remained stretched out on the floor between our feet.

When I was seventeen I hadn't even met Harry. I had only been on three dates in my life. Harry had sisters five and six years older than Ivy who still wouldn't have known one end of a boy from the other. Yet Ivy had come across to us the day we moved in, the way I remember my mother, while she was still able, calling on new neighbours, with a drum of salt for luck.

'I'm in number 8,' she'd said. Up close I realized how tiny she really was, five feet perhaps, if she stood on her tiptoes. 'Pop over some day and we'll have a cup of tea.'

Then, as when she answered the door today, her face was made up as though for a movie set.

Ivy shifted a little in her seat, dropping to one knee to keep her skirt from riding up as she reached down to remove the handle of the rattle from George's mouth. The baby watched her, thought about crying, lower jaw making a lateral grinding motion. Unbidden, an image formed of his hard little gums on Ivy's seventeen-year-old nipples. I blinked, focused my mind on the baby's bottle I had seen in a pot on the cooker when Ivy was taking me on a tour of her house while we waited for the kettle to boil.

The cooker was an English Electric. The house was the reverse of ours, everything to their right that was to our left.

She had showed me the baby's room, at the back of the house, to the left of the bathroom. She had to switch on the light, though it was early afternoon and the sky was not at all overcast. North-facing. Which meant – it hadn't crossed my mind before – our back must face south. The light, as electric light in daytime often does, seemed to take away from rather than add to the room, falling on a cot with one side down, satin-trimmed blankets folded on a junior chest of drawers.

'We're going to put a carpet in here,' Ivy said, tapping her toe on the lino, which covered this and every floor in the house, this and every house in the street. 'And Denis is going to paper the first Saturday he's off.'

Papering other people's houses, she had already told me, was Denis's job. Papering and painting. I had seen him coming down the street in the evenings with a brown paper parcel under his arm. His overalls, I assumed, because there was never a drop of paint or paste that I had seen anywhere on his clothes. Denis was nineteen. He had a swallow tattooed on the back of one hand, an expression, in the photograph on the mantelpiece, like an exercise book on the first day of school, folded open.

'And this,' said Ivy, squeezing past me to the next door, 'is our room.'

'Lovely,' I said from the landing.

My mother had a rule about not getting too friendly too soon. 'Because people get bored without change and where is there to go after best friends?' So I stayed on the threshold of Ivy and Denis's room. Ivy, with George asleep in the crook of her arm, smoothed in passing the rumpled foot of the bed. (The pillows and headboard were behind the door and I was spared that added intimacy.) My eye followed Ivy, past the wardrobe and the chest of drawers to the bedroom window, and followed her eye the thirty feet across the street to the inevitable conclusion of her view. I could see the alarm clock on my own bedside table. I could nearly read the hands.

'Is that the kettle?' I said and was running down the echoing stairs ahead of her.

George awoke and cried.

★

We sat in the living room, drinking tea, watching George use his elbows and heels to propel himself and the towel across the floor.

'Well,' Ivy broke the silence and smiled, 'we hope we'll be seeing a lot of you, don't we, George?'

'I still don't understand why we had to move,' Harry said.

'Quit *you* moving,' I told him.

I was trying to put a dressing on the knuckle of his ring finger. Bed spring. He had been on his back on the lino in the rear bedroom, tightening the screws of the bed frame, when the spring caught him. He hadn't grumbled about shifting the furniture up till then.

'It's brighter in the back room,' I repeated. He winced. 'Sorry.'

'It was brighter in the back room last Saturday when we decided on the front.'

I felt each word as a more or less forceful breath on the exposed slope of my shoulder.

'You're still moving,' I told him. The gauze shifted, blood ran down between his fingers and dripped on the bathroom floor. I raised his hand and stemmed the flow with the tip of my tongue. Harry placed his other hand under my hair, on the back of my neck, and turned me around so that the bathroom sink was pressing into my kidneys. I managed in turning to nudge the door with a toe, shutting the world out, us in. The smallest room. 'You're *still* moving.'

The house to our right, number 3, was the Watsons'. He was a riveter in the shipyard. They had a boy of four and a girl of two. Mrs Watson was pregnant with her third. I knew this even though Mrs Watson was not yet showing and she herself had so far done no more than pass the time of day with me. I knew this and much besides thanks to the return visit which Ivy Moore paid me the following Thursday.

'I hope we're not late,' she said, as though I'd asked her, settling George on the floor, herself on the settee. 'You have the place looking lovely.'

I knew that the Robertsons, whose house attached to Ivy and Denis's, were 'fifty easy', with one son in America and another, Graham, in his early teens still at home: a 'pet', according to Ivy, who would run messages for you down to the main-road shops if ever you were stuck. I knew that there were lovely people called Quinn further down on our side of the street and that opposite them was a foreign man by the name of Headache.

'Headache?' I managed for the first time in minutes to get a word in.

Ivy's expression did not change.

'That's what Denis says he's called. Andy Headache. I'm heart scared to speak to him. There's something awfully stern-looking about him.'

I met this foreigner a few days later. The workmen had been round to tar the footpaths. He and his wife were walking towards me up the middle of the road. She was carrying a long metal pole, he a matching base in one hand and in the other a cage wrapped in newspaper.

He was not in the least bit stern, but had a wide smile, high cheekbones, almond-shaped eyes. Andy Headache, needless to say, was not his real name. András Hideg, or as he introduced himself, 'Hidek, Undrash'. It was – he was – Hungarian. He had come here the year before last to escape the Russians. He had originally intended carrying on to Boston, but . . . His wife smiled. His wife's name was Jill. She was a local girl, my own age, round-faced. She did most of the talking.

'Even in Hungary,' she said of the surname love had landed her with, 'it is pretty unusual.'

I asked her what it meant exactly.

'Cold.'

Perhaps I smiled. (Cold, I was thinking. Headache.) Her husband leaned in towards me a touch, frowning. His words were heavily accented.

'And what does it mean "Falloon"?' he asked.

'Falloon?' I had never since I had known Harry given it a single thought. I was flustered. 'I haven't a clue.'

András Hideg's frown deepened as he considered my reply, then he shrugged the wings of his nose, the thick tips of his eyebrows. The effect, I had to admit, was a little severe. A bird cheeped a question from inside the cage. Jill laughed.

'I keep telling him English names don't really mean anything.'

The following Wednesday I ran into Ivy. She had had George down at the doctor's. She had chosen a crisp white blouse for this, a fitted marigold skirt. She asked was I all right for tomorrow afternoon. I apologized, saying I had to go and visit an aunt across town.

'Not to worry,' Ivy said. 'We can always make it another day.'

'Yes,' I said, though clearly without conviction. Ivy's eyes lost a little of their brightness.

'Unless, of course, you don't want to *bother*.'

'No, no, I do,' I said, trying to make good the fault. Bother was a big word here. There was a fine line between avoiding getting too friendly too quickly and appearing stuck up, and it didn't do to be thought stuck up.

Ivy was pleased.

'Oh, good,' she said.

*

The last remaining empty house, on the left adjoining ours, was sold at the start of May. The buyers were a couple called Fraser with twin girls in primary one. The first I was aware of their moving in was seeing the two girls skipping down the front path one afternoon when I returned from the shops on the main road. I had been away less than an hour, there couldn't have been a big lot to move. The girls told me their names, Emily and Audrey, then skipped back up the path and in the front door. Emily had a ponytail, Audrey's hair was in bunches. The heels of their shoes were worn almost flat.

(The girls, I noticed over the next days, wore their uniforms out of school as well as in. Even at the weekend they had on them their wee white shirts and grey pinafores.)

Inside and before taking my coat off, I went to the kitchen cupboard looking for the salt. The drum was nearly two-thirds empty. How could two people use so much salt in such a short time? And then I remembered, one evening, Harry running into the kitchen from the backyard, a look of panic on his face. 'Quick, quick,' pulling open the cupboard doors, 'salt.' Slugs. Harry, it turned out, had a horror of them. Amazing the things you could date a person for two and a half years and not yet know.

I was still searching for a smaller container to pour the salt into when I heard Ivy's voice out the front of number 7 and I knew I was too late now anyway.

It was an unfortunate association, the salt and the slugs and the new next-door neighbours, and one not helped by my first meeting, the following day, with the twins' father. Mr Fraser had a sty, which shouldn't, I know, have made the slightest difference, though it did for some reason, it just did. This was a man who I would never be able to look squarely in the eye. His name was Russell. His wife was Noreen. She came out on to the doorstep to say hello, then said sorry, she had the pan on, and she went back to the kitchen and that was the last I saw of her for weeks, though I heard her sometimes, moving about on the other side of the kitchen wall from me. Sometimes too I heard their toilet flush, so that I would blush imagining Harry's moans and mine resounding in rooms so recently empty, and even still on occasion I would come over all self-conscious when perched on our own toilet seat. (To hear me talk you'd think I'd been brought up in a palace and not a two-up, two-down, but either the walls were thinner here or the air there was thicker with other sound.) Courting constipation, I trained myself to wait for the sound of their front door shutting on Noreen taking the twins to school, half an hour after Russell had gone to work.

Harry left for work a good twenty minutes before Russell Fraser, at twenty-five to eight. It was a one-mile walk to the bus terminus by public footpath, left out of the street along what we called the high road, as a consequence of, left again, the one joining it to the main road into town being signposted Low Road. At the opposite end of the street, however, next to McParland's, number 24, a wire fence had been tramped down and from here a rough track ran a diagonal three-quarters of a mile across fields to a patch of waste ground behind the main-road shops. If it had rained at all in the previous seven days, this path was a quagmire. If there had been no rain, each step you took beat up a cloud of orange dust.

Artie kept promising that the Corporation would reroute the buses to within a hundred yards of us once the district was fully developed. Artie still came round the odd time, though his work on the street was finished long since. He was checking on the progress of the next block of streets, now under construction. Some day the land between the high road, the low road and the main road would all have been filled in.

'Yous are like Adam's ribs in the Bible,' said Artie, inflating both our importance and Adam's sacrifice.

To be honest, I didn't care for Artie any more than I did back when he was showing us round the house, but weekdays at home, I was finding, could be a bit samey when you had been used to going out to work, and any visitor to the street was a distraction. It did seem to be the street Artie visited. He parked his car halfway down, lit a cigarette, one foot on the runner-board, an elbow resting on the roof. He sought out no one in particular, but talked to whoever chanced to be passing. And surprising numbers of women from the street did just chance to be. Like I said, weekdays at home could be a bit samey.

He kept on about how lovely the new houses were and swore blind he told us at the time we should wait to buy, which of course got the women here going.

'Listen to him!'

'God forgive you!'

Even I couldn't help myself joining in the chorus.

'*Twenty-five down, twenty-five to pay.* That's all you ever told us.'

Artie laughed, at ease in the company of women. I didn't doubt but that there were streets in the four corners of the city where Artie parked his car and leaned on the roof smoking a cigarette, where the same sort of banter was exchanged, day and daily. Maybe it was tiredness that first day I met him, maybe it was that, despite the teenager I saw backing a pram out of the door across the street, viewing a house had made me feel ridiculously young, but whatever it was it had led me to misjudge Artie's age. He was probably not much more than thirty-five. Ivy asked me one day as his car was pulling out of the street whether I thought he was married. I told her I had never thought about it one way or the other and Ivy cast a sideways look at me.

'Gosh,' she said, 'it's the first thing I always ask myself.'

When I recalled this conversation later the word that really stuck in my head was 'always'.

I noticed that I didn't let on to Harry about Artie calling. Men, I thought, must puzzle over what their women did while they were at work. (I had puzzled about it myself before I was married.) It didn't do to be giving them undue cause for concern, even though Harry had never struck me as one of life's worriers on that score. I didn't believe he could have known many girls before he met me. I hadn't asked, just as he had not asked me about boys. Perhaps only people with no experience could have no curiosity. Those who asked most, I'd found, were those with most to tell.

Harry asked me, at five past five, coming in the back door, going straight to the sink and scrubbing his hands, over the sound of running water, one eye already trying to locate the towel, how my day was.

Shops, I told him. He reached for the towel. Stew, I told him, going to the pot and lifting the lid.

'Smells good,' he said, kissing my forehead on his way into the living room, and both of us were happy.

Harry was a boilermaker. It was one of the things I loved most about my husband, his skill, his trade. Either he was made for it or it had shaped him, for I couldn't imagine the one without the other, though I teased him the night I met him, at a friend's twenty-first: what did that mean, boilermaker? And, well, he said, I make boilers and things, with such a serious expression that I wanted to take hold of his face and kiss him.

Months later I asked him, side-stepping for the moment a particular question of his, what a boilermaker *really* made. Enough to keep you, was his reply.

And say I didn't want kept? Say I wanted to carry on working?

We were going to have a brand-new house, he said. Making a home out of that would be job enough for any woman.

I didn't believe him for a moment about the brand-new house, but I was in love, so I said, all right, that'll be my job.

There was an ad running then in the newspapers for a Home Furnishing Investment Plan. 'Why spoil the ship for a ha'porth of tar?'

Some days I would go from room to room, with my vacuum and my duster and my tin of polish, and feel like the chief engineer, alert to every speck of dirt that might foul up the vessel's smooth running. Other days I spent half my morning on the floor of our bedroom, listening to the distant sounds of building work, becalmed.

There were four churches within walking distance of the street. (I remembered reading this in the estate agent's description.) Harry and I were not as regular in our attendance as we might have been, nevertheless on a Sunday late in July we managed to get ourselves out in time for the ten o'clock service at the church we preferred. It was day three of a mini heatwave. The sun had seemed to rise this morning fully charged. The path by McParland's would be impossible. Harry and I stuck to the longer, paved route, past houses in several states of incompletion, past the new telephone box awaiting its phone. We came upon Ivy, wearing her white cloche hat and a button-through mint-green dress, halfway down the Low Road. She was resting a hand against the wall of one of the big houses and waved with the other when she saw us.

'Oh, thank goodness you came along,' she said, though she could hardly have been standing there too long undetected at that time on a sunny Sunday morning.

The rubber tip had come off one of her high heels. She was afraid if she let go of the pole she'd fall and break her neck. Harry found the heel-tip, nail intact, several yards back, in the footpath's softened tarmacadam. He held the nail in place while tapping the heel against the wall.

'There,' he said and returned the shoe to Ivy. 'That ought to hold it.'

Ivy was still uncertain, taking a few steps, pausing to glance down at her upturned heel, taking a few steps more, pausing again. At some point she asked (asked as she was already doing it) could she take my arm. Her hip, even in heels, came no higher than the middle of my thigh, bumping it as we walked. My skirt and its lining moved out of sync. Horrible feeling.

'Which church is it you go to?' she wanted to know. I said the name.

'Isn't that a bit of luck,' said Ivy. It was the same church as hers. 'We can all sit together.'

Ivy had her shoe off again in church, during the prayers of intercession, pressing the heel against the back of the pew. My lowered head inclined towards hers. She smiled at me as she wriggled her foot back into the shoe. I shut my eyes quickly.

I could hardly believe the gusto with which she belted out the next hymn, as though she had been absorbing holiness during the prayers, instead of fiddling with her feet. Even the minister seemed to be trying to locate her in the ranks of singing faces.

Guide me O Thou great Je-he-ho vah

Leaving church, I let Ivy get left side of Harry before slipping round to the right and holding tight to his arm. The sun was warm against my cheek. I closed my eyes, enjoying the sensation of being led by Harry, listening to him listening to Ivy's ceaseless chatter. My Denis this and my Denis that and what all her Denis wasn't going to do in their house.

'I see,' said Harry and, 'Boys-a-boys.'

I tightened my fingers around his upper arm. I felt the muscle flex. I heard Ivy, breathless from keeping pace, return to the subject of how *long* she was standing at that wall before we rescued her.

'Boys-a-boys,' Harry said.

I fell into a kind of sleepwalk beside my husband. I was on one of the imaginary expeditions my mother and I used to make together, just the two of us, through jungles and forests, conjuring all kinds of weird and wonderful animals and birds, their colours, their calls, beneath the canopy of trees. My mother had a bad accident when she was a girl, walking was difficult for her, but she would not let the fact that she was not able physically stop her seeing the world. The imagination, she always maintained, was the best form of transport known to woman or man.

For a few moments when I opened my eyes again I was startled by the glare. We had just turned into the street. Denis was walking George down the footpath towards us. The baby's legs bent in at the ankles, his father hoisted him straight by the hands. Ivy quickened her pace and I sensed a brief adjustment to Harry's weight, as though his sleeve was being lightly tugged and had now been released.

'Georgie, Georgie,' Ivy singsonged. 'Here I am. Home again, home again, jiggedy-jig.'

'Right, then,' Harry said meaninglessly and disengaged his arm from mine.

'Right, then.' I sent his words straight back.

He looked at me.

'What?' he asked, as if he genuinely didn't know.

After lunch, a roast of silverside which neither of us had much appetite for in the heat, I was in the living room when I saw a car pull up across the way. A little black roundy car. Don't ask me the make of the thing. Not one of 'our' cars, that's for certain. There were five on the street. I knew them all by sight and sound.

A grey-haired couple unpacked themselves from the doors either side and stood for a moment, looking around them like they had never seen so many houses in the one place. Or maybe they were just searching for a door number. Country people, I decided anyway, their clothes dark, their faces ruddy.

Oh, my, their faces.

The man was bending to unlatch the gate of number 8. He placed a hand on the woman's back as she passed through.

Ivy opened the door, just long enough for them to step inside and for me to be certain that these big ungainly people were her parents.

I won't deny I took a smidgen of pleasure from the comparison.

At half past five the car was away. The street was empty. The sun shone hard. Through open windows, the sound of wirelesses, gramophones, the odd television set.

At twenty minutes to six, the door to number 18 opened and Andy Hideg brought a kitchen chair out to the south-facing front of his house. I knew this because I was watching him. I sensed other people were watching him. A kitchen chair outside the front of the house was perhaps too close for comfort to what many of them, like me, had left behind. They were watching, as I was, to see how a chair looked here.

No, not on the path – in the garden . . . only not so close to the street . . . *There*. That was all right. Wasn't it?

Andy Hideg rotated the chair a touch, till seat and sun were aligned, then steadied the legs on the garden's baked earth. Folded small under one arm was a newspaper, which he now unfurled and settled himself to read.

He wasn't from here, of course, but Jill was. I couldn't believe she hadn't said something to spare him the embarrassment.

In fact, Andy seemed perfectly at his ease. There was no air moving inside the living room where I stood looking out. There could be no air moving in any of the other living rooms. A quarter of an hour passed. Mr and Mrs Nixon came out of number 12 and conferred about something in the corner of their garden, then he – Tom was his name – walked to the end of the path, hands in suit-pants pockets, whistling, and Valerie, his wife, bending her knees by degrees underneath her full skirt, and as though she would spring up at the slightest murmur of consternation, arranged herself on the doorstep. The earth didn't open. Still whistling, Tom walked back up the path and sat down beside her. Lightning didn't strike. Soon, half the doors on that side of the street were open. Ivy's door opened. Ivy appeared in it in cap-sleeved gingham and as though there had been no little black roundy car anywhere near the street.

'Harry,' I shouted, 'bring the stools from the dinette, we're going outside.'

The following Sunday, the same weather and at the same time, the same thing happened. First Andy and Jill, then the Nixons, then the rest of us. Out into the gardens. The lovely couple called Quinn, even Russell and Noreen Fraser. Their children, the Watsons' children, all the other children, ran back and forth in the street, a rubber ball bouncing between them, its arc closely followed by a wire-haired terrier I couldn't remember seeing before: up . . . and down, up . . . and down.

In the distance, the tips of twin church spires, idle factory chimneys, the cluttering of the skyline towards the city centre, a three-quarter-mile walk and a bus ride away.

I loved this street. I loved our house.

Our house:

Hall mat, tan coir, from Noble Bros on the main road. On the wall to the left, a joined VW of coat pegs, red balls on black stalks, bought from Nobles', mounted by Harry, though unused as a rule, as too many coats impeded the opening of the front door; on the wall to the right, a mirror, moulded plaster frame, leaves and berries, a wedding present from my Aunt Mildred, my mother's youngest sister. Through door to: dark-grey moquette armchair, one of two (the other faced it across the room), making up, with the three-seater settee beneath the window, the Chesterfield suite, from the Co-op on the instalment plan. Either side of the second chair, a radiogram, possibly from the Co-op too, probably on the instalment plan as well, a wedding present from my father, and an occasional table said to have been in Harry's family 'for generations'. Opposite the settee, a hearth rug, burgundy with navy and gold motif, a hearth set and matching coal scuttle (all Nobles'), a mantel clock from the girls I used to work with, a delft cat, 'Souvenir of the Isle of Man', souvenir of our honeymoon, a Busy Lizzie in a plastic pot. Through kitchen door, right to: G-Plan dinette table and chairs, present from Harry's parents; long, low china cabinet, mahogany, double doors (Harry's sisters), containing a twenty-four-piece dinner service, 'Spring Meadow' flowers on white, from Harry's boilermaker colleagues (I tried to imagine them going into the shop to buy it, and failed), a canteen of stainless Sheffield steel cutlery, a set of sherry glasses, still in their gift box ('with love, Auntie Betty and Uncle Bob'), five-sixths of a set of hi-ball glasses that had only ever had milk in them and lemonade; above the cabinet, in a gilt frame, a print of a girl on a cliff, wind at her back, hand to her hair, looking out to sea; on the chimney breast a shilling calendar, from a gypsy woman who came round selling door-to-door and which we would never have bought, Harry said, if it had been him opened the door to her instead of me.

Whenever I attempted this mental inventory, I rarely even made it into the kitchen. So many things and so many still to buy. Every second day it seemed another delivery van arrived in the street: carpets for number 17, a wardrobe for number 10.

I was passing the newsagent's down on the main road one wet and windy mid-autumn morning when my eye was caught by a postcard taped to the window. *Wanted: Young Lady for Typing and Filing.* I had typed, I had filed, I was not what you would have called old, I read on. *Mon–Thurs, a.m. only. Attractive rates.* Christmas would soon be with us. *Interested?* I was. *Ring* . . . I memorized the number and after queuing for a quarter of an hour at the telephone outside the Savings Bank, dialled it.

A man answered, gruff, indistinct. I had to ask him three times for the address, so that I was surprised when he said he still wanted to interview me.

'Can you come now?'

'Now?'

'Is now no good?'

I thought of all the other young ladies who would pass the newsagent's window today.

'No,' I said, 'now's fine.'

The address turned out to be a double-fronted Edwardian villa, a damp mile along the road away from the city, the cause of the man's gruffness and indistinctness to be a pipe, which did not budge from the corner of his mouth while he was introducing himself. Mr O'Neill. Mid-forties, fifty maybe, not tall, though with what my mother would have called a military bearing, eyes watery and a little sore-looking: pipe smoke, I supposed. The last two fingers of his right hand – he masked them slightly with the first two – were as pale and slender as a ten-year-old child's.

We talked in a room to one side of the panelled, polish-smelling hallway: a formal dining room with a silver service laid out for cleaning on a walnut sideboard. Mr O'Neill asked me where I lived and nodded unconvincingly at my reply.

'The houses have only been up a lot of months,' I told him. 'It's really not that far.'

A large truck drove at no little speed up the driveway and along the side of the house, causing the cutlery to vibrate on the sideboard. Mr O'Neill's pipe was moving up and down and I realized he was still talking to me.

'I'm sorry,' I said. Steam brakes sounded from somewhere at the rear of the house. 'I missed that.'

'Timber.'

'I see.'

'The yard's out the back. And the office. I'd take you, but the mud.'

A woman came, straight out of *Homes and Gardens* it seemed, into the room, smiled at me, and tiptoed out again leaving an impression of pearls.

'Do you have boots?' Mr O'Neill asked. I told him I could get them, but he had half turned away, searching himself and the floor. Finding a book of matches, apparently under his thigh, he relit the pipe, watched it a moment or two, nodded. 'And how's the typing?'

'Excellent,' I said, without exaggerating too much.

The cutlery vibrated as another lorry rumbled by, headed for the main road. The pipe smoke drifted in fingers towards me. It had at the back of it a farmyard tang. Mr O'Neill stood up. The interview was over. Out in the hallway again I saw the *Homes and Gardens* woman on the stairs, a bicycle tyre's inner tubing slack around her wrists, like wool to be wound. Mr O'Neill opened the front door and offered me his right hand. I slipped my own hand in and out, afraid of crushing his withered fingers.

'When can you start?'

'Monday?'

'You cannot indeed,' Harry said.

'What do you mean, I cannot indeed? Who says I can't?'

'I do, that's who.'

'Oh, Harry, come off it.'

We were facing each other, in the armchairs, across the living room. I wanted to laugh at how silly we must look, but Harry's foot was tap-tap-tapping on the lino and the moment for laughing passed.

'I don't see what the problem is.'

'*That's* what the problem is.'

'What, for heaven's sake?'

'That you don't see it.'

'Ho-rry,' I had half a Honey out when my mouth overrode me, 'it's just a couple of hours a day. To help us out.'

'Who says we need help?' He was as near to shouting as damn it. 'Ivy?'

'Oh, look, now you're being . . .' I realized with a fleeting chill that I was reluctant to say ridiculous, '. . . unfair.'

It had got dark while we had been sitting there. I didn't want to stand up to get the light. I didn't want him to stand up either. I didn't want there to be any less space between us for the time being. I needed to think. The Frasers' gate clacked open, clacked shut. Sound of key searching for lock. Door being closed at second attempt. Rain.

'You're not going out to work there and that's the end of it,' Harry said, so that I was uncertain which he objected to most, the general principle or this particular job. He had in fact been quite calm, open to persuasion I'd thought, until I told him I had already called at the house.

'You did what? *Anybody* could have seen you going in.'

'It's a timber yard.'

'It's the man's home, you said it yourself.'

'I was in his dining room, for ten minutes.'

'I don't care, you shouldn't have gone.'

'His wife was there the whole time.'

Well, thereabouts, I told myself.

'Was she now.'

He wasn't prepared to let this make a difference. That was when I had said I had agreed to start on Monday. That was when it really got out of hand.

It was the night for the Pink Paraffin man. We had been sitting for maybe half an hour in silence and in darkness when the van turned into the street.

'Pee-yink!' The van boy's voice unravelled like a streamer as the van rolled past our door to a slow halt. Harry got up and went out to the cupboard under the sink for the paraffin can.

While he was gone I asked myself what he could possibly do should I decide to take the job with Mr O'Neill against his wishes. He was hardly going to walk out the door on me.

Was he?

I went to the window. Harry was third in the queue at the back of the van, passing the empty can from one hand to the other, squinting into the rain, which continued to fall, spangling in the streetlight.

I remembered how much I liked the look of him when he didn't know he was being watched. I remembered fixing my eyes on the back of his head as my father walked me up the aisle.

Next morning I walked to our local phone box and rang Mr O'Neill. He was no less and no more gruff than the day before. I really didn't hear much of what he said distinctly, though it was me was the cause of the trouble this time, apologizing all the while he was speaking. My palms were sticky when I replaced the handset.

On my way back to the house I met Ivy with George, now graduated to a pushchair. Ivy asked me was everything all right. I surprised myself by blurting out the whole story. Ivy surprised me even more by taking Harry's part. Actually, she could have taught Harry a thing or two.

'How did you think he was going to react?' she asked me. 'If our fellas had wanted mill girls I'm sure they could have found them.'

Mill girls! This was the woman who wondered whether every man she met was married, who pawed *my* husband when she thought I wasn't looking.

Maybe Ivy's problem was that she couldn't trust herself.

A few weeks into the New Year, I was in the waiting room of Dr Campbell's surgery down on the Low Road. The surgery was a lightly made-over 1920s family house. Reception was a hatch squeezed under the staircase, the waiting room had picture rails, a polished wooden fire surround. A dozen mismatched chairs followed the run of the walls around a low table. The woman with the appointment before mine had just been called up (the actual surgery was on the first floor) when the door half opened. Graham Robertson, Ivy's next-door neighbours' boy, slipped in, saw me, and dropped into the seat nearest the door.

'Hello,' I said. He jerked his chin towards me in reply. He wasn't wearing his uniform, though the schools had been back over a fortnight.

Ivy had already told me he had been having problems. Eric and Alma, his mummy and daddy, had moved him miles from his school when they came to our street to live. (Eric had been a plumber on the building site. He didn't even talk it over with Alma, just drew the money from the bank one day and put down the deposit.) They thought it would be better if they got Graham into a school closer at hand, but wires got crossed, or letters went astray. He turned up at the new school and found he hadn't been added to the roll. A full term passed before his parents discovered he had been leaving the house in the morning and sitting in a swing park. By then he had fallen so far behind he had been transferred again to what was, in effect, a school for slow learners. He learned slower.

Alma, said Ivy, was at her wit's end. But what could you do? She sighed in sympathy. He'd soon be fifteen.

Now there was a frightening thought, he was closer in age to Ivy than Ivy was to me. Maybe that was why she found him such a pet. He had never so much as opened his mouth to me.

'Have you not been well?' I asked now, more out of spite than politeness. He shook his head at his hands. He appeared to be trying to pull off one of his fingers. Obviously it demanded his full attention.

The woman with the appointment ahead of me had left a not-too-ancient *Tatler* face up on the table. I was leafing through it, with every page less aware of my neighbour's sullen presence, when I saw a face I recognized: pipe in mouth, local businessman Mr John O'Neill, at the something-or-other Masonic Ladies' Night. (I asked myself how I could ever have thought of those eyes as watery.) Next to him was the woman who had smiled at me in his dining room. Her name was Janet O'Neill. Miss. She was John O'Neill's sister.

I had an urge to tear the page from the magazine, to bury it in a bin somewhere very far away, in case Harry should ever be in the waiting room and chance upon it, but this was overtaken by an even greater urge. I leaped from my seat, pushed past Graham Robertson's outstretched legs and ran out to the toilet to be sick.

Harry's and my unexpected present to each other. A Christmas baby.

A girl. Six pounds ten ounces. Little red imploded face, a swatch of black hair, barely attached. Penelope, for my great-grandmother. Penny-lope for fun. Plain Penny for short.

We had re-papered the front bedroom, ducklings and teddy

bears, though for the first few months the cot stayed in the back bedroom with us.

I thought I had never before known what it meant to love. Not just the baby, but Harry too. Even in the first days of our marriage I never loved him like this. Sometimes, sitting with Penny in my lap, trying to lasso her roving arm with the rolled sleeve of a matinée jacket, I imagined Harry in the noise and heat of his work, boilermaking, and my heart ached to breaking.

Time too seemed altered, the days so full of event that it was scarcely credible that the gap between their beginnings and endings could be counted in mere hours, yet still the weeks stacked up intolerably fast.

Penny was the third baby born on the street. Many of the neighbours walked behind the pram with Harry and me to the christening, even some like the Quinns and McGuinnesses whose consciences would let them accompany us no further than the church door. It was one of those days you can get here, whatever the season, of no real weather at all, the sky a white too uniform to be called cloudy. Not cold, not warm, just not bad. The pram was the pram Ivy had for George. Silver Cross. Cream carriage, maroon hood, chrome frame and fittings. Harry and Denis had come to an arrangement while I was still in the hospital. Denis, Ivy had told me, spent his whole Friday night with the pram upturned on newspapers in the backyard, cleaning and polishing and oiling. The morning of the christening, the chrome gleamed like brand new, there wasn't a peep out of the springs. It was hard to know who looked the prouder, us or Denis.

'There's not many like him in half a dozen,' Ivy said later, when the neighbours had been and gone out of our front room and she and I were in the kitchen washing the sandwich plates. Denis was up the garden with George, bent to his son's height. (At two, George was a solid child who already gave the impression that he would not grow tall.) Together they searched the untidy grass.

George had appeared in the front room an hour before, bawling.

'Sojer!'

Everything was sojers with George just now. He was never without a toy soldier of one sort or another in his hand. Cavalrymen were his favourites, but frankly he wasn't too fussy as long as it was in uniform. I was on a bus into town with him and Ivy when the conductor came to collect our fares. 'Sojer!' George shouted, delighted, and made a grab for the man's hat.

'Sojer!' he struggled through the tears in our front room. Crying was not becoming in many children, but least of all in George. He aged years, his features lost all alignment, nose above eyebrows, lip below chin. He was crying that sore, his hands fluttering here and there about his face, Ivy thought he might have poked himself in the eye or even swallowed one of the wee plastic men. Denis it was who interpreted the single repeated word to mean that George had lost this particular sojer while playing out our back.

'He'll look there all night if need be,' said Ivy of Denis. She lifted a Spring Meadow teacup from the drainer, dried it carefully, inside then out. 'God love him.'

I turned from the sink, emboldening myself to make a joke about her going to be needing her pram back, but my tongue was stayed by the grim set of Ivy's face.

'Here it's!' Denis shouted and I looked quickly out the window.

'Sojer!' shouted George, clapping the heels of his hands. 'Sojer!'

★

It was around this time that I began seriously to wonder about Ivy Moore. To be specific, I wondered how much hers was a marriage born of necessity rather than of love. I called to mind the wedding photograph on her mantelpiece: Ivy petite and perfect and very probably pregnant. Why else would a sixteen-year-old want to tie herself down? If, that is, marriage had tied Ivy down.

I was out, with Penny asleep in the pram, doing a bit of shopping on the main road a fortnight after the christening when I saw George in his pushchair outside Watt's the butcher's.

'Hello, Georgie,' I said. George pressed himself back in his seat, kicking up his feet, chuckling.

Graham Robertson stood a few steps along the sawdusty footpath, unwrapping a Milky Bar. It was late morning. Graham wore a jerkin and a green sweater with wooden buttons at the neck.

'No school today?'

'Half term.'

It might have occurred to me that I hadn't noticed any other kids about, but I wasn't really paying him a lot of heed. I was too busy looking into the butcher's, past the marbled carcasses, to see could I spot Ivy. Graham broke off a square of white chocolate and gave it to George. I realized that Ivy wasn't in the butcher's.

'Where's his mummy?'

'Home,' said Graham.

He might have lost a little of his lumpiness, but this was still one surly wee boy. I managed to winkle out of him that Ivy had asked him to run a couple of messages for her. It was just too much effort to discover whether she had asked him to take George too or if he had offered. George, it must be said, with the Milky Bar in one hand and a Crusader on horseback in the other, did not appear at all discontented.

Even so.

I returned home along the high road. While I was still some way off, a man came out of our street, turning right, away from me. We were walking into a breeze, he had his coat collar up, his head down, a hat held in place by a hand on the brim. Penny was starting to wake. Her blanket slipped to one side. I reached down to rearrange it. Up ahead, the man leaped a good six inches in the air. He flicked out one foot then dragged it on the ground, twisting to look back at the footpath: Artie, I might almost have said, if I'd ever known Artie to walk anywhere. Still dragging his foot, the man turned into the next street. Penny ground her fists into her eyes, moving her head from side to side on the pillow. She was due a feed, she looked angry.

A car flashed past. I straightened up, turned about, caught only the back of the car as it rounded the corner on to the Low Road, but I saw enough to be pretty certain it was Artie's.

What on earth could he have been up to, parking in one street and visiting another: visiting *our* street?

I thought of Graham Robertson outside the butcher's, feeding George a Milky Bar, and I suspected I knew the answer.

Only I had no one I could talk to, to tell me I wasn't imagining things. I mean if it had been anyone else but Ivy I was wondering about I'd have asked Ivy herself. Harry was the obvious person and once or twice, lying beside him after making love, I was on the point of broaching the subject, but I could never quite overcome the worry that he would round on me, raising himself on his elbow:

'Is this the kind of talk that goes on behind our backs?'

Anyway, I had no need of reassurance. My suspicion grew,

there were things going on across the road that were just not right.

Be on your guard, I counselled myself, as if loose morals were a contagion of the imagination, or like something vile lurking beneath the fallen leaves for the unwary to step in. Be on your guard.

Almost the sole preoccupation of the winter months in any house I had ever lived in was keeping warm. It was no less of a preoccupation here, though thanks to the builders the task had been made a little easier. The fire remained the focus. It was to the fire that Harry went first thing in the morning and last thing at night and it was to the fire, I was reminded, that I had to administer countless times in between, opening, closing, raking, collecting ashes, polishing the brass surround, so that at moments I glimpsed a world in which a house was no more than a shelter for the hearth. At the back of the fire was the boiler, which gave us our hot water, and further up the chimney (this was the innovation of our houses) a fan had been added to blow air through two adjustable vents, one high on the dinette wall, the other just above the skirting in the front bedroom. The water tank was in the hot press on the landing, though it could also be accessed by way of a cupboard to the right as you went into the back bedroom. When the fire had been going long enough, the tank was almost too hot to touch and then some of the heat given off could be directed into the bedroom by angling open the cupboard doors.

For back-up we had a paraffin heater, shaped like a small grandfather clock, with a door on the front for getting at the wick and a handle on the top for carrying it from room to room as required.

That first winter of Penny's, Harry came home late one evening with a new fitting for the bathroom light, a plate with three electric elements which fitted around the bulb: to keep the room warm while I was bathing the baby.

'Thank you,' I said. I felt as though I was standing under an invisible shower of heat. 'It's brilliant.'

'But remember,' he told me, 'it's electric, so use it sparingly.'

The third week of March, ten days since we'd last lit the paraffin heater, there was a severe cold snap. Penny woke us at six on the Saturday morning, wailing. I switched on her light and saw water running in a straight line across the ceiling and down the wall into her cot.

'Oh, my God,' I shouted, going to her, kicking up water from the lino. 'Harry!'

Penny's little sleep suit, I was relieved to discover as I lifted her out, was not too wet, though drips had fallen on to her hair and face. She grizzled into my shoulder.

'There, there,' I told her at the same moment as Harry turned out the light.

'Are you out of your mind?' he said and already his feet sounded on the stairs. 'You'll fuse the whole flipping house.'

Penny, plunged anew into darkness, bawled.

When the electric and the water were switched off and every pot in the house had been lined up with the kitchen basin at the foot of the wall where the cot had stood, Harry said he was going to run down to Andy Hideg's.

I had dug out the candles we had been keeping under the stairs for just such an emergency.

'What do you want to be running down there for?'

'We need someone to look at the plumbing, don't we?'

'Harry, Andy isn't a plumber, he's a traveller.'

'In plumbing supplies, it's the one line of business.'

This was ridiculous.

'What about Eric Robertson?' I said

Harry looked out into the street where day was still struggling to appear. Someone was already up and about in number 6.

'Oh, yeah, I forgot about Eric.'

Forgot my foot, you didn't forget what a person was. Harry's problem was he was afraid of looking stupid to someone Eric's age. Eric and Alma could be mother and father to half the married couples on the street.

Harry went back upstairs. I heard him moving pots around, then for a few minutes I heard nothing more. I went out into the hallway.

'Harry?'

'Right,' he said, pushing past me in the gloom. 'Right, I'm going.'

I lit the rest of the candles, got the fire going properly. Harry returned carrying the front lamp off a bicycle. Behind him Eric Robertson carried a torch and a long cloth bag full of tools. Their shadows were thrown back on to the living-room wall, bending at right angles where they met the ceiling.

'Alma says you're to go on over to the house with the baby,' said Eric. 'Keep yourselves warm.'

I told him I didn't want to be putting the two of them to any more trouble, but he insisted.

'Dear knows how long we'll be fixing this.'

His pyjama jacket was sticking out from the bottom of his sweater. He gave off a stale, bed smell and I was embarrassed to realize I must do the same.

Alma was still in her housecoat. She brought me straight

through to the kitchen, telling me to make myself at home, which of course wouldn't be difficult. I had never been in this kitchen before but could still have found my way around it blindfolded. The hatch of the Houseproud was down, as my own would normally have been, to make a shelf on which were laid cups, saucers and sideplates, a pan loaf and a block of margarine. (There were, though, I noticed, other plates mounted on the walls between the cupboards and appliances, with bits of verse on them, a recipe for soda bread, shamrock and shillelagh, a portrait of Edward VIII. Such were the things that made one house begin to look unlike another.) Alma opened the cupboard next to the sink. On the upper shelf was a splintered crate with potatoes, soup vegetables wrapped in newspaper, on the lower shelf a sewing box from which she took a length of plaited wool. She dangled this in front of Penny, who looked at it a little uncertainly then reached out her hands. The instant she had hold of the wool, Alma without the least fuss lifted her out of my arms.

'Now,' she said to me, 'sit down. Eat.'

'You've done that before,' I said watching her with Penny in her lap.

'Not as much as I'd like,' she said.

She had three grandchildren, she told me, two of whom she had never seen to hold. When I had finished my breakfast she fetched me the photographs. A boy with short blond hair, missing teeth, trying to hug a rabbit. A girl with teeth only where the boy had none. Another girl, Penny's age or size, in the arms of a fine-looking dark-haired man who wore a patterned shirt open at the collar and untucked from his trousers.

'Bobby's in Pittsburgh seven years this summer.'

Bobby looked as though he could without effort charm the

birds from the trees. And yet at the same time he was clearly Graham's brother, his features a template for what Graham's might become as they acquired definition. More difficult, though, was imagining Graham's face ever being lit by the spark that made Bobby's face handsome.

It was well after ten o'clock before Eric returned from our house. Alma and I had not moved from the kitchen. Penny had not let go of the wool plait. We had not seen hide nor hair of Graham.

'Not too much damage,' said Eric. His smell now was atticky, of corners never ventured into. 'A mop and a bucket and a wee bit of paper and it'll be as right as rain.'

I laughed. He looked at me quizzically then opened his mouth, a silent 'oh'.

Footsteps above our heads in the bathroom. I gathered Penny up.

'I can't thank you enough,' I said as the toilet seat slammed down.

Eric was a little optimistic. We had to strip two entire widths of duckling-and-teddy-bear paper off the front bedroom walls, damaging a third in the process beyond repair, and roll up the lino to let the boards dry underneath. Penny's cot came back into our room. The next weekend when we went looking for replacement wallpaper we were told that the line had been discontinued.

Harry and I quarrelled outside the shop. He was all for buying three rolls of something similar – Penny, he argued, was only six months old, she was hardly going to notice – but I wouldn't hear of it.

'Would you rather I stripped the whole room?'

'Yes,' I said, 'I would.'

'Right,' he said, managing to turn it into wrong, 'I'll strip the darned thing, but I haven't the time to do it now and we're not all going to stay in that back room until I do.'

And so Harry and I wound up in the front bedroom again. No mishaps in the dismantling and reassembling of the bed, no fooling around up against the bathroom sink, and months later still no new paper on the walls.

Eric Robertson appeared on our doorstep one evening in early summer with a television in a wheelbarrow. He didn't once rest the barrow on the ground the whole time he was talking to me.

He wanted to know would we like the lend of the TV for a time. He said he offered it to Ivy Moore, but she already had one. I started to say it was very kind of him, when Harry, coming out to the hall, asked over my shoulder why Eric was looking rid of it.

Eric's cheek twitched. He hadn't had his wash and shave. His jaw was plum-coloured and slack with a mould of fine white bristles. He rolled his hands around the barrow's rubber handles.

'The wee fella,' was all he said as he executed a tight U-turn and started back down the path.

'Punishment,' Ivy elaborated when I called on her the following afternoon. (Ivy couldn't resist a little dig. 'You finally remembered the way across?' she said.) Eric had gone to two more houses before relenting and wheeling the television back home.

'Punishment for what?' I asked.

Ivy set her teacup down, called into the living room.

'George?'

'Yes?'

'Nothing.' She leaned towards me. 'He wrote a word.'

'He wrote a what?'

'A word, in ink, on the back of one of the antimacassars.'

'In the name of heavens,' I said as Ivy poured us a warm-up. 'In ink?'

It was like something a child would do, though actually, I was a little relieved to hear the wee fella could write at all.

George was making vroom-vrooming sounds in the living room. Penny was fast asleep in her carrycot. A starling alighted on Ivy's washing line and swung back and forth. Ivy was watching me closely, making her decision.

'You know what word I'm talking about, don't you?'

I got a sudden hot prickle at the top of my breastbone. I brought the cup up in front of my face to disguise the flush I felt rushing up my neck. Ivy was leaning in still further, her neat little bust resting on the tabletop. I wanted to stand up, grab Penny's carrycot, fly, but there was no time to get away. Ivy's eyes were wide, her teeth bit into her lip as she began forming the word.

'Oh, God,' I said. The tea trembled in my cup. I was looking into the damp hole of the vowel, so bottomless seeming I barely heard it close. Ivy sat back, smiling, George vroom-vroomed, the starling on the washing line preened itself.

'Imagine,' said Ivy and it was nearly as bad a word as the one that preceded it.

Harry was clambering over the broken fence at the bottom of the street as I left Ivy's. He caught me up, took the carrycot from me.

'Well, did you find out what that was all about with the television set?' he said when we were inside.

'I forgot to ask,' I said, hurrying into the kitchen, fumbling with my apron strings. Harry followed me to the door.

'Forgot to ask? I thought that's what you were going over there for?'

I switched on the radio and Harry let the subject drop.

Some days afterwards I had put Penny down for a nap and was in the middle of making a shopping list when a movement outside the kitchen window distracted me. Starling. I watched it for a time flit from coal bunker to bin lid to bunker and back. I started counting the rows of bricks above the bunker, I counted the bricks in each row. I contemplated calculating the number of bricks that had gone into the making of the whole house and then I have no idea where I went, but the next thing I was aware of was rain hitting the kitchen window. The sky had clouded over, the bird was nowhere to be seen. I had a cramp in my right hand from gripping the pen. The shaft had ploughed two red furrows in the pads of my middle finger and thumb. I shook my hand and it was then as the pen fell across the envelope on which I had started the shopping list that I saw that word written, not once, not twice, but three times, in capital letters.

For a moment I couldn't think what to do, but stared at the envelope as at a confession I had signed. A great sadness hollowed out my chest and I was certain I had cut myself off for ever from the person I was when I got out of bed this morning. The next instant, though, I was on my feet and rooting in the larder for the kitchen matches. I tore the envelope to shreds and heaped them on a saucer. I placed a lit match under the pile and set the saucer in the sink. When the fire had burnt itself out I ran the tap, sluicing the ashes down the plug hole. I scoured the saucer and held it to the light as I dried it to ensure that nothing of the burn mark remained. Then I took another used envelope from the drawer in the Houseproud and sat down to start the shopping list again. The window was open, the remaining smoke drifted away, the kitchen was exactly as it had been half an hour before, and I was exactly as I had been, except for this: I was wet like I could hardly believe.

I paid special attention to Penny when she woke. I told her as I changed her what a beautiful baby she was. I told her her mummy loved her more than any other mummy loved any other little girl. I told her I'd never ever stop loving her like I loved her today. I told her I'd never ever leave her.

Then I dressed her in her red corduroy pinafore and a cardigan Harry's sister knitted and I popped her in the pram, shoved a couple of a slices of bread in their waxed wrapper into the pocket of my short raincoat, and went out.

If you took a right on the Low Road instead of a left, you came after a quarter of an hour or so to a rutted, hedged-in road leading to a farm. On the last bend before the farmhouse, a gate had been let in the hedge and beyond this a hundred yards lay a pond with ducks. There was nothing to say you could or couldn't enter, just a sign reminding you to please shut the gate. This was where most people from our streets had in mind when they said they were going for a walk. This was where I took Penny. The sun had broken through again. Bees bumped against the tall grasses lining the path down to the water. The ducks looked like they were expecting us. One hopped out on to land and shook itself. I propped Penny up in the pram. She pointed at the duck, at the flies scooting over the surface of the water, at everything else that moved. She gurgled. I gave her a half slice of bread and she pulled it to pieces. She forgot about the ducks, I forgot about my earlier emptiness, pretty much.

It was already half past four by the time we turned into the street again. The twins watched from number 7's garden as I pushed open the gate; side by side, hands behind their backs.

'Hello, Mrs Falloon,' they said.

'Hello Emily. Hello, Audrey.'

'We're waiting on our daddy,' Emily said.

'We're going to have beans on toast,' said Audrey.

'That'll be nice,' I said, but didn't think, then remembered I hadn't done a single thing about Harry's dinner. There was no way I felt like trailing down to the shops now. I unstrapped Penny from the pram just inside the front door. She came out bottom heavy. I had potatoes in the vegetable basket and a big bunch of scallions; there had been a full pound of butter bought the day before yesterday.

'Your daddy can have a plate of champ,' I told Penny as I laid her down to change her again. 'Many's the person would be glad of less.'

Harry could hardly believe his eyes. He parted the mashed potato with his knife, lifted up huge forkfuls for a look underneath.

'There's no meat,' he said.

'You don't need meat with champ. It's a meal in itself.'

Harry's expression was more perplexed than angry.

'A sausage,' he said. He flattened the champ with the back of his fork until it reached the rim of the plate. 'A couple of bits of bacon.'

I set down my own fork and lifted Penny from the high-chair on to my lap. To tell you the truth, I'd had just about all I could take for one night of Harry and his complaining.

'Go out there and have a look in the kitchen. If you find anything resembling a sausage or a bit of bacon you're welcome to it.'

Harry folded more butter into the potato and scallions, ate

a couple of mouthfuls, sipped his glass of milk. He would only speak when he had thought this all through properly.

'Why have you nothing in?'

Penny was reaching for the handle of my fork, I pushed the plate away from her. She made do with the end of the tablecloth.

'There wasn't enough left in the housekeeping,' I lied with ease.

'How was there not enough? You said you were all right yesterday.'

I had forgotten, I did.

'Well yesterday I thought I was, but we were running low on baby food and then I needed You-Know-Whats for myself.'

Harry ceased eating. I bent to take the tablecloth from Penny's mouth, but knew without looking that he was staring at me, trying to work out dates. I wasn't due for another four or five days.

'If I'd taken that job, that time,' I started but didn't finish.

Harry spoke with his mouth full.

'Now what's the point of bringing that up? Sure wouldn't you have had to have left it anyway when you had Penny?'

'I might have been able to put a bit aside, for when things got tight.'

Harry let his knife drop, nothing but angry now.

'Can we have an end to this? Things are not tight. You ran out of housekeeping one week, the day before pay day.'

He pinched the bridge of his nose, both elbows on the table.

'There are tinned pears there,' I told him, 'and a wee drop of cream.'

I got into bed that night with my pants on under my nightie, keeping up the act. I was still getting into bed like that eight nights later.

'That can't be normal, can it?' Harry said.

By the tenth night I was as desperate as he was. For perhaps the first time in our married life, I fucked my husband.

I hadn't actually thought it would be possible, but I had begun to daydream about having another baby. Noreen Fraser was expecting again, so was Elizabeth Watson. Jill Hideg had had two in under two years. Throughout the autumn and winter I was half prepared at every moment to find myself pregnant again. It got to the point where I was wondering if there was a reason why nothing was happening. I said as much eventually to Ivy.

'You should consider yourself lucky,' she said. 'Half the women in the world are praying for a pill to stop it.'

'Ivy!'

'Well it's true.'

'True doesn't make it right.'

And Ivy said, like Methuselah's mother, 'Oh, Stella.'

I kept my thoughts to myself after that and carried on doing what I had always done, trusting to nature to take its course.

April. The third anniversary of our moving in. One thousand one hundred days, all but, looking out the kitchen window at two hundred and ninety-two and a half square feet of concrete path and grass. I decided to do something about the garden. I started one day while Harry was at work. I had a vague memory of us owning a spade, but for the life of me I couldn't think where it might be, and then I saw the long-handled shovel we used for getting coal from the back of the bunker and I told myself I could make do with that. I had been intending to work from a sketch, but in the end I just walked down the path, tapped the ground in a few places this side and that – eenie-meenie-minie-mo – then stepped on to the grass and thrust the shovel . . . half in. The handle, when I let go, leaned at an unimpressive angle. Only then did I realize how much earth was contained in even a fraction of two hundred and ninety-two and a half square feet. Penny had carried on up the path and was sitting on the grass dismembering daisies. I wondered did she need changed. I wondered did I have enough clean nappies for the day.

I had picked Penny up and was almost at the back door when I asked myself what sort of a person I had become that I couldn't see a thing I had started through to its conclusion.

'Never say can't until you've tried,' I told Penny, jigging her against my hip in time to the words.

My mother was thirteen when she had her accident, on an escalator in one of the big department stores in town. She was in hospital four months. They took away the whole front part of her left foot. My grandparents were contacted by a solicitor acting for the department store. There had been litter on the steps of the escalator, a fault in the emergency-stop mechanism. The directors of the store were willing to pay my mother a sum of money in consideration of her injuries. A significant sum, my grandparents clearly thought.

'It would set you up for life,' my grandfather told her. I had never met him, but I imagined him in this story holding a hat. 'You wouldn't have to worry about being . . .' *a cripple* was what he was trying not to say, '. . . being forced to go out to work like the rest of us.'

He seemed relieved at having extricated himself. My grandmother too was cheered.

'Just think,' she said, 'a life of leisure.'

My mother could think of nothing worse. She was thirteen years of age. Leisure had no meaning for her, except maybe boredom. Leisure was sitting in the house on a rainy summer's afternoon. Leisure was willing the clock to speed up, a tram to crash – God forgive her – out on the road, the hills to turn to volcanoes – God forgive her even more – and erupt on to the city.

In this she was no different from the rest of the thirteen-year-olds she knew and, foot or no foot, she would prefer to remain as much like the rest of them as possible, thank you very much.

When my grandparents had left her bedside, my mother asked the nurse for an envelope, paper and a fountain pen. Two days after she posted her letter, the solicitor acting for the department store called to see her. My mother put a proposition to him. Instead of a lump-sum compensation, the department store would give my mother a job – commensurate with her talents, not the condition of her limbs – said job to be guaranteed for life, or until such times as my mother married and decided to have a family, in which case a pension equal to half her salary would be paid up to the age of natural retirement.

The solicitor laughed. He had never heard of such a thing. But my mother had. The boy who until the previous week had been in the bed two along from her had lost one of his hands when he touched a broken power cable lying in a field. My mother heard every word of the settlement he was offered.

'I can't go back and tell the directors of the store this,' the solicitor said.

And my mother said, 'Try.'

I dug through the afternoon with the blunted coal shovel. I made three flowerbeds, one along the back of the garden, one midway down either side of the path. I was head to toe mud. Penny too. I ran a bath – the water was barely lukewarm, I had to boil several kettles – and got into it with my daughter.

We splashed about in the filthy water. I wiggled my toes. Penny laughed. I wiggled them more. She clapped her hands. I wiggled my toes like fury. Tears streamed down my face.

My mother worked for over fifteen years in the accounts department of the store where she had her accident, at the end of which time she married the man who came to her office twice a day with the mail. I was the last of three children she brought up. People would stop me on the street and tell me my mother was a great woman altogether. She never had a day without pain. Phantom pain, which she said was the worst kind. She left the house less and less as I grew older. She put on weight. We still went on our imaginary explorations, but her heart wasn't in it. Her heart in fact was under terrible strain. She died when I was sixteen.

Sometimes lately I had thought that my mother had tried too hard to convince people she was happy, convince herself maybe. Sometimes lately I had thought with dread about my own life ending before I was quite middle-aged, before I knew what it was all about.

The day after the digging, I pushed the pram to the shops on the main road and I picked out a dozen plants from the stall in front of the greengrocer's, loading them on the rack between the pram wheels. I hadn't a clue what half of the plants were and the wee boy who helped out in the greengrocer's wasn't much of a help at all. Most of the plants were dead within the fortnight. I dug them up and planted new ones. Trial and error. By the next spring, I told myself, I'd have got it right.

It didn't strike me as too great a presumption to imagine that I would actually be here next spring.

Months passed and still nothing happened to suggest otherwise. We spent a blustery week in a caravan on the east coast, walking down to the beach in the mornings in sandals and Aran sweaters. Penny had her second birthday. The clocks went back. On the Sunday nearest the anniversary of my mother's death, the Sunday after Hallowe'en, Harry and I paid for the floral arrangement in front of the pulpit in the church we went to. The minister, waiting as ever by the doors at the end of the service, thanked me as we were leaving, pressed Harry's hand and mine. Ivy, who had turned twenty and got a new coat for it, asked us were we sure we weren't too grand to walk with her now we were so thick with the vicar. We carpeted the living room and bedrooms, rented a television set. The Frasers discovered they were expecting their fourth child and put their house up for sale.

The weather turned cold. Turned colder.

I couldn't get heat into me. I was on a bus out of town, four weeks before Christmas. There were puddles on the floor between the seats. On the window side of me Penny pushed and pulled a soft fingernail through the condensation from her own breath. Across the aisle an elderly woman in a plastic rain hat lit a cigarette. Her hands were mustard and blue, they shook, but when she drew on the cigarette, the woman smiled. I had never smoked, never wanted to, but I wondered now whether the smoke that the woman swallowed was warming. I wondered about pipe smoke, about the taste of it in a person's mouth, or – given all that would follow from the next thought it arrived with little fanfare – in the mouth of a person kissing that person. I was still watching the elderly woman across the aisle remove the cigarette from her mouth with a blue and mustard hand, use her lips to direct smoke into her lap, still listening to Penny talking to the squiggles she was making. I had not so much as shifted in my seat, but my imagination had leaped.

How many infidelities have come about because a body just couldn't find a way to get warm?

From that moment on, at any given hour of the day or night, wherever I was, whatever I gave the outward appearance of doing, there was every likelihood that I was thinking about sleeping with another man. Other men. I made a mental list. Honest to God, my mind was a sewer. I was only thankful that I didn't have the opportunity to act on its promptings.

And then, towards the end of January, Harry awoke with a sore throat.

He sat at the breakfast table, hand to his neck, looking miserable. He couldn't swallow his porridge, he couldn't swallow his toast, he could barely even swallow his tea. I made him stand up under the dinette light. With my index finger on his teeth I forced down his lower jaw. I was on my tiptoes.

'Say Ah.'

'Aaaah.'

'Ugh.' His throat was a mess. I sat him back down and moulded my hand to his forehead. 'You're very hot.'

Penny was in the bathroom on her own. I heard her trying to flush the toilet. And trying and trying. I went out to the hall and shouted up the stairs at her to leave it be and to come down for her breakfast.

She looked upset.

'Mummy,' she said, 'it's number twos.'

When I returned to the kitchen, Harry had his overcoat on and his packed lunch under his arm.

'Where on earth do you think you're going?' I asked him. It had been snowing for much of the previous two days. 'You'll catch your death.'

He didn't answer, but took from the drainer the medicine bottle he used for his milk and filled it from the bottle on the sideboard.

'Harry, you're not going into work like that.'

'I'll be OK,' he said. He bent to kiss me, his breath was atrocious. I put my hands on his chest, to keep him from coming any closer as much as to prevent him leaving the house.

'You're not well, you should be in your bed.'

But he was already out the back door. It was still dark outside. The wind would have skinned you. Fresh snow had fallen overnight. A silent second opened between his feet touching the surface and the definite crunch of their meeting the frozen snow below. Penny was tugging at the sleeve of my housecoat.

'Mummy,' she said, 'flush it now!'

The wind blew the door shut.

Harry was home again before lunchtime. His foreman had told him he was daft even to have left the house. I didn't say I told you so, he was too wretched as it was. He could hardly speak at all, hardly raise his hands to undo his shirt buttons. I pulled the curtains and helped him into bed. He was asleep before I had returned with the paraffin heater. An hour later when I looked in on him, though, he was tossing and turning. The blankets and sheets were soaking. He was burning up.

I went straight back down the stairs and put on my coat. I took Penny across the road and left her with Ivy and then hurried as fast as I was able in the snow to the phone box to call the doctor.

'Tonsils,' Dr Campbell said, packing his things back into his bag.

Harry was calmer now after whatever it was the doctor had given him when he first came in. Dr Campbell was approaching retirement, a lean, stooping Scot with whitening hair and – the one thing that stuck in my mind when I was talking to him on the phone – full, purple lips. It was, though, maybe six months since I had last seen him – Penny mostly went to the nurse – and I was struck immediately by the change in him. His hands, always big, seemed enormous, ungainly, as he struggled with the clasp on his bag. His face too had swollen. The pores looked like pencil marks in dough. His full lips were wet and slack.

I couldn't believe Dr Campbell had ever been on my list.

I couldn't believe I was thinking about that at a time like this.

'They're going to have to come out,' he said and Harry moaned, though whether in distress from the tonsils or at the thought of an operation, I couldn't say. 'Pack a case for him, we'll see if we can get him in tonight.'

After Dr Campbell had gone, I sat on the edge of the bed and stroked my husband's hair.

'Hospital?' he said hoarsely, unhappily.

'There, there,' I said. 'Try not to speak.'

The hospital sent an actual ambulance for him, or half for him, as there was already one other patient inside, an elderly man who stared out in some confusion from the open rear doors. Harry was wrapped in a hospital blanket and guided from the house by an ambulanceman. It was teatime. Neighbours had come out on to their steps, framed in the light from their hallways. Penny cried, big inconsolable sobs, as the rear doors were closed and the ambulance drove off slowly through the slush, taking her daddy away.

'It's all right,' I told her, 'Daddy's just got a bad throat. He'll be home again in no time.'

When nothing of the ambulance remained to be seen, the eyes of the neighbours slid round to me. I smiled bravely, led my daughter back along the path and in the front door.

Penny and I played with her farmyard animals in front of the fire and soon she had forgotten all about her tears. Still, when she could finally fight sleep no longer and I was carrying her up the stairs, she told me she wanted to sleep in our bed. I laid her inside with a water bottle, singing as I moved about the room. She asked me to get into bed with her and I said in a minute, sweetheart. I saw her crooked index finger above the covers: one minute. It toppled on to the double-stitched blanket trim. I backed, still singing, towards the door then faded out.

Downstairs again, I sat on the settee and folded my hands in my lap. In six and a half years of nights – two thousand three hundred and seventy something – this was the first I had spent without a husband. After all the fierce fantasizing, I didn't know what to do on my own. I went on sitting on the settee.

I was woken by a tapping at the front window. The room appeared to me on its side. My head was on the arm of the settee. I had drooled on to the moquette. My neck was stiff. It was twenty-five to nine. The window was tapped again. I tried to fix my hair as I walked into the hallway, too disoriented even to get my hopes up. Which was as well.

Graham Robertson had already started back towards the gate when I opened the door. He said something to me over his shoulder. I didn't get a word of it.

'Sorry?' I said, pulling my cardigan closed at the throat. He turned to face me.

'My da says do you want your coal in.'

For some reason I looked across the road. The Robertsons' front door was shut, though the hall light was on.

'Did he tell you to rap the window as well?' I asked.

'Wee Penny,' Graham said and I thought then there was no way he'd have had the gumption to have reasoned it through himself. 'My da said she might be sleeping.'

'It'd take more than a knock at the door to wake her once she's over,' I said. 'But tell your daddy thanks for thinking about me. I'm all right for coal for the night.'

He turned and carried on out the gate.

'And thank you for coming over,' I called after him. Graham grunted. I was laughing as I closed the front door. Back in the living room, the fire had, in fact, more or less gone out. I lifted the lid off the coal scuttle. Half empty. Well, wasn't I the stupid one, looking a gift horse in the mouth? What with having to wrap myself up before braving the coal bunker, it took me the best part of an hour to get a decent fire going again and by then all I wanted to do was go to bed. I closed the fire up and laid a lid of slack over the coals. At the top of the stairs I took the door off the paraffin heater and blew down the chimney to extinguish its ring of blue flame. I didn't even bother cleaning my teeth.

Penny woke me.

'Your *face* smells.'

She was supporting herself on arms folded on the very edge of the mattress. Our heads were an inch apart. I felt weak from nameless dreaming. She crossed and uncrossed her eyes.

'Poo-ee,' she said and reached out to close my mouth.

I worked my arms free from the covers, wanting to catch hold of her and lift her back into bed with me, but she ran off giggling. She had dressed herself, or at least had tried to. As she disappeared round the bedroom door I caught a glimpse of her Sunday frock, flapping at the back, tights only half pulled up.

'Careful,' I shouted at the same moment as her run stumbled into a fall. 'Penny?'

I was out of bed in an instant, calling her name a second time, panicked by her silence. She was sitting in the landing when I reached it, the empty tights lying where she was catapulted from them. She looked embarrassed more than anything. I examined her forehead, her teeth, her knees. Not a bump or a scratch, thank God. There was a small rip in the hem of her dress, but I decided not to say anything and run the risk of upsetting her. As it was her lip had begun belatedly to tremble.

'I poked you and you didn't get up,' she said and I saw then, by the steely blue rectangle of the bathroom windowpane, that the morning was well advanced.

'Mummy was very tired,' I told her and the thought appeared to delight her, as though it had not occurred to her until now that I went to bed for the reason she did. It only lasted a few moments, but when she tilted her head to look at me I imagined she was seeing, for the first time, not Mummy, but another person with needs and moods and good thoughts and bad thoughts. We are the same, her expression said, you are just bigger.

She started giggling again. I snatched one of her feet to my mouth and blew air, hard, against the kidney-smooth sole. *Blarge*. She shrieked. I snatched up the other foot, blarged it. Penny laughed uncontrollably.

The hospital was way on the other side of town. Having woken so late, it was a race to get there in time for afternoon visiting. We had to change buses in the city centre. There was sleet in the air. It really was a horrible winter. Penny became cranky on the long walk from the hospital gates to the wards. I got us lost twice in the confusion of corridors. We arrived at Harry's ward by way of countless Nissen huts and – God only knows how – the kitchens, with their sickly smell of boiled milk and almond sponge.

The nurse at the door of ward 28 informed us that Harry had not come round from the anaesthetic. I asked her could we see him anyway. (I was sure that was his bed at the far end of the room with the curtains drawn around it.) I told her how far we had come. The nurse was not interested. 'Rules,' she said and, when I kept at her to let us in, 'Sister!'

'All right, all right,' I said, grabbing Penny by the hand as the Sister hove into view. 'Forget it.'

We wandered the Nissen huts a while until we found the gates, just in time to see a bus pulling away from the stop. I checked the timetable, twenty minutes to the next one. A cold, cold wind blew down the road that the bus would come.

By the time we got home we had less than three hours before we had to head out again for the evening visit.

Harry didn't say a lot, not surprisingly. More surprisingly, perhaps, since no one had been gouging away at the back of my throat, neither did I. Penny covered for me. She was up on the bed beside her daddy. She was telling him a story she 'read' from a *Radio Times* she had found on his locker. There was a talking cat in the story. The cat's name was George. There was, I noted, a mummy cat who didn't get out of bed in the morning. This weaving in of the events of her day was something she had started doing only lately. Harry combed her hair with his fingers while she prattled on. I told her to be careful of her shoe buckles on the bedspread. Soon the bell was ringing for us to leave. I kissed Harry's forehead (there were people watching) and told him I would see him tomorrow afternoon. I regretted saying this as soon as I was out of the ward. Penny was limp with tiredness and dejection at having to leave. I could hardly face the prospect of going through all this with her twice again tomorrow, but then I could hardly run back and tell my sick husband I had changed my mind about visiting him.

Ivy came to the rescue. She offered to mind Penny for a few hours to let me get to the hospital on my own. I was less tense, Harry was more talkative. He told me it was true what everyone said, they really did feed you jelly and ice cream after your operation. He told me not to come the next afternoon. I said I'd see, but he insisted, evenings were more than enough and anyway he'd be home in a couple of days. He squeezed my hand as he said this. All at once I realized what an outlandish thing it was to lie in bed in public and before I could stop myself I was remembering the feeling of wriggling my fingers into the opening of Harry's pyjama trousers, rubbing the pliancy out of him.

I laid my other hand on his and returned the pressure.

'Just you be sure and get well soon.'

'You'll never guess who was round while you were out,' said Ivy.

'Who?'

'Guess.'

'Cliff Richard.'

'Oh, go on, guess properly.'

'I haven't got a clue,' I said, and to Penny, who was struggling to put on her mitts, 'You have to open your hand right up.'

'Artie.'

'*Artie?*'

There had been murmurings this last while that building was to start soon at the end of the street, where the track to the shops currently began. Not that Artie needed an excuse.

'You were just away,' said Ivy and smiled at the remembrance of something. 'He's a terrible cod.'

She hadn't even the grace to blush.

'Artie,' said Penny. 'Artie, Artie, Artie.'

Ivy made two bunches of my daughter's hair.

'Took a bit of a shine to this one,' she said. 'Gave you sixpence, didn't he, pet?'

Penny nodded, silent on the instant, secret out. I realized why she wasn't able to open her hand to fit it in her mitt.

'He was actually in the house?' I asked.

'Listen to you,' said Ivy. '*Actually* we stood on the doorstep chatting, but what if he had come in? It's not a crime, you know.'

I took the sixpenny bit from Penny and told her she could have it back when we got home.

'He was asking after you.' Ivy's tone was teasing. I tutted.

'Artie wouldn't remember me.'

'Oh, I don't know about that.'

Ivy was walking ahead of us to the back door. I was sure she was exaggerating the swing of her hips.

'Lucky man, that Harry,' she said, taking off Artie's voice.

'He never said that.'

'He did so.'

'Artie, Artie, Artie,' Penny piped up, her pleasure in the name getting the better of her coyness.

'Lucky man,' said Ivy, herself again, 'apart from the tonsils.'

'You didn't tell Artie he was in hospital, did you?'

I didn't know what difference I imagined it would make if she had told him.

'Well, what else would I be doing looking after Penny?' Ivy said, then afraid perhaps that I was over-reacting (my mouth might indeed have been open), gave me a gentle shove. 'I'm only playing. You know that, don't you? I'm only playing.'

I told Penny that she wasn't to let on to her daddy about Artie and the sixpence. I told her it would only annoy him, because he was in hospital and couldn't give her money himself.

When I returned to the hospital that evening with Penny, however, it was a listless Harry I found. I asked him had he been asleep and he shook his head. I asked him had he eaten and he said (I could just about hear him) a bit. Penny 'read' him a story from an old *Football Monthly*. I was ready to intervene should she find a way of working in Artie's name, but I need not have worried. Even so, Harry's smile was a long time coming. I stopped at the nurse's desk on the way out, the same nurse who was on duty the first day I tried to visit. I told her I was concerned about my husband. He looked a little feverish. The nurse explained that patients sometimes got hot and uncomfortable when there were too many visitors on the ward. I began to ask her to let me speak to the Sister, when I was interrupted by the *whoosh* of sudden vomiting from the ward behind me. I turned my head to see a woman visitor jump back from a bed just inside the door, thick, Lucozade-coloured bile webbing the fingers of her right hand. I didn't see the patient who had been sick, but I heard the surge of the next wave battering his chest and throat.

'Hu-ah,' he said.

'Nurse!' shouted a man three beds down on the opposite side of the ward.

'Nurse!' shouted Harry and then he too sat forward and was sick.

I phoned the hospital first thing the next morning to be told that my husband's ward had been isolated. Precaution only. No visitors were to be permitted until the nature and source of the outbreak had been determined. Walking back to the house, I could scarcely believe what I had heard. How could anyone get sick in a hospital? I was angry for my poor ill husband. And then slowly, unfairly I knew, but could do nothing to stop it, I discovered I was angry with him. If anyone could get sick in a hospital, as sure as God it would have to be Harry. Too much jelly and ice cream, I wouldn't have been surprised.

My feet were going mad itching. Chilblains. All that tramping across town in the cold and wet. I was going to have to bathe my feet with vinegar.

I didn't tell anyone about the ban on visitors. I didn't leave the house again the rest of the day. This might have been, I realize, a mistake. I kept the fire stoked. I was possibly the only person in the city that bitter night who was too hot to sleep. I didn't even have the excuse of unconsciousness for the thoughts I entertained. The following day I asked Ivy if she could mind Penny again for a couple of hours. When I called across to drop her off after lunch I was even clutching a bag of fruit. At a safe distance from the street, I took an orange from the bag and peeled it as I walked. I concentrated on each separated segment, counting my chews, from one to – how many was it? twenty-one, twenty-two? – from succulence to less than string. In this way I avoided thinking about where I was going.

By the time I had carefully chewed and swallowed the whole fruit, licked a hanky and wiped the juice from between my fingers, I was already more than halfway down the road to John O'Neill's timber yard. I dared myself on and didn't turn around until I was practically at the open gates.

I froze.

John O'Neill, complete with pipe, was walking a flat-footed golden retriever along the footpath towards me.

I was aware, while trying not to look at him too directly, of having to make a brief adjustment to my mental image of him, though the world and all that was in it seemed pinched and diminished these gruesome winter days. He wore a checked shirt and tweed tie under a thick crew-neck sweater and fawn duffel coat. The ends of his corduroy trousers were stuffed into water boots whose small size recalled to me his lame hand. The hand with which he was attempting to rein in his golden retriever. The dog lunged across the footpath between us, reared up, front paws treading the air before my midriff.

'Heel, Lady,' John O'Neill said and the dog's paws hit the ground flat once more as it turned towards its master's voice then scrabbled up his thigh. 'Heel.'

'I'm very sorry,' I said. The lead was tangled around John O'Neill's legs. He told me – stepping over the lead, over the dog, over the lead the other way – there was nothing for me to be sorry about.

I walked on, head down, stopped after ten or so yards to cross the road. John O'Neill was standing in his gateway, looking back at me. He frowned, concentrating, then said, stringing out the initial letter, 'Stella, isn't it?'

A gap opened in the traffic. I didn't cross.

'Yes.'

'Well, well.'

He took the pipe from his mouth. Lady whimpered.

'I think someone wants in the house,' I said.

John O'Neill looked at the lead wrapped around his wrist, looked at the dog on the other end of it.

'My sister's,' he said. 'She's not been well.'

'Oh, dear,' I said and he waved a hand to indicate it was nothing serious. I thought of Harry quarantined in his hospital bed. I turned my head towards the road.

'So,' said John O'Neill, 'how has everything been with you all this time?'

I focused on a point midway between the cars, rushing into and out of town, and the drive.

'I have a little girl now.'

'Congratulations,' he said and I began to cry.

Once, when I was twelve years old, I fainted in the school playground. It was a game we girls played, holding our breath, having someone slap us on the back. Someone slapped me, I went down and didn't get up. The caretaker was called, then a teacher, then the nurse. I was told this afterwards. All I remembered was coming to in what I feared at first from the thickness of the smoke was hell, but turned out to be the staff room. I tried to rise from the armchair across which I had been laid. A woman teacher, hand on my forehead, pressed me back.

'Rest,' she said.

I closed my eyes. I rested. It was lovely.

I opened my eyes, dabbed almost dry, in John O'Neill's panelled hallway. I wouldn't let him invite me further into the house.

'I feel silly enough as it is,' I said. 'I should just go home.'

Lady ran up and down the hallway, claws snickering on the parquet floor at each U-turn. Janet O'Neill's voice sounded distantly, but distinctly concerned, from above. Her brother took four steps up from the hallway, shouted it was only him. The dog pounded past him, its tail thumping against every second or third spindle. John O'Neill returned to my level. His regard was not unkind, though it was unwavering. I felt I had to give him an explanation.

'It's my husband,' I said. 'He's in the hospital. It was only his tonsils, but now there's this bug he's picked up and . . .' And I was running out of words here, afraid if I said much more I would make myself cry again. 'I just had to get out on my own a while for a walk.'

He nodded, something like 'this is reasonable', or 'you don't have to explain'.

And suddenly, as I felt it begin to depart, I was aware of the tension that had been building up inside me for days.

I exhaled deeply, letting my shoulders rise and fall.

'Well, thank you,' I said.

'I'm not sure I've done anything yet,' he said. 'You could at least let me make sure you get home OK.'

I told him I was all right to go home on my own, but he wouldn't hear of me walking. He went to the door and flagged down the driver of one of his lorries.

I followed him outside.

'No, honestly,' I said and really, really meant it.

'I insist. Now,' he said, 'address?'

I mumbled it. He listened with his head inclined, straining to catch street name and door number.

'*Five*, did you say?' I nodded. He turned to the driver. 'Did you get that?'

'Number 5,' said the driver.

John O'Neill handed me up into the passenger's seat. I felt the air cold where I stretched to make the step.

The driver's name was Thomas. There was something a little odd about his build, he had tied the cushion off an armchair to the driver's seat to bring him up level with the steering wheel. He smelt of damp wood, hard work. I explained to him as soon as we were out on the main road that I really was perfectly fine.

'Good,' he said and kept on driving. Right off the main road, right at length again, along streets that did not exist when Harry and I first made this journey on foot. The tension had not gone completely. I felt it regroup in my shoulders, in my jaw. But above all else I felt the beginnings of shame.

I persuaded Thomas to set me down short of the street corner. A little fresh air, I said, before I went in. Thomas leaned across me to open the door. It was a long way for a man of his size, his arm rested briefly on my legs. I sidled along the seat and clambered out.

'Thank you.'

He looked at me a moment standing at the kerb, shook his head, then banged the door shut. The lorry performed a wrenching three-point turn, leaving behind a cloud of sawdust and exhaust fumes. I realized I was still clutching the remains of the bag of fruit.

I handed the bag to Ivy.

'Wouldn't let you in?' she asked me and when I told her again, 'What do you mean he's took sick?'

I swear you'd have thought from her tone I was making it up.

'Oh, look,' I said, 'it's only a bug, it's not going to kill him.'

I was crouching, trying to get Penny's coat on her. Penny was trying to pick up a stub of crayon from the floor. I tugged her by the sleeve. By the arm, I suppose. Penny howled.

'Stop it,' I shouted. 'Stop it or I'll give you something to really cry about.'

'Stella?' Ivy asked and I looked up at my neighbour's frightened face and I thought, as I had not thought since the first days after I moved here, that she was barely a grown woman herself. 'Are you sure you're all right?'

I hugged Penny to quiet her.

'I'll be fine.'

Penny called out to me twice in the first hour after I put her to bed, fretting about her daddy, but when I looked in on her a few minutes after nine on my way from the bathroom she was dead to the world. That would be her now till seven o'clock tomorrow morning, with any luck. I had washed a load of her little socks and tights in the sink and left them in a basin on the draining board to hang out in the morning. There was a pair of my nylons in there. I had taken them off when I was standing at the sink. Pantie girdle too. I hadn't even looked to see what state it was in, though in my head I had imagined all the folly of the afternoon concentrated there darkly. I dragged them this way and that in the soapy water with the chapped wooden tongs, I picked them up and let them drop, making sloppy grey waves. I overdid it a little maybe. I ceased to remember that this act of cleansing was something I had set myself to perform. I grew sulky, felt a faint stirring of rebelliousness at the tops of my thighs.

By the time I switched off the kitchen light, every last drop of remorse had been wrung out of me. I flopped on to the settee, looking at the bare legs sticking out of my skirt, at the ripe red berries of my itching feet.

Apart from the trip to the bathroom I hadn't moved in over an hour.

I turned the television on. Watched a while, went across and changed it to the other channel. Turned it off. I looked again at my bare legs sticking out of my skirt. I thought about where my bare legs ended, about John O'Neill handing me up into the lorry. The seconds passed scratchily on the mantelpiece clock. Something in the kitchen – the fridge? the cooker? I never knew which – clacked. Electricity, I told myself, keeping itself entertained. Race you from the socket to the element. Water rumbled in an upstairs pipe disapprovingly. I made of my skirt a tent to hide my legs in, blowing hot air through the fabric on to my knees.

I caught my breath. A car had come into the street, slow from taking the corner, past number 1, past number 3. It did not pick up speed as it passed the front of our house, might even, I thought, have been slowing down more . . . I strained to hear . . . Stopping?

The night all at once was an uproar of incidental noises. I couldn't make out anything distinctly, couldn't decide whether there was a car out there at all. Pulling my legs from beneath my skirt, I went round the back of the settee and placed my ear against the blind. That was an engine, surely, ticking over? I dropped to my hands and knees and slipped a couple of knuckles between the sill and the blind's wooden hem. Slowly, slowly. A front door opened down the street. Tinkle of milk bottles on tiled step. The door closed, I counted to ten, flexed my fingers. Slowly.

Streetlight. That's all I saw. I shifted my weight, changed perspective. Streetlight *and* something now, something hunched and dark. I increased the gap I was looking through until it was the width of the letterbox and the something had revealed itself to be an outcrop of number 7's hedge. My knees were stiff. I used the back of the settee to help myself up and had just hobbled round to my seat when there was a soft knock at the door. The skin prickled in my underarms, as though I was erupting out of myself. I knew if I was to look down I would see my nipples against my blouse. I hadn't moved from the settee. The knock was repeated, soft still, but insistent. As quickly as they came, the goose bumps went and I felt once more self-contained. I walked to the hall doorway where I listened for sounds of Penny stirring then remembering myself I crossed the living room and closed the door to the kitchen and the basin with the nylons and pants to be hung on the line.

By the third knock I was already reaching out for the front-door knob. I knew what I was doing.

'Oh,' I said. 'Hello.'

McGovern

OUT-OF-TOWN CHARM – IN-TOWN CONVENIENCE

*A most attractive 'four-in-block' terrace house enjoying
an excellent location*

ACCOMMODATION COMPRISES:
Entrance hall into:
Lounge: 11'4" × 10' 10" Tiled fireplace.
Kitchen: 11'2" × 6'0" Single-drainer sink unit with mixer
taps. 'Alflow' water heating system. Access to understair
storage.
Dinette: 11'2" × 9'10"

FIRST FLOOR:
Landing: Hot press, copper cylinder. Access to roof space.
Bedroom 1: 11'2" × 11'0"
Bedroom 2: 11'2" × 9'10" Range of built-in cupboards.
Bedroom 3: 7'10" × 7'8" Built-in cupboard.
Bathroom: White suite. Electric heater.

OUTSIDE:
Neat garden to front. Rear garden in lawn and
flowerbeds.

*Situated in one of our fastest growing 'suburbs', this mid-
terrace property is in perfect order and ready for immediate
occupation by those requiring a modern labour-saving home in
a first-class residential locality. (Direct bus service pending.)*

*Satisfactory reason for disposal. Further particulars
from Agents.*

'Margaret!'

'What?'

'C'm'ere.'

'Where?'

'Here.'

'Coming.'

'Quick!'

'Coming.'

'Look.'

'Oh.'

Youngsters.

Skipping.

Girls and boys, ten or more of them, some tall, some small, happed up in gabardines and anoraks, in a line facing our house, not seeing us, not focusing on anything but the ropes that are as often above, below and behind them as they are in front. Some jump feet together, some two-step their rope, right foot, left foot. If they stumble they start again without missing a second beat, right foot, left foot, feet together. The daylight is fading, mist swarms high up about the orange globes of the street lamps. Down where the mouths are, puffs of breath issue forth, like steam from an engine in full flight, as ten or more ropes whip through the air, nick off the ribbed roadway.

'Do you think it's a display?' Margaret whispers. 'A greeting?'

I shake my head, at a loss. Whatever it is, it is extraordinary.

We stand side by side at the window, hardly daring to move.

∽

'Rodney?'

Deep breath. Hold it. Hold it. Hold it.

'Rodney, are you in there?'

Let it go.

'No.'

'Why haven't you the light on?'

'Haven't I the light on?'

'Quit acting the lig.'

I opened the bathroom door. Margaret had just taken her heated rollers out. Her hair, here and there, still described the shape of them. Her hair was more grey now than brown. She had talked about dyeing. I – and this was not a stage, an age, I ever thought I would get to in my life – liked it just the way it was.

'What were you doing in there?'

She squeezed past me, reaching for the light cord. Her dress was not done up at the back.

'Looking out the window,' I told her.

The window was still on the latch, specks of ash clung to the frosted glass. There was two and there was two and then there was four.

'You were smoking,' she said and pulled the window shut.

'Smoking and looking out the window.'

It was on the tip of my tongue to ask her did she remember the skipping craze, back when we moved in, but I couldn't imagine myself what brought it to mind and I didn't want her thinking I was being maudlin. She leaned over the wash-hand basin to clean her teeth, holding her hair steady with her left hand. I zipped up her dress as she straightened and replaced her toothbrush.

'You don't have to hide it from me, you know. It was you wanted to stop.'

She was right. I had wanted to stop smoking. Did stop, overnight. Willpower. Told the whole street. Told Hideg.

74

Margaret squirted a haze of Tweed and stepped into it as I walked backwards out the bathroom door.

'No one will think any the less of you for going back on them.'

'I'm not back on them,' I said from the boxroom.

'Rodney!'

'What?'

The Tweed preceded her.

'There isn't time.'

I carried on with what I was doing, sharpening a 2B pencil.

'There's plenty of time, it's only ten.'

'Ten past ten and we've to be there at half past. Ten past ten and you're not dressed.'

I walked up to the party wall, turning the shade of the floor-standing Anglepoise with the palm of my right hand and pressing the button with my thumb. I stopped, I stooped, my nose an inch from the plaster.

Margaret switched the lamp off again, got left side of me and pushed with her shoulder.

'Come on,' she said and I submitted to her shoving. 'Rhodesia'll still be there in the morning.'

'The Sudan, actually.'

'Wherever.'

The year before last, our fifth year in the house, I had finally got around to stripping the two remaining bedrooms. (I had stripped the one with the baby paper before Margaret and I even moved in.) There was a slight discoloration in the plaster towards the top of the boxroom's party wall, a foot and a half left of centre. Something about the shape – I drew around it in pencil the better to see it and, yes, I was right – it looked a bit like Greenland. I tried to recall the maps we had at school that rolled down to cover entire walls. I drew a rough circle,

bottom right of the discoloration: Iceland. After a few
moments' thought and a few moments more judging the angle
of the diagonal I wanted to follow, I sketched an oval, a foot
from the circle, to represent this lump of a place.

'I hope you're not going to forget you've to paper over
that,' Margaret had said when she came up a couple of hours
later to see how I was getting on with the stripping. I had a
vague Isle of Man in by now, a big-bottomed approximation
of Britain.

'Don't worry, don't worry,' I said.

Next day on the way from work I stopped at the central
library and borrowed *The Times Atlas of the World.*

What did the two of us want with three bedrooms?

'What's keeping you now?' Margaret called from the living
room. 'See if you're at that blinking map?'

'My black shoes need polishing.'

'Wear your new tan ones.'

'The tan ones won't go with the grey trousers.'

'Put on your green trousers.'

'The green trousers aren't ironed. Anyway I'm wearing my
navy blazer.'

'Rodney,' Margaret came to the foot of the stairs and looked
to where I stood at the top, holding my shoes, 'it is now
twenty-two minutes past.'

'Maybe you're right,' I said and began unbuckling my belt.
'Maybe I should change into the green ones. Is the ironing
board still up?'

'No,' Margaret said, though not, from her tone, in answer
to my question about the ironing board. 'You'll wear what
you have on you. Give me your shoes down till I brush them.
And would you for God's sake hurry up?'

There was a further slight delay while I searched behind the chest of drawers for the back of a cufflink, another while I took the year-old bank statement I found there to the safe-keeping of a Clarks shoe box – Margaret was on the front doorstep, stamping her feet – and then at a shade after a quarter to eleven and with a bottle of Teacher's under my arm, I stepped out into the glittering street with my wife in the direction of number 18, where the Hidegs were hosting their traditional Old Year's Night party.

Every first of January I resolved not to spend another thirty-first of December in their house, but Hideg was indefatigable. The groundwork commenced the week after his Hallowe'en party, and even when I should have known enough to expect it, year after year I was caught unprepared.

'Rodney, made any plans for the New Year?'

'Well, it's still a bit early for . . . Plans? No, not exactly.'

'That's good.' Rubbing his hands. 'Allow me then to book you and Margaret both.'

'Is it a big thing where he comes from?' I asked Margaret as we carried on down the street, as I must have asked her a hundred times before. 'Or does he think it's a big thing with us?'

'Give over,' Margaret said then shouted, stepping off the kerb with me into the road, to Mr and Mrs Quinn from number 15, who were getting into their car, who were escaping the street. 'Happy New Year, Mrs Quinn. Happy New Year, Mr Quinn.'

'Happy New Year,' they both shouted back. Nice people, the Quinns. Lucky people. I saluted with the bottle of whisky.

'Teacher's!' Hideg said when I handed him the bottle a minute later. It could hardly have been a surprise, I brought a bottle of Teacher's every year. 'Excellent.'

Jill busied into the hall (what on earth was she wearing?) and took our coats.

'Is it starting to freeze?' she asked. She had to hitch up her dress to climb the stairs without tripping.

The Hideg children – one boy, one girl – would have been packed off as usual to Jill's parents, his room become a cloak depository, hers a temporary home for the bird cages.

Hideg and his blinking birds. To hear him sometimes you would have thought he was a world authority, but I'd got him all right at Hallowe'en. Had him driven near to distraction asking him about the Wydoo.

'The Wydoo?' he was saying, hunting through his *Jumbo Book of Birds of the World*. 'The *Wydoo*? Where did you hear of this bird?'

'In the song, of course,' I said and sang it. 'Wydoo birds suddenly appear, every time you are near . . .'

'Rodney,' Hideg slammed the book shut. His nostrils twitched, his eyebrows twitched. 'You're very funny.'

'Come in,' he urged us now, pushing the living-room door. 'Come in.'

The room was blue with smoke. I waved at the party guests waving to me, from the cushions and arms of the chairs and settee, waving to me from out of the clusters they had formed by the television in one far corner and record player in the other.

So many people. When Hideg shoved the furniture back it was as though the walls themselves were pushed further apart, as though *space* was bent.

I took them all in without, as it were, differentiating them. Fellow residents, my brain said, neighbours, though there were invariably a few wild-card invitees in amongst us.

'We were just beginning to worry,' Hideg said. Since last I

was here he had wired up wall lights either side of the fireplace and done away with the overhead light entirely. I supposed the idea was to make the room more 'atmospheric', but if you asked me it would have destroyed your eyes.

'Smoke bothering you?' Hideg asked. I must have been peering. 'How long is it now?'

Margaret was by my side. I didn't look at her.

'Seven months,' I said and Hideg said, 'Good, good. Drink?'

'Well,' I said when he had gone.

It *was* seven months. Seven months since I had read the article in a *Lancet* someone had left on the train, saying that American researchers had proved the link between cigarettes and lung cancer. The Royal College of Physicians were preparing their own report. I had been telling anyone who would listen to me that one day very soon there would be a warning printed on their cigarette packets.

I told my own doctor.

'I'll take my chances,' he said, flicking ash. 'Thank you.'

Jill was downstairs again. Margaret joined Ann McGuinness in admiring her dress. Jill's dress, now that I got a proper look at it, was equal parts puffs and ribbons and ruches, from neck to wrist and waist. The hem was practically trailing on the floor. I didn't see what there was to admire. The cluster of guests by the record player broke up in laughter as Ray Coniff gave way to the moronic strains of 'Back Home', the England World Cup song. I wandered towards the kitchen doorway. Hideg put a glass in my hand as he passed coming the other way. He raised his own glass to within a whisker of mine. Hideg never clinked glasses. Bad luck. Some Hungarian superstition.

'Egészségére!' he said, as he had to, at least once, to every guest every year.

'Cheers.'

There was a good spread laid out on the countertop and the gate-legged dining table. There was always a good spread at the Hidegs'. Pavlova, flan, apple tart, trifle, mounds of sausage rolls and sandwiches. Pickled silverskin onions, cucumber slices and bright yellow cauliflorets followed one another round the compartments of a stainless-steel carousel, the box for which stood on its end under the table. Lundofte. The draining board was straining under the weight of bottles and glasses. Of course, everyone had brought something, but still, you had to wonder how Hideg did it. And not only at New Year either. It was a plumbing supplier's he travelled for, not a distillery. Some people just liked giving parties, Margaret said. They saved up for them the way other people saved up for holidays.

Four male voices, Hideg's prominent among them, were roaring along now to the England record, achieving the nigh-on impossible in making footballers sound tuneful.

'Oh, God,' I said into my glass.

'I see someone else is full of the festive spirit.'

Caroline – Mrs Stitt – stood on the kitchen side of the doorway. A ruptured strip of Sellotape on the frame directly overhead might well have once held mistletoe.

'Is it the cigarettes? Hard staying off?'

Christ, I really had told the whole street. Caroline – Mrs Stitt – was one of those neighbours I seemed to be able to go six months or more without seeing. In fact, I had seen her so rarely in all the years I had been living here that even now I was unsure what I should call her, Caroline, Mrs Stitt. Tonight, as on the previous dozen or so occasions when we had spoken, I got around the problem by not calling her anything at all.

'Nice Christmas?' I asked.

'Only a man could ask a woman that,' she said.

'Ha-ha.' That's exactly the way my laugh came out.

'If you're not running round the shops, you're running round the kitchen. See kids? They're a flaming curse.'

'I'll take your word for it,' I said, but she had turned talking over her shoulder to Ivy Moore, whose dress, for all there was of it, might have been stitched together out of the few scraps left from the making of Jill's.

'Denis minding George?'

'Just till midnight, then we'll swap.'

Ivy raised herself on tiptoes to get a smile in at me.

'Everything all right with Rodney?' she asked as though I was Rodney's brother, or even her boy George's.

'Getting better by the minute,' I said. 'Getting better by the minute.'

The cats' chorus rejects had wandered, way down in their boots, from England to the Wild West, Lee Marvin country. Did I know where hell was? they asked, redundantly. It was eleven o'clock, thirty minutes (according to Hideg tradition) to supper, sixty minutes to 1971, the proper start to the new decade whose advent had been proclaimed so raucously inaccurately in this very spot twelve months ago.

I would not have thought at the beginning of the last decade that I would be seeing in this one in the city. We were market-townsfolk then, Margaret and I, born and bored. Oh, were we bored. There was not much theatre in a market town, not much chance to take in an orchestra, see more than the one new film a month.

Still, Margaret's mother would say, the city was no place to be bringing up youngsters. I would look at Margaret. Will you tell her or will I?

'You're right there, Mummy,' was all she ever said to her.

To me she said it would be a sin to leave her mother on her own. Margaret's mother was a widow at the age of thirty-five. She lived till she was seventy-three. When her affairs were settled, I asked Margaret what there was to keep us in our market town now.

'Find us a house, then,' she told me. And by the next week I had.

'Just come in,' said the estate agent. ('Artie, for dear sake. Call me Artie.') He showed me the brochure. Inside terrace, royal-blue door, Bakelite number 5. With the nail of his ring finger, Artie dislodged a flake of dry skin from his hairline and transported it below the table. 'Lovely house, lovely area.'

'So why's it so cheap?' Margaret had asked me when I brought the brochure home. She didn't appear quite as delighted as I'd imagined.

'The people are emigrating. Probably got their tickets bought, need a quick sale.'

Margaret continued to examine the brochure, chewing her lip as though our good fortune was somehow ill-gotten.

'Handy to buses and the city centre,' I carried on, putting on the funny voice I used when I wanted to kid on I was somebody other than me, somebody like an estate agent. 'Very quiet neighbours.'

De-dang-de-dang-de-dang-de-dang-de-dang.

I was in the kitchen of our neighbours Hideg and Jill, hoping for a second helping of flan, when the hand bell was rung. Jill was a supply teacher. The bell was her signal that we were into the last two minutes of the old year. I gave up on the flan and refilled my glass ahead of the rush, so that by the time the one-minute warning was rung I had actually managed to find a seat – not an arm, not a perch – a seat directly in front of the throbbing, retina-scalding spectacle that was *The Andy Stewart Hogmanay Special*, beamed on to the Hidegs' eighteen-inch colour television screen.

I made room for Margaret as she located me through the bodies moving back in from the kitchen and hallway, though there was no time for her to sit down, because Andy Stewart himself (who I discovered to be an orange-faced gentleman) had started the countdown, which was taken up by every voice in the Hidegs' living room.

'. . . nine, eight, seven . . .'

Jill was crouched with one ruched and ribboned arm around the television set as though she owned not just the box but its contents, as though Andy was doing this all for us.

'. . . five, four, three . . .' Hideg blocked Andy out, faced us . . . 'two, one,' and crossed his arms in front of his chest, offering his open hands. We all followed suit. We formed a raggedy ring, which straggled over settee and chairs, over occasional tables become mini Manhattans of tight-packed glasses, and sang 'Auld Lang Syne'.

'Happy New Year,' we told one another. Margaret kissed me.

'Happy New Year, love,' she whispered. She looked sad.

'How many of those have you had?' I asked, with a nod to her half-empty glass.

Too much drink always made Margaret blue. Her only answer was to shake her head. Which I took to indicate the opposite of what she thought it did.

At some point – I didn't wear a watch outside work, the TV was off, the Hidegs' wall clock had no numerals and in any case may have stopped – the conversation turned to politics.

I was in the chair before the television. The Teacher's bottle was on the unit holding the record player to my right, a jug of water beside it. People were looking disappointed. (We were, as they say, mixed company.) They were looking at me disappointed. I was wagging my finger. Slowly the realization dawned that the reason the conversation had turned towards politics was because I was steering it.

I stopped wagging my finger.

'Well that's my opinion, anyhow,' I said. I got the impression I had been talking at some length. Margaret, no doubt, wherever she had got to, would have said what's new in that, but the fact of the matter was that most people needed to have things explained to them. They were not in the habit of thinking for themselves.

The living-room walls had contracted once more to the dimensions of the other end-terraces on the street. You could even see a bit of carpet. Dark, dark blue to swallow up stains and show up potato crisps. Jill, at the front door, called goodnight to departing guests. For a few moments more, no one in the living room said anything, then Hideg, who I did not recall having noticed while I talked, sat forward in his chair.

'Interesting,' he said, which was Hideg for I don't agree with a word you say. 'But you know we should not get carried away.'

Caroline Stitt and her husband, whose name, supposing I ever knew it, escaped me, made their excuses and left.

'After all, we are not talking Hungary in '56. Some rioting, a bomb or two, now and then a gun battle. No, this is not at all like in Hungary. This time next year, you will see, everything will have settled down again.'

A few of the neighbours who remained in the living room nodded. From one came a muttered 'God willing'. I seemed to remember Hideg saying last year that it was already over. My brain had just suggested I let it rest when my mouth said,

'You're missing the point.' There was a loud familiar sigh, which I chose to ignore. 'Missing the point entirely.'

'Rodney.' Margaret had come in from the hallway carrying the coats. 'Time we were off.'

'In a minute,' I said and Margaret dropped my coat on the settee and left.

Hideg laughed. 'You and I,' he said, 'we could talk the whole night.'

This time I resisted the temptation to tell him that we might talk all night, but only one of us would talk sense. Everyone else was making ready to go home. He gave me my coat.

'A lovely night,' he said, to me, to whomever else was within earshot, and then, as though this had been an experimental get-together, 'Yes, we must do it again.'

Margaret was already at our gate by the time I reached the end of the Hidegs' path. She let herself in, switched on the hall light, leaving the door ajar for me. The Quinns' car was parked in front of their house again. Nice people, the Quinns. A cat hunched between the rear wheels, all eyes and radar ears. Nice cat.

'Puss,' I said and bent my knees slightly the better to see under the car. 'Puss, puss.'

I pitched forward and, shooting my hand out to break my fall, stubbed my thumb on the road. The cat fled. I used the back of the car to help myself up.

A door shut at the far end of the street. I didn't think anyone could have seen me, but to be on the safe side I scowled down at the roadway, as though at a pothole or a patch of ice, dragging my foot backwards and forwards over the surface.

★

'Looking out the window again?' Margaret asked from out of the darkness of the bedroom, her voice muffled by the covers.

'I thought you were asleep,' I said, turning out the landing light. I had been in the house the best part of an hour. The sky outside the bathroom window was already brightening.

'I smelt the smoke,' she said. 'I don't know why you have to keep pretending.'

I took my trousers off and sat on the bed. My thumb throbbed.

'You know why,' I said. 'They'd never let me hear the end of it.'

Margaret turned in the bed towards me. 'Who's they?'

'Hideg . . . everyone. They'd try to make me look ridiculous.'

Margaret said nothing and after a second turned away again. I folded my trousers, matching the creases as best I could with only one good thumb, and laid them over the cushion of the dressing-table chair. The street was entirely silent. In the room next door the Sudan awaited the drawing of its eighth and final land border. (Wot, no break between here and Niger?)

'Margaret?' I said and when she didn't answer the first time I said it again. 'Margaret? Can we please do something else next Old Year's Night?'

∞

'Margaret?'

'I'm in the kitchen.'

'There's a pluck in this polo neck.'

'A what?'

'A pluck, in my white polo neck.'

'Your new one?'

'It must have caught on something.'

86

'I told you to be careful.'

'I was being careful.'

I fingered the little puff of nylon thread, traced the pucker that ran out in a straight line on either side.

'Well, take it off and give it down here,' Margaret called from the kitchen. 'And for God's sake don't fiddle with it.'

'I won't,' I said and stopped. My hair crackled as I tugged the polo neck clear of my head. It wouldn't have surprised me if the flaw had been in the thing when Margaret brought it home. She got it through a woman she worked with whose sister worked in a factory shop.

'Are you sure that stuff would be all right?' I'd asked her when she suggested it.

'Rodney, they don't look any different from other clothes. Half the town's probably running around in them only you don't know it.'

Margaret was sitting by the fireplace when I came into the living room, sewing box already on her lap. The television was on, the volume turned low. I stood by Margaret's chair following the pictures with her. Some underwater thing. Fish, vivid as glass ornaments, cut through a turquoise sea. It was like discovering television for the first time, getting colour.

'You shouldn't wear a string vest under this,' Margaret said, eventually turning her eyes from the screen, via me, to the polo neck. 'You'll look like a candlewick bedspread.'

'It's too cold to wear without a vest.'

'Wear one of your other ones.'

'I thought they were all thrown out,' I said and went to the Christmas tree, reaching in to the aluminium trunk and bending a white-fringed branch into a more natural shape.

'Who would throw them out?' Margaret asked, but I didn't reply. The simple truth was I preferred string vests. There was something comfortingly scientific about their trapped-air warmth.

'What time are we expected at?' I said instead.

'Same time as every year.'

Margaret lifted her glasses case down from the mantelpiece. 'The Hallowe'en party was earlier than usual.'

'There was no truce at Hallowe'en.'

'Pity there's one now,' I said and Margaret narrowed her eyes at me. 'Joke. Honest.'

It was, of course, no laughing matter. To say things had taken a turn for the worse of late would have been the understatement of the year now ending. Every day of the last three hundred and sixty-five seemed to top the one before in awfulness. As ever at the year's close, pious hopes were being expressed that the horror would finally hit home and that next year would be an improvement.

I am afraid I had no such hopes. Somewhere deep down people in this city, this country, did not like one another.

The water on the television fizzed as though a tablet had been dropped in the top. A shark twisted through the pinking turmoil. Margaret bent over my polo neck fishing for the source of the pluck with the point of a needle. Little by little the nylon puff disappeared, like breath drawn in and held.

'There.'

'Teacher's! Excellent!' Hideg took the bottle from me in the hallway.

'Just for a change,' I said.

He placed a foot on the stairs. A tiny orange tab with an italic *f* was stitched into the waistband of his blue slacks. For Farah, not factory shop.

'Jill? Rodney and Margaret are here.'

A bird squawked.

'Come in,' Hideg said to us. 'Come in.'

The living room was the usual ferocious fug, though when my eyes had acclimatized I wondered whether, the unofficial truce notwithstanding, there weren't a few less guests than last New Year. Even with the earlier starting time, the Hallowe'en party had been a quiet affair, though there again Hallowe'en was not Hallowe'en since they brought in the fireworks ban.

The turnover in neighbours hadn't helped. The Quinns, of course, wouldn't have been here even if they hadn't moved out, but the McGuinnesses definitely would have, the Kellys too.

This was not a violent part of town. Until recently I would not even have said it was a flag-waving part of town. Besides, the Nixons who had upped and left for England at the start of November might not have been expected to take the same exception to the flags that were now being flown in the streets round about, but loss of nerve at times like these could be viral.

I could only see one set of the new neighbours in Hideg's front room. Blake, you called them, Paul and Annette. She used to run the mile, only just missed out on a bronze in the last Empire Games but two. Commonwealth Games. Blake wasn't the name she ran under then. Blake wasn't even the name she ran under when she got married the summer after those games. This was a second marriage for the two of them. They had a sports shop together on one of the main roads heading north out of the city. The papers were full of pictures when it opened.

Far be it from me to do my own street down, but you would have thought owning a shop and with the name she had (used to have) they could have afforded somewhere a bit grander than here. Or maybe this was what happened when there were divorces with alimony and what have you to pay out. I saw a couple of boys playing in the garden the odd Saturday with Billy, Annette and Paul's Jack Russell pup. I had never enquired, but I had a feeling they were his. They certainly didn't look like they wanted for anything.

Hideg handed me an amber tumbler.

'Egészségére!'

I recognized the tumblers from the TV. Shell or someone was giving them away, ten tokens a glass, a token for every pound's worth of petrol.

'Tell me if that's enough water,' Hideg said and walked away before I'd had a chance to taste it.

'Thanks,' I said brightly to his back. Paul Blake's black moustache rose at the points, either side of his mouth, where it began the descent to his chin. I took this for a smile. I smiled back. He held up an amber tumbler as though for my inspection.

'I'm an ice man myself,' he said. 'Cleaner taste, I always think.'

I was guessing he did not really want to talk about whisky and that this exchange was intended only as a base camp. I opted for non-committal.

'I suppose it's what you're used with.'

'I suppose so,' he said.

We swallowed whisky, looked to see where our wives had got to and, finding there were no obvious roads out, turned back towards each other. Another drink, then:

(Him) 'No White Christmas again, then.'

(Me) 'Only on BBC2, ha-ha.'

'Same old bunch of repeats.'

'Christmas Day?'

He shook his head. 'Desperate. We switched it off altogether and played a game of rummy.'

'*Scrabble*,' I said. 'Me and Margaret.'

'*Scrabble*,' he said, with an air of wistfulness.

'Oh, we love a game. I've often said to Margaret, give me a game of *Scrabble* or a good book and I could do without the television altogether.'

His moustache (maybe I was being a little harsh earlier: it was the fashion, after all) rose at the corners, higher than before and for longer.

'You can't beat a good book.'

'You cannot.'

'Biography.'

'History.'

'Thrillers.'

'Mm.'

We drank, let people pass, held to our places.

'Do you mind me asking,' he said, and I knew what was coming, 'what it is that you do?'

I spied a small enamel forget-me-not in the lapel of his broad-checked jacket. Freemason.

'I drive trains,' I told him.

'A train driver?' He managed to pass his surprise off as the every-boy's-dream variety. 'I don't think I ever met a train driver before.'

'What people don't understand,' I said, 'is the time it gives you for thinking.'

'Oh, we're all big thinkers here,' Hideg interjected point-lessly, en route to the kitchen. Paul Blake availed of the opportunity to laugh. I could have let this go, but I had grown too fed up of people's incredulity at what they (not I) considered the gap between my interests and my living.

'There you are, alone in your cab, no other traffic to distract you and a vast panorama opening before you.'

I had mostly worked the suburban line since moving to the city, vast panorama was maybe overstating it, but the point stood.

'I hadn't thought of it like that,' Paul Blake said and sounded genuinely chastened. 'Makes working in a shop seem very dull.'

He took a box of Senior Service from his jacket pocket.

'Smoke?'

He lit up as I shook my head.

'Annette's at me all the time to quit,' he said, 'but I say to her, I've been on them since I was a teenager, what am I going to do?'

'I know how you feel. I was on them myself from I was twelve.' I had not had so much as a puff in six and a half weeks. 'There's no answer only willpower.'

He looked at the end of his cigarette, then into his glass, glum.

'Of course,' I said quickly, 'you'd know all about willpower, running your own business.'

In the kitchen for a refill, I spotted – and gave a wide berth to – Ivy Moore. I had just seen Denis in the living room. Clearly they considered George to be old enough, at thirteen, to look after himself for the night.

Ivy was in full flow. I noticed her hands as she talked, touching forearms, shoulders, her fingers at moments hovering around her listeners' kidneys. She leaned in whispering, drew back, laughed with complete abandon. The woman was incapable of moderate emotion. I remembered her, the day we got the keys for the house, practically weeping when I met her in the street.

'Be happy there.' I was holding a drum of salt she had pressed upon me. 'Oh, be sure and be happy, won't you.'

Margaret found me close to the breakfast bar. She had been talking to Annette Blake.

'They seem a very friendly couple.'

'Yes,' I said. I was examining two plates at either end of the countertop. Each had squat hollow columns of puff pastry, filled on one plate with whipped cream and mandarin orange, and on the other with what appeared to be condensed chicken soup flecked with ham.

'It might be nice, some Saturday night . . .'

I nodded. Vols-au-vents? I'd read about them, *Sunday Times* supplement, or somewhere.

'. . . have them over, him and her.'

I looked at my wife. We had lived in this street for going on nine years and this was the first time she had suggested having people over. We had been married for almost twenty-five years and I could have counted on the fingers of one hand the number of times we had had guests on a Saturday night. I wondered whether Margaret's head wasn't a little turned by Annette Blake.

I touched her cheek with my fingertips, stroked behind her ear lobe with its tiny gold sleeper.

'She lost one last year,' she said in an undertone. I didn't need to ask her who. I didn't need to ask her what.

'Ah,' I said.

I wasn't the one started it. I wasn't even in the room. The bell had been rung, the toast drunk, 'Auld Lang Syne' sung and I had gone to the bathroom – the chicken and ham vols-au-vents, I feared – and by the time I came down the whole room had erupted in argument. *Arguments*, I should say, those who were unable to get a word into the main one having discontented themselves, each other, with a little local variation. Heads were shaken, fingers pointed, faces thrust into faces. It had occurred to me earlier that though the numbers might have been down on previous years, I could not remember ever having seen so much drink lined up on the draining board.

Someone was saying disintegration, someone else reunification. I heard independence, capitulation, direct rule. I heard Hideg say, in his Hideg way, 'Yes, but let us have some perspective, we are not talking about Bangladesh.'

I wondered sometimes whether Hideg had actually escaped from Hungary after the Rising, as he said, or whether the Russians had simply turned a blind eye to his going so as not to have to put up with having to listen to him all these years.

More than once lately, watching or reading about some new enormity, I had caught myself thinking what will Hideg say to that? I told myself that all I wanted was for him to take what was going on here seriously, admit that things were getting right out of control and never mind Hungary '56, or Vietnam, or Bangladesh or wherever else just happened to be in the news at that moment.

These were not circumstances in which I could take pleasure in being proved right.

Margaret was standing over by the fireplace with Annette and Paul Blake, watching me closely, them anxiously. With so much bait I knew she thought it was only a matter of time before I bit, showing her up in front of Annette and Paul. A fellow could have been hurt by such lack of faith. The Stitts, on either side of me, were leaning in to bicker with one another. I heard 'hands tied behind their backs', I heard 'gloves off', 'hell in a handcart', before I closed my ears to the clamour.

'Coats?' I called and Margaret looked as though she might kiss me.

∽

'Rodney?'

'What?'

'Enough.'

'Oh. Margaret,' I said, 'relax. Paul knows I'm only joking.'

Paul Blake, it was true, was not laughing, but really I was disinclined to care. We were in the Hidegs' dining . . . area, I suppose was all you could call the eating end of a knock-through. It was a quarter to eleven on the last day of another perfectly bloody year. Even I had not imagined twelve months ago that things could have got quite so hairy. This was more or less exactly what I had just said to Paul Blake. Paul now sported a thick black beard and sideburns to go with his black moustache. It was not a look, I wouldn't have thought, calculated to bring the customers in, and from what I gathered Paul could ill afford to be turning people away from his shop just now.

'Hmph,' he said and turned his back to light, with a none-too-steady hand, what must have been his twentieth Senior Service of the night. Margaret shook her head at me, but she could shake all she liked, it wasn't as if she couldn't have predicted how things were likely to go.

I had told her this evening at dinner Hideg had turned the Blakes against me.

She carried on eating, looking off towards the window, though there was nothing to see there except our reflections dining al fresco under a stark white light.

'You're not denying it.'

She swallowed, drank from her glass of milk, riming the down on her top lip.

'There's no point,' she said at last.

'Then I'm right.'

'That's not what I said.'

'Well that's what I heard.'

I looked at Margaret watching the husband and wife in the window not talking to one another. He moved his mouth and I said, 'That's a lovely pork fillet.'

'Watt's.' Margaret let fall the name of the butcher then faced me. 'Why would Hideg want to do a thing like that?'

'You tell me,' I said.

The plain fact was that Paul and Annette had been giving us the cold shoulder for months. There had been a night, beginning of March, they had called over. All perfectly civilized. We played rummy, whist, chase the ace. We didn't touch the *Scrabble* in the end.

'Oh, God, *Scrabble*,' said Annette when she spied the box on the sideboard. 'I'm an absolute dummy at *Scrabble*.'

And Margaret said – I never did pull her up about it – 'I know what you mean, but Rodney likes it.'

Annette, all in all, was not quite what I had hoped. She had taken up athletics at school, she said, to get out of something she liked less. Middle-distance running was not a passion, just a thing she turned out to be good at. And then too her Commonwealth Games fourth *was* a long time ago.

'Of course,' said Margaret. Of course.

Still, a not unpleasant evening. Before they left I had taken Paul up to the boxroom.

'Hold on,' I said at the door and went ahead to adjust the Anglepoise. 'Ready.'

I showed him how I worked out the scale from the atlas, marking on the wall the four points of a territory – extreme north, south, east and west – and drawing between them freehand. I had been on the South Sea Islands then for the best part of six months. Fiji, Tonga, Samoa, the Ratak Group and Rajik Group, some of them even on my scale little bigger than dots.

'How many nights a week did you say you spend doing this?'

He shook his head. He seemed impressed.

I had thought a fortnight, three weeks, maybe a little more – let them get Easter out of the way – they would return the invitation. Since when, nothing. Not even a Christmas card.

'Some people just don't send the way we do,' said Margaret. And some people had someone like Hideg bending their ears.

It was only when Hideg opened the door to us tonight that the penny finally dropped, or should I say the *pin*, a brand-new-looking forget-me-not in the middle of his paisley tie.

That was why he and Paul were suddenly so thick: it was the solid bond of masonry.

I had already spotted a couple more forget-me-nots on the jackets of this year's wild-card guests. I even thought one of them was giving me the handshake when Hideg introduced us. I had pulled my hand away before I realized the man had something the matter with his fingers.

'I'm terribly sorry,' I said and the man, O'Neill I think you called him – what with the shock, I'd hardly taken it in – the man told me I wasn't to let it worry me.

'It's been happening all my life. I'm used to it by now.'

He hadn't hung around too long after that. I hoped it was because he wasn't enjoying himself, I mean I hoped he *was*, but if he wasn't I hoped it wasn't just because of me.

97

('It's been happening all my life,' he did say. 'I'm used to it by now.')

'Refill?'

Hideg.

'Not just yet.'

Hideg went to take the glass from my hand anyway. He wasn't really paying attention to me.

I placed my free hand on top of the glass and, saying I said I'm fine, yanked it towards me. Hideg gave a start and looked at me as though just realizing who I was.

'Rodney.'

'Hideg.'

'I'm sorry,' he said. 'I missed-heard you.'

Seventeen years he had been living in this country. I went to correct him, but his gaze was wandering again. Fine, let him talk like a foreigner all his life. And then as I tried to remember was it really O'Neill you called the man with the gammy hand, tried too while I was about it to remember (the garbage you overheard at work) the surname of the woman to whom Neil Sedaka was singing, as loud at the back of the house as at the front now that there was an arch where the fireplace used to be, 'Oh, Carol', Paul Blake, standing where Hideg's gaze had come to rest at the far end of the room, reached out for a curtain as though for support and clutching only air collapsed.

'Bloody hell,' said Hideg, and Ivy Moore, helpfully, screamed.

'He's having a heart attack!'

Annette, coming from nowhere, just as she did in the Commonwealth Games, elbowed past me, reaching her husband before even Hideg did.

'Paul?' Nothing. 'Paul!'

Paul from the floor answered her with a groan.

'He just dropped,' said Ivy and let her arms flop by her side by way of illustration.

Paul groaned again, closer to speech.

'Open his shirt,' said Hideg, but Paul with Annette's assistance was already struggling to stand.

'Mo,' he gasped, breathed deep, gasped again, 'kay.'

He didn't look OK, leaning both hands on the table's edge, nudging a platter of mixed sandwiches with his whitened knuckles, while Annette rubbed his shoulders. He had cut a lip in the fall and the blood from it was weaving a glistening line through his beard.

'You had us terrified there,' said Ivy, herself resting a hand on the table.

Everyone was now either in the dining area or in the archway. Neil Sedaka stretched out the last note of his hymn to Carol . . . *King* was her name. I hadn't moved since Hideg attempted to refill my glass.

'He's been taking these turns,' Annette said. 'The doctor has him on tablets.'

Hideg, who was in the act of pouring a large measure of brandy, now set bottle and glass out of Paul's reach.

I sniffed the air and had just opened my mouth to ask was something burning when Paul Blake, barking with pain, jerked upright and beat his chest with one hand while tugging with the other at the front of his shirt.

'He's going again,' said Ivy, stepping back from the table into Margaret, who blanched.

But it was a false alarm. To the sound of a shirt button hitting a plate, Paul had got his shirt open and retrieved from it a squashed but still smouldering Senior Service.

The something burning was chest hair.

'Bloody cigarette,' Paul Blake said and Hideg said he had heard me say they could kill you, but didn't know I'd meant that way.

Which for Hideg was pretty funny, though the laughter that everyone joined in went on a little too long, as if it was fuelled by something more needful than enjoyment of the joke. Indeed, unlike Paul who insisted he didn't need to go home, was soon in fact requesting another drink, the night never really recovered. At one point I found myself in a conversation about previous years' parties, which was always a bad sign. Tom McParland reckoned they started, on a much smaller scale, we were to understand, before the street was opened up beside his house, for he remembered an impromptu reprise the winter of the really bad snow, tipsy races across the waste ground on makeshift sleds. He bent almost double as he tried to describe for those of us who weren't there Ann McGuinness on a tin tray, yards from everyone else, beating her heels in the snow, shouting over the top of her head, Push me, push me!

There was a silence. Had anybody had word from Ann or Hugh? Michael and Patricia Kelly? The Quinns? The mood dipped again.

'They've been after Paul this months for protection money,' Margaret whispered, for no other reason than that the light was out.

Nineteen seventy-three was two hours and forty-five minutes old. There were still people abroad on the street, but Margaret and I were back to back in bed.

'Who's been after him?' I asked. 'And who told you?'

'Ivy Moore,' Margaret answered the second question first, but I was too impatient to listen to any more.

'Honestly, Margaret,' I said.

'No,' she said, 'listen. Ivy was talking to Annette. They threatened to bomb the shop unless he paid them and then as soon as he gave in they started asking for more.'

'Rumours,' I said. Margaret talked over me.

'He's told them he doesn't have any more, but they don't care. That's why he's on the tablets. That's why we've hardly seen him.'

Someone walked past the front of the house, whistling now through their lips, now through their teeth. I thought it was the tricky vocal part from 'Oh, Carol', but I could have been wrong. Margaret rolled over. I felt her breath on my neck where it emerged from the covers. She must have raised her head. She must have been watching for a reaction from me. I considered reminding her that Ivy Moore was the person who told her that the woman who lived here before us lost all her hair in a single night. Instead I listened to the whistler, out of the street by this time but still audible, and in a very few moments I had genuinely forgotten that Margaret was examining the back of my head until I felt her own head hit the pillow again, her entire body turn away.

Actually, even allowing for its source, the story about Paul and the protection money was all too easy to believe. These were days when anything, you felt, could happen to anybody in this city. Tinker, tailor, soldier, sailor, rich man, bearded shop-owning man . . . me.

Long after Margaret was asleep I lay and thought of Paul Blake, of the worry he must have been going through, the terror. I thought too about the words Margaret and I had at dinner and what I had come out with about Hideg turning Paul and Annette against me. The last thoughts I had that New Year's morning were of my own vanity and foolishness.

I resolved, I resolved, I resolved, I resolved.

∽

'Margaret!'

I pushed the front door shut and pulled the curtain across it
to keep the heat in, even though we would be leaving again any
minute. I placed the car keys in their drawer in the telephone
table and went through the living room to the kitchen.

No Margaret. I called her name again as I sloughed the tight
brown bag from the neck of the Teacher's bottle and picked
at the price tag with my thumbnail.

'Margaret?'

Margaret's brother, Jim, was away to his son in Guernsey
for the holidays so he hadn't called, as he normally did, on
Christmas Eve. Jim it was brought us the whisky I brought to
Hideg's on Old Year's Night. It was near nine tonight before
I remembered and had to jump in the car to drive to the
off-licence.

'Margaret?'

The price tag came off the bottle in three sections, each
more reluctant than the last. I looked at my hand as I finished
rolling the pieces into a jagged excuse for a ball and I wondered
did I detect a slight tremor.

It must have been years since I had last had to go out on to
that main road at night. I had driven through after dark, but
driving through didn't prepare you. It was not an experience
I'd want to repeat in a hurry. The only premises that didn't
have their shutters down were the off-licence and the hot-food
bar, the Chuck Wagon, on the same side of the street. Crowd
of young lads in denims and tartan scarves milling around on
the footpath between the two, chip papers everywhere, broken

glass in the gutter where I first tried to park, so that I ended up having to drive on a hundred yards and walk back through the mêlée.

The language was nothing ordinary. Eff this, eff that, eff in the middle of other words. The letter F itself had been spray-painted in red over the first two letters of Chuck.

While I was standing outside the off-licence, waiting for someone of the staff to hurry up and answer the buzzer to let me in the security gate, a youngster in a denim jacket, trousers halfway up his shins, came and stood at my side. He had a pound note in his hand.

'Mister,' he said, 'will you go in for us?'

'What?'

He couldn't have been more than twelve.

'The offie. Go in for us, will you? Them ones there' – a nod to the older boys – 'are being sly. Go ahead. It's New Year's Eve.'

'I will not indeed,' I said and he wandered off a way, not, I thought, greatly surprised. As I closed the security gate behind me, I saw the boy stop another man and again be refused. Someone shouted he was an effing double-u. There was laughter. The boy shrugged, passed his pound from one hand to the other, looked up the street.

My leg brushed against the radiator in the dinette. It was roasting.

'Margaret?'

I went back into the living room, opened the fire's glass door with the tongs and nudged the air regulator to low. No tremor at all.

George Moore and his girlfriend were in the off-licence. I was in the queue, inching towards the till and the spirits bottles behind, when I caught sight of them by the beer cans in the shop's system of convex mirrors. It was the girlfriend I recognized, straggly dyed-blonde hair, a half a foot taller than George.

(George, from the first I had ever seen him, last in a line of skipping children, was always a good half-foot shorter than most of the rest.)

I craned my neck, looking down the shop to make sure I wasn't mistaken, at the same moment that George, selection made, began walking towards the queue. He wore a yellow tartan scarf knotted at his throat. The tins in his left hand said Long Life, the tins in his right, Colt 45. I turned away, but he had already seen me.

Now what did I do?

The wee fella was barely sixteen. The sign on the door said strictly no service to persons under the age of twenty-one. I allowed my gaze to wander towards the convex mirror and of course George Moore and his girlfriend were watching me in it. George smiled at me. Maybe it was the mirror that turned the smile into a leer. The till drawer chinged open and shut, I took another baby-step closer to having to make a decision.

Already, though, I was beginning to suspect that there was no decision to make. George Moore was barely sixteen, George Moore, despite his big blonde girlfriend, despite his carefully shaped and tended bum-fluff moustache, *looked* barely sixteen. If the off-licence had a policy (for it was not the law which prevented them selling to persons under twenty-one) then the off-licence staff should be the ones to enforce it. Yes.

Ching went the till. Open and – ching – shut.

'Yes?'

The sales assistant who was to serve me wore glasses with lenses the colour of an iced-up river. An iced-up city river. Lenses so thick you could have skated on them. In fact going by the scratches someone already had.

'A bottle of Teacher's, please.'

'Ten, twenty or forty ounce?' the assistant said, on the turn, seeming to find his way to the whisky by touch rather than by sight.

'Forty.'

I couldn't help it, I glanced at the mirror again. George and his girlfriend were still watching, so intently that a gap had opened between them and the person in front of them in the queue. Another customer filled the gap and it occurred to me that they were going to hang back until they could get this particular sales assistant to serve them.

Which meant, in all likelihood, it was not me they'd been staring at all this time.

'Next,' shouted a second sales assistant and the man at my back stepped around me and set two dumpies of Guinness bottles on the counter.

'That's two ninety-five.' The short-sighted assistant adjusted his spectacles and took my five-pound note. 'Sorry,' he said, 'no pounds.' He counted the change into my hand, watching every coin. 'Five is three, three-fifty, four, four-fifty, -sixty, -seventy, -eighty, -ninety, and ten is five pounds.'

I began to think it possible that George Moore would get served after all. My heart sank at the thought of meeting the parents in less than an hour's time. Did I tell them? Did I not? Did they know already? Did they care?

Ching, ching.

'Who's next there?' shouted a third assistant. A woman with satin button earrings excused herself as she passed me and asked the assistant for a bottle of Pernod and twenty Bel Air.

I took the brown bag with my whisky in it and headed, without a backward look, towards the door. The buzzer sounded to let me out.

'Happy New Year, Mr McGovern,' George called as I reached for the handle.

I stared for a moment at the enormous male genitals, sprayed, the same colour as the F in Chuck, on the shutter of Watt's the butcher's across the way. The glans had been adapted into a trilby hat and a grin added halfway down the shaft. I turned.

The sales assistant who had served me peered at George and from George to me. Even through those glasses there was surely no way George could be taken for twenty-one.

'And to Mrs McGovern,' George added. His girlfriend smiled. The assistant peered harder.

Don't look at me, I wanted to say. But look he did, waiting for my response. I knew what would happen if I opened my mouth to say anything other than 'This boy is under-age.' I wish I could say a thousand thoughts raced through my mind. Only one did. I wanted to get through that crowd of yobs and into my car and home.

'Happy New Year, George,' I muttered, validating him.

Out on the street the child in the denim jacket stood with both hands in his pockets. For the first time, I thought, he was genuinely forlorn.

I walked into the hallway and climbed to the third stair.

'Margaret?'

'I said, I'm in the bathroom,' she called back.

'I'm sorry, I didn't hear you.'

I had carried on up to the top of the stairs. I listened outside the bathroom. There was no lock on the door.

'Can I come in?'

'No!'

In the early days of our marriage I would have known exactly what that meant. Peeing in one another's presence was fine, but not the other. Of late, however, our intimacies had contracted ever closer to our double bed. My wife's ablutions were an increasing mystery to me.

I trod quietly across the landing to the boxroom, but suddenly hadn't the heart for the bays and inlets of the Bellinghausen and Weddell seas and I went instead to check the radiator in our room. Hot, hot, hot. (My new hobby, Margaret called the central heating.) I had not taken off my car coat since returning from the off-licence, in spite of the heat. Oddly, given, one, that I knew Denis and Ivy Moore would be there and, two, what I had so recently seen, I was impatient to get to Hideg's party. Or maybe what I mean is that I was impatient to have a drink.

I crossed to the window, and found an angle from which to look up the street towards number 18. There were lights on in every window, the front door was open. I was distracted by several Stitt brothers passing on the far side of the road kicking a ball between them. I didn't know for certain how many of them there were in total. (I didn't know half the children I saw running up and down this street any more.) Three here, but there was at least a fourth, possibly a fifth. These three – eleven, twelve and thirteen maybe – were eating lollipops while they kicked their football. Lollipops in December. Football at – I checked my watch – after ten o'clock.

'Margaret!'

'Quit your yelling,' Margaret said, coming in the bedroom

door, looking past rather than at me. She was in her housecoat. The skirt and blouse she had been wearing when I left for the off-licence were on hangers, which she carried across to the wardrobe.

'You're not dressed.'

'I'm not going.'

'You're not what?'

'I'm not going.'

'How can you not go?'

'Watch me.'

She pulled back the bedclothes and, still in her housecoat, climbed into bed.

'I don't understand,' I said. Margaret gave me a look as though I had said something unintentionally funny. 'You were all right when I went out.'

For reply she let go an exasperated sigh. I sat on the edge of the bed. She drew the blankets up to the housecoat's lacy collar.

'It's you,' she said at length.

'Me?'

'And,' Margaret pursued her own train of thought, 'I wasn't all right when you left. I'm never all right on Old Year's Night. How can I be when I've been worrying about you from the moment I woke?'

There ought to have been something more to say than what I did say, but for the life of me I couldn't think what.

'Me?'

'Yes, Rodney, you. You spoil it for me every year, the way you get on over there.'

I tried to think how it was I did 'get on' over there.

'The year before last was OK, wasn't it?' I asked her. Or was I thinking of the year before that?

Margaret shook her lowered head. She shook tears from her lowered eyelids. I was so astonished that when one tear landed on the back of my hand I could do nothing for a moment but sit and watch it roll, swell, and break against my coarse black back-of-the-hand hair.

'Oh!' said Margaret and pressed her fingertips against her eyes. I knew that Oh. Part 'look at me', part 'look what you made me do'.

I reached for her, was impeded slightly by the seam of my car coat cutting into my underarms, but kept on reaching out until my arms were right around her and her head rested on my shoulder.

'Darling,' I said, shifting now that I had hold of her to ease the burn-like pain in my armpits, 'I'm sorry.'

Margaret made a light fist and struck it without force against my back. She was shaking her head again.

'I'm fifty,' she said. I told her I was too. She said, 'I have great big tufts of hair all over me.'

It was such an extraordinary thing for her to come out with that, despite myself, I laughed. When she struck my back the second time, I felt it. She pulled away from me, tugging at the housecoat's collar.

'Oh, my good God, Margaret.'

Her neck, low down on the right-hand side, was scraped and raw.

'How did you do that?' I asked, though I knew her answer before she gave it.

'Shaving.'

I leaned across and kissed the rawness. I swung my legs on to the bed and laid her back against the pillow.

'Sweetheart, sweetheart.'

'Don't say it,' Margaret told me, tensing.

'What?'

'Don't ask me if that's what this is all about.'

'I wouldn't dream of it,' I whispered into her hair and as I said it so I did indeed cease to dream of it.

'I get myself so worked up worrying about you, I don't know what I'm doing half the time,' she said. 'Imagine me trying to shave.'

'If you want,' I said, 'you can borrow my Old Spice.'

I got up off the bed and went to the wardrobe. I took out the skirt she was wearing earlier, but passed over the blouse in favour of her cream one with the high neck. As I turned back towards her I suddenly stopped.

'I like going to Jill and Hideg's,' I said, with the force of revelation.

And Margaret, who in more than a quarter of a century of marriage I had never known to swear, said through the last of her tears, 'Well, you've a bloody funny way of showing it.'

∞

'Rodney?'

'Two minutes.'

'You said two minutes ten minutes ago.'

'I was only having you on then.'

'How do I know you're not having me on now?'

'You don't, but I'm not.'

'That man,' Margaret said to herself, I presumed, though I yelled to her through the boxroom door, 'I can hear you, *that woman*.'

I leaned against the frame of the uncurtained window. A blustery day out, spring looking over its shoulder at winter. A Post Office van was pulled up next to the telegraph pole in front of number 9. Two Post Office engineers, old hand, new hand, donkey jackets buttoned to the neck, stood in the shelter of the open rear doors, pouring themselves tea from an enamel pot. They had a Tupperware jug of milk, a little bowl of sugar. The inside of the van was half kitchen, half giant toolbox. A young lad glanced at them as he passed, coming from the newer houses, fingertips wedged in slit pockets, shoulder-length hair sailing behind him on the wind. I couldn't remember seeing him before. I didn't imagine I'd see him again. He glanced into our car sitting low on its suspension, hard by the kerb at the bottom of the path, lampshades crushed against the rear windscreen, bundles of bedding topped off with books on the back seat, and instinctively he veered in towards the garden walls.

It was a sensible precaution.

I tried to imagine driving a car laden with explosives, not being able to find a parking space, pulling it up to the kerbside in any old street, walking away. It was as good an explanation as any for the car that exploded outside the Chuck Wagon, the car abandoned with hazard lights flashing, boot ticking, in the driveway of O'Neill's timber yard.

I had recognized the man at once when I saw him interviewed on the TV. The windows were gone from the front of his house. The window frames were gone. One side of the roof had collapsed. Out the back the wood in the stores was still ablaze.

'At my age,' he had said, 'you have to ask yourself is it worth trying to start again.'

He was at a guess sixty. He looked, more than anything else, disappointed.

Alma Robertson was polishing her living-room window brasses, elbows going like fury – like she'd just had word there was to be an eleven o'clock inspection. She paused for breath, caught sight of me, pulled a face: 'Terrible sad.' I made a face back. 'Isn't it just?'

I lit a cigarette, the last of ten I bought a week ago. I never was that heavy a smoker. Alma kneaded her lower back. The engineers clasped their white Pyrex cups, eating chocolate snowballs, heads tilted right back looking up at the telegraph pole. A car with L-plates turned – too wide – into the bottom of the street. I performed a neat turn of my own to face the newly papered boxroom wall. Crown Vinyl P85832, a Rorschach test in shades of pink. I saw giant butterflies against the white background, a devil in a bow tie. I saw what would have been a perfect colour for the Common Market countries lying underneath.

It was my one big regret that I hadn't got round to colouring my continents. Oceans and ice caps, that was as far as I'd got.

'You can't cover this up,' Hideg had said and could not have sounded more outraged if he had created it himself. 'It's a work of art.'

'Oh, I don't know about that.'

Hideg shook his head, stepped back, heavily, for a better view.

'A work of art.'

This was after one o'clock in the morning, New Year's Day just gone. We were neither of us the soberest and we were still working our way through the quarter of a bottle of Teacher's we had brought across the road from Hideg's party.

Margaret hadn't come with us. I was in the bad books with her because I had let it slip (Hideg was already talking about next year's Hallowe'en party) that we were selling the house. *Thinking* of selling, said Margaret, who was superstitious that way, though of course the damage had already been done.

Hideg was affronted. He flung an arm as wide as the presence of neighbours would allow, which is to say wider than he might have in years gone by.

'Why would you want to leave all this?'

Because there were no cinemas or theatres left to go to; because my wife had never really felt she belonged here; because we were not city people when all was said and done and even this was too much city for us; because this was not a place we would have wished to grow old in; because, though you might not have been aware there was a contest, you won, Hideg, I lost my nerve.

'He needs a bigger wall,' Paul Blake said across the top of his glass. 'For the solar system.'

I wondered how often quips like that had been made behind my back, though of course now it was made to my face I had no option but to stand there and take the laughter.

Hideg didn't so much as smile.

'You'll have to show me this famous wall of yours.'

Jesus, Hideg, I thought, I'd have to draw you a map just to show you where our house is on the street.

'I'll try and book you in,' I said. 'This is our busy season.'

Hideg threaded his arm through mine.

'But you're open now, are you not?'

In our kitchen, ten minutes later, hunting for the cut-glass whisky tumblers I'd last seen the day we moved in, I was conscious of Hideg's appraisal of the cupboard doors (red Formica), the cushioned flooring, of every last pin in the pin saucer . . .

The *pin saucer*? When did Margaret and I acquire a pin saucer? When did those words come to seem as perfectly wed as our own two names?

I was reminded of the moment in my childhood, visiting a

primary-school friend's house, when I discovered that the dinner table, chairs, settee and wireless in my own family's house weren't *the* at all, but *a, some*: versions rather than the definitive articles and, what was worse, that there was no way of telling whether they were the right versions. Standing in the kitchen of number 5 under Hideg's roving eye, I didn't know that I had had a day free from anxiety in all the years since.

The cut-glass tumblers were at the very back of the very last cupboard I looked in. They came out with difficulty and with another memory attached: Margaret and I arguing the night her brother – he of the whisky for Christmas – gave us them as a housewarming present.

'They're horrendous.'

'They're a gift.'

'They're not real crystal.'

I wiped them inside and out with a linen tea towel, held them up to the light, as if checking I'd got all the dust. Actually, they weren't that bad-looking.

With Jim's glass in one hand, Jim's bottle in the other, I asked Hideg at the top of the stairs to excuse me if I didn't give him a drum roll. I used my backside to open the boxroom door, my chin to flick on the overhead light.

For a minute or two Hideg was motionless save for the quick movement of glass to mouth, silent save for the sound of sipping and breath departing by his nose.

He hates it, I thought. He loves it. He's waiting for a suitable moment to make his excuse and leave.

Another quick movement of the arm, another sip, a long nasal exhalation, then he said the thing about it being a work of art and I said, 'Oh, I don't know about that.'

When he was through repeating himself, he complimented

me on my Hungary and pointed out with a thick fingernail Budapest and the city of his birth, near the broad Y of borders where Hungary, Yugoslavia and Romania all meet. He sniffed. I worried he was going to cry.

The first siren of the city's year wee-wawed distantly. I took a drink. The room tilted. I closed and opened my eyes. Hideg said something I didn't quite catch.

'Sorry?'

He was still looking at the wall. I was focusing on the back of his head. There was a spot of pink there, like the seat of a small explosion from which wisps of grey curled out and away.

'I said,' he said to somewhere about the Kalahari, 'why have we never been able to get on together?'

I realized I had in fact heard him the first time. Even the second time, though, I wasn't ready for it. I shrugged to his back.

'Jill says we are too alike.' *Jill* says? So they had talked about me. Me and him. Us. 'But I don't believe that like-and-like stuff, except maybe in the science lab.'

Those last few words were so Hideg. No situation was too inauspicious for him not to parade a little of his knowledge. Was he trying to score points even now, reminding me he had been (*claimed* to have been) a university student in another life?

We were alike all right.

'We should have been the best of friends,' I said then caught myself on. 'Better neighbours, anyway.'

'That's for sure.'

Hideg turned and, forgetting himself – or perhaps reminding himself he had now spent more of his adult life here than there – clicked his cut-glass tumbler on mine.

'I thought that was bad luck.'

'Only with beer,' he said, 'between you and me. But it's a better story.'

'Ege-shay-shay?' I struggled to remember the toast.

'Egészségédre,' Hideg said. 'Your health.'

'Rodney!'

'I know.'

'That's five minutes already.'

'I know.'

'As long as you know,' Margaret sarked.

Margaret had said it was up to me whether I covered the wall or not. I didn't have to think about it for too long.

'We don't want anything getting in the way of a sale.'

I had taken a few pictures with the Instamatic. They looked like nothing, if I was being honest, though the blue of the seas was nice.

At the last moment before starting to paper, I dug out an old bit of crimson crayon from the tin ('The Tin') with the Sellotape and parcel string in it, and knelt by the bottom left-hand corner of the wall, between Chile and the Maria Theresa Reef.

'The World by Rodney McGovern,' I wrote and added the dates: 'October 1968 – March 1975'.

Well, it was more than most people left.

Alma had moved on to the brasses in the front bedroom, Garrulous Graham's room. Garruless. Garruleast. The older of the Post Office engineers rinsed the empty cups with water hot from a flask. I opened the window to stub my cigarette on the sill. The men whirled round, saw me, saw I was harmless, nodded. The learner driver was reversing round the corner by number 24. Stalled, restarted the engine, stalled it again. The engine revved.

Margaret shouted.

'For the last time, Rodney!'

Tan

EASILY RUN, CENTRALLY HEATED TERRACE RESIDENCE

ACCOMMODATION COMPRISES:
Entrance hall into:
Lounge: 11′4″ × 10′10″ Tiled fireplace. 'Rayburn' glass-fronted fire.
Kitchen: 11′2″ × 6′0″ Single-drainer sink unit with mixer taps. Range of recently fitted high and low cupboards. Access to understair storage.
Dinette: 11′2″ × 9′10″

FIRST FLOOR:
Landing: Hot press, copper cylinder and immersion heater. Access to roof space.
Bedroom 1: 11′2″ × 11′0″
Bedroom 2: 11′2″ × 9′10″ Range of built-in cupboards.
Bedroom 3: 7′10″ × 7′8″ Built-in cupboard.
Bathroom: White suite. Electric heater.

OUTSIDE:
Concrete paths and shared alleyway. Pleasant, well-tended gardens.

Solid-fuel central heating. Thermostatic valves to radiators and hot-water tank. Fitted Venetian blinds. Good decorative order throughout.

Don't believe us – have a look yourself!

It's the balloons that stick in my mind.

We were crouched on the stairs, my mother, my father, my little sisters and me, as the paper plate started to come through the letterbox, bent into a long U-shape. We could hear the people on the other side of the door, but apart from the two fingers pushing back the flap of the letterbox, we could not see them. The landing light was on, but the one in the hallway was not. The only other light was from the lamppost outside. In my memory it comes in with the paper plate through the letterbox. That was how I was able to tell, even though it was bent out of shape, that the plate had a blue trim and a pattern of clustered balloons, red, orange, yellow.

The letterbox flap resisted, the plate buckled a little more. I breathed the sharp smell of my mother's underarm, where the top of my head nestled. My pyjama jacket had come untucked and she tried to push the ends into the waistband of the trousers. Her fingers were cold and they trembled.

A length of cane slid along one side of the plate and pushed the flap to the full extent of its hinges. The cane was from our own garden. Only this morning – or perhaps it was yesterday, I had woken out of my night's sleep into this, I didn't know whether I was on one side of midnight or the other – I had helped my father transplant sunflowers and tie the stalks to lengths of cane with twist-its. Even without their blooms the sunflowers did not look like any other plants on the street.

A woman stopped at the garden wall to look at us.

'It isn't a vegetable patch,' she said.

'They're sunflowers,' said my father.

'I don't know what you're used with,' the woman carried on over the top of him, 'but if you want to grow vegetables in this country get an allotment.'

The plate tipped forward, more than halfway through now,

and then there was a second, stronger smell, a *stink*. My sisters pinched their noses, my father began softly to cry, drowned by the sound of feet running down the front path, of laughter, long-held, escaping, the letterbox snapping shut.

I watched the smeared plate follow its cargo to the hall carpet and already I knew that we would not talk about this, inside the house or out, any more than we talked about the piss-filled milk bottles left on the doorstep night after night, about the eggs thrown, about the uprooted plants the sunflowers were intended to replace. We would clean up again in silence and under cover of darkness and when the street awoke the neighbours would find us as we were when they – or most of them – went to sleep. Only in this way could we go on living among them, by not letting them see what was done to us.

I was seven that night spent on the stairs, but a very bright seven. You know what us Chink kids are like. Who's to say I didn't think those things?

'Hey, you, yella bake. Is this here the way your ma's fanny goes?'

Little fingers trailing his mouth into a long, joyless grin, mates smirking beside him and behind.

'What would you know?'

Lets go the corners of his mouth, pulls his fingers into fists. 'What do you mean, what would I know?'

'I mean,' I said, seeing nowhere in the playground to run, but thinking if I could keep this up till the bell went I was doing OK, 'what would you know?'

And that was the last I said before he hit me. A big dig under the ribs. The wind went out of me. My breakfast followed.

'I know your ma buys Rice Krispies.'

A few days later the same blond boy caught me up on the way from school. He wore his tie in an enormous knot. His jumper hung like a sling from his waist.

'Seriously,' he said. 'What way do they go, Chinky fannies?'

He said it was all right to call him Tit. His proper name was Roy. Roy Stitt. If he didn't like you, or didn't know you well enough, he'd take the head off you for calling him Tit. Or Roy's. He hated Roy's far more than Tit.

'Never mind me in school,' he said. 'See me in school? All's I do is rake. It's this fucking name. It's either rake or act the hard man.'

And he hit me a dig that had no power in it.

'I'm telling you, Tan, you don't know how lucky you are.'

He said he'd see me around. It would have been hard for him to miss me: he lived at the bottom of my street, though he had a whole pile of older brothers he preferred to knock about with. (Their hair was less fair the taller they got.) Then one day I was sitting on the kerb at my end of the street, firing stones at the kerb opposite, and he came walking up and sat down and started firing stones with me.

'Where're your brothers the day?'

'Fuck knows.'

He fired a round stone that clanged against the lamp-post's metal door.

'Fancy going for a dander?' he said.

We never said let's be friends.

We walked to school at the same time as one another every morning. We walked home at the same time every afternoon. When we were eleven we left primary school and went to different schools down the town, but we still caught the bus together, kept seats coming home, sitting either side of the aisle with our backs to the windows, our feet up, on the lookout for the inspector getting on.

In the evenings if it wasn't raining we dandered the streets. There were twelve streets in all round our way. Tit and I walked every inch of them time after time, after time.

One morning while we were standing in the bus shelter on the main road Tit pulled out a black marker. I let on I wasn't looking at what he was writing. He let on he couldn't care either way.

Tit'n'Tan.

He drew a scroll around it, like the scrolls you'd see on paramilitary wall paintings right across the city, like we were a two-man army ourselves.

FTA, he wrote underneath. Fuck them all.

I was lucky not to get a hiding next time my mother was down the town.

'Right there in the bus shelter. Our name,' she said. 'What will people think when they see it?'

'How many Tans do you think there are around here?' my father added.

Not as many as there are Tits, that's for sure.

'What?' he said.

'Nothing.'

My father had spent much of his life here and in England, but up until the year she married him my mother lived in Hong Kong, a city ten times the size of this, a hundred times as varied. English was one of four languages she spoke, but sometimes she had difficulty understanding people here ('what is it they *do* to words?') so that she began to doubt her own intelligence and lapsed into something close to pidgin.

One day when she was at home with a sick headache there was a knock at the door. She almost didn't answer, but the knocking went on and on, louder and louder, and in the end she could bear it no more.

A man stood on the step. The doorstep was not a place where my mother expected to see a man in the daytime other than one who wanted to sell her something. And this man had a thick ginger moustache and wore a green hat with a feather in the band, a grey sports jacket over a purple shirt and a brown and orange tie. My mother wanted to shield her eyes. Even before he opened his mouth she felt at a disadvantage. She would have bought whatever he had to offer just to be spared having to look at him.

But the man was not interested in selling. He said he had come to see the house. My mother asked him what for, but he already had one foot in the hall. He tapped the skirting board as he passed through with the side of his ox-blood brogue. He walked into the living room and flicked the light switch up and down. My mother turned to close the front door, changed her mind, and came into the living room as the man exited to the kitchen.

'Please,' she said and he said, 'These units in long?'

'Please,' my mother said again. Her head was throbbing. 'Husband not home.'

'That a fact?' The man had a pair of glasses in his hand that he held up to his eyes as he opened the cupboard door over the sink and looked inside. His face said he didn't care much for what he saw. He returned the glasses to his breast pocket, left the cupboard door ajar.

My mother had to stretch to close it. The man had started on the cupboards under the sink. She laid a hand on his sleeve.

'I must ask you, leave now.'

The man looked at her hand, shook his arm and rubbed his sleeve where she had touched it.

'Listen,' he said, 'I took time out of work to come here. Are you going to let me look around or not?'

He was walking back through the living room with my mother behind him.

'Why?' she kept asking. '*Why?*'

He stopped in the hallway with his foot on the bottom stair.

'You're not in bloody China now, you know. You want to sell this place you've got to let people in to view it.'

'Sell?' my mother said.

'Number 5?' the man asked.

'Yes, number 5, but not for sale.'

'Oh, for God's sake,' said the man and carried on up the stairs.

Through the open front door my mother saw Mrs Moore come down her path. She ran outside waving her arms. 'Help,' she said. 'Make him leave.'

They found the man trying out the bathroom taps.

'You the translator?' he asked Mrs Moore and flushed the toilet.

'What do you think you're playing at?' she asked him back.

He pulled from his inside pocket a sheet of newspaper folded in four. The property page. He pointed to a small ad. My mother caught sight of the address as Mrs Moore read aloud.

'Inside terrace house, no reasonable offer refused. (Death in family.)'

My mother fainted.

'What, really fainted? Like fell right down on the ground?'

I had been giving Tit the edited highlights.

'*Yeah*. Well, against the wall anyway,' I said, wondering now whether there'd actually be room to faint with three people in our bathroom. 'Sort of slid down it.'

I let my head loll, my tongue hang loose.

'That's wild,' Tit said. 'Bet your man felt wick.'

These were very carefully edited highlights, no mention of death in the family. I was playing it strictly for laughs. Tit laughed, so that was OK.

Next time I saw him, though, he told me that if anyone did give our family serious grief he'd knock their melt in. What was I going to say? That I used to see his big brother Sid creeping away from our doorstep at dead of night doing up his flies? That the party plate that carried the shit through our letterbox when I was a kid was identical to the ones I saw sitting in a box by his own bin the other year when his ma had a big kitchen clearout?

'Dead on,' I said.

We had dandered to the limit of the twelve streets tonight and squeezed through the gap where the houses ended and the electricity transformer had not quite begun, feeling our way along the railings until we came out at the manky old pond next to the haunted farm. We lobbed rocks into the dark water. *Plump.* We argued over the water's depth.

'You could drown a horse.'

'You couldn't drown a cat.'

'Bollocks.'

'Bollocks you.'

'Donkey bollocks you.'

'Elephant bollocks.'

'King Kong bollocks.'

'Tyrannosaurus Rex bollocks.'

'*Puff the Magic Dragon bollocks.*'

'Ha! Loser.'

'Loser how?'

'Tyrannosaurus Rex is bigger than Puff the Magic Dragon any day.'

'Bollocks.'

We were not always such energetic conversationalists. Often at the end of an evening I could not remember a single thing we had said. We spat a lot.

For a change of scenery we would walk down the Low Road and out on to the main road. We wrote our names. Tit'n'Tan. On bollards, on shutters, on rubbish bins bracketed to lamp-posts, in shorthand on the brackets themselves. T'n'T.

Dynamite.

'Know where's mad?' Tit said to me this other night, replacing the lid of the black marker.

'Where?'

'Fucking Iran.'

Iran had been in the news for the past three or four years. I wondered whether he had not been watching till now.

'See even doing this?' Tit had his red and purple markers out. 'They'd cut your hands off.'

Our names on this occasion were to be wrapped in a flag entirely of Tit's devising. Next thing we'd be getting our own national anthem.

'It's not like we're doing anyone any harm,' I said.

Tit paused, looked at me, turned again to colour in the background of his flag.

'Cunts.'

I spat.

'They wouldn't put up with us at all,' he said.

★

'Speak to him,' my mother urged my father. 'It's everywhere I look now. Tan, Tan, Tan. Like a finger pointing back at us.'

∞

The smiling, red-haired girl from my French class had just offered to undo her bra when my father appeared at my side telling me we were going to build a snooker room.

We were big fans of *Pot Black*, the two of us, but really there was a time and a place.

'Dad,' I said, 'not now.'

'Come on,' he said. 'A hobby will help occupy your hands.'

Clearly he hadn't seen the red-haired girl in her underwear. *I* couldn't see her now. I squeezed my eyes, blinked them open.

My father made a grab for the bed covers.

'Come on, up, up! Let's get to work.'

It was eight o'clock, the second week of the school holidays. Only the willing girl from my French class was a dream. I held the covers tight until my father had left the room, until I could move in bed without risk of part of me snapping off, then I walked out on to the landing in the yellow satin Adidas shorts that were my summer pyjamas.

'You're not serious? A snooker room?' I called over the banister. 'Where?'

My father came out of the front bedroom behind me carrying a saw. I had no idea where he could have got it. I had never in my life known my father to use a saw. In his other hand he held a tape measure and he tossed me this as we went back into the boxroom.

'Here,' he said, pointing with the saw at the door of the built-in cupboard.

Even more than snooker on TV, my father liked comedy programmes. He fancied he was a bit of a joker himself.

(He was the storeman in the cash and carry my mother managed. I had heard him when he was at work, speeding around on his bashed-up forklift, whistling the same song over and over. 'Starman'. That's how funny he was.)

I was still too sleepy to raise a laugh. I looked at the bedclothes and thought about wrapping myself in them again. I thought about the dream I'd been having that prevented me getting out of bed straight away.

My father had opened the cupboard door and was gathering armfuls of clothes on hangers. I panicked. This was my cupboard. There were things in there I did not want anyone, least of all my father, to see. My father threw clothes and hangers across the bed. I didn't even ask now what he was doing. I started to empty the bottom of the cupboard, where I kept my school bag and shoe boxes and magazines.

'Let me,' I said. 'I'll call you when I've finished.'

'No need to call.'

I could have been storing guns in there for all the notice my father took. He had already begun sawing into one end of the clothes rail.

'Wait,' I said. 'Wait. Where are the plans?'

Sawdust coated the last plastic bag, which I removed and clutched to my chest.

He made a sound of mock indignation. 'Fathers don't need plans. It's all part of our knowledge.' He tapped the side of his head. 'It's an instinct.'

This bit at least was a joke. He sent me into the front bedroom, where I found a jotter with all the measurements written neatly in pencil. A staircase so long and so wide to run at such and such an angle from the floor of the boxroom cupboard to the roof space. Only thing was, it wasn't my father's handwriting.

Of course not, he told me. The Watsons next door had built a staircase in their cupboard, the measurements were the same. Like the tools, which for the rest of the day and the days that followed miraculously appeared at the precise moment they became essential to the task in hand.

I didn't mind having to work. The weather wasn't up to much.

'There are no seasons guaranteed in this country,' my father told me on the third morning, over the sound of his own drilling. 'November, April, July ... always be prepared to entertain yourself indoors.'

The weather was duff and Tit was away. Half the street was away. The Twelfth Fortnight. Light a bonfire to celebrate going to Torremolinos. We never went anywhere. We were saving for a family trip to Hong Kong, or that at least was what my sisters and I had been told.

Mrs Moore returned from her holiday every year the colour of Bombay duck. She had a sun lamp upstairs, which all through the spring rimmed the front bedroom window ultra-violet, turning the blinds into a great big blank screen. It was hard not to project on to it thoughts of what she was up to – or down to – behind the blinds.

Since the previous summer there had been a painting on one wall of the Moores' bedroom of a dark-haired woman. The first day I saw it, lying on my bed, chin resting on the windowsill, I had mistaken it for Mrs Moore herself looking back at me. It was a week before I dared peek across the street again. The woman in the painting had bare shoulders, a long slender neck, one arm bent behind her head. Dancing maybe, or something else entirely.

A short time later, I had conducted an experiment. I closed the Venetian blind then tilted it open, millimetre by millimetre, until the painting had just come into clear view. I placed a football on the windowsill with a book behind it to keep it from rolling off. Then I went out. I messed around in the garden and on the footpath, I kicked a can into the road and followed after it, kicking again. When I had reached the Moores' wall, I glanced up at my own window. I couldn't make out the ball at all.

Yes.

It was only when I was coming out of our alleyway the next day, still feeling pleased with myself, that I noticed the identical tilt of the blinds in the Robertsons' big front bedroom.

I knew from Tit that this was Graham's room. 'Graham the bin-hoker', as Tit called him. Graham worked for the council, sweeping streets.

'I don't care if he does get paid for it,' Tit said, 'he still hokes bins.'

Tit told me he remembered the Robertsons getting their Venetians. The house played peek-a-boo as one at a time the old yellowed roll blinds came off and the aluminium ones went up in their place. He told me he had been looking from our side of the road, from on top of our wall, and had seen right into the big front bedroom. There were pennants and things on the wall like a kid would have.

'Worse than that,' he said, lowering his voice, 'there were pictures of wee lads beside his bed.'

'What sort of wee lads?'

'Just wee lads, in their school uniforms and stuff.'

Our wall was about two feet high. If this had all happened before I came here to live, Tit couldn't have been a lot taller himself.

'Sure, there's no way you could have seen that much.'

'Who said I seen it all? The fella that did the blinds was a mate of my da's. I heard him saying.'

'Aye,' I said. 'Right.'

Tit spat. 'So don't believe me.'

I had never known whether to believe him or not, but it made my skin crawl anyway as I stood at the end of the alley to think Graham might be behind his lightly tilted blinds looking out.

Never mind what I was doing in my own small room. I was fourteen then, I had a recently acquired masturbation regime to maintain and a bedroom opposite a painting of a bare-shouldered Spanish woman and all that that suggested. Graham Robertson was pushing forty.

After the guts of five days working, my father and I had the staircase completed into the roof space. My mother and sisters took turns walking up it, my sisters holding on to my father's shirt, because there was as yet no back to the stairs, so that you could see between them into the main stairwell.

At the top of the steps a new light switch had been connected and a bare bulb shone on a causeway of chipboard leading back to the original trapdoor entrance above the landing. My father now covered this trapdoor too. When he had hammered in the final nail he smiled with real pride and satisfaction. I smiled back at him across the causeway. It was late in the afternoon. He said that would do us for the day. Tomorrow we would start in again refreshed.

The next morning, though, started out sunny and got sunnier. It was hot under the eaves, much too hot to work. The day after that was another belter and the day after that Tit was home and the cash and carry had reopened.

Long into the autumn, if I opened the cupboard door in my

room, I could look into the hall below. My father boarded it in eventually. I begged him while he was at it, as I had been begging him since I was seven years old, to strip the pink patterned paper off the walls in my room, but whatever the paper was glued on with it threatened to take the plaster with it and in the end he slapped a couple of rolls of woodchip over the top and painted it white. We didn't get round to finishing flooring the roof space. We didn't get a snooker table. I wasn't holding my breath waiting on us ever getting to Hong Kong.

My mother had a sister in the east of the city. She and my uncle owned a restaurant called – guess what? – the Far East. One Sunday a month we crossed town to see them. Some Sundays other relatives, from up the north coast, came to join us. A section of the restaurant was reserved for family and friends. Sunday nights were quiet nights for restaurants here anyway. For most things. A few young men walked in out of the dark and sat at the tables nearest the door waiting for takeaways. I think they were disturbed to see so many of us in one place – there could be fifteen, twenty, sometimes more – and I imagined them waking in sweats from dreams where their world was reversed and they were the odd men out, the curiosities.

I enjoyed these Sunday nights, though in many ways I felt less like myself with my cousins than I did with Tit. I enjoyed the wonton noodles. I enjoyed the smell of the French cigarettes my uncle smoked and listening to the grown-ups talk. At times of the year, perhaps for the benefit of all of us cousins, the talk was of the long, long-ago, ancestors and other ancient stuff – completely mad, some of it – taller than Tit's tales. Mostly though they gossiped about their own old days.

My aunt had no end of stories about my mother, who said

that if there weren't impressionable teenagers present she could have told plenty of stories back.

'Tell us,' we impressionable teenagers said. 'Tell us.'

A story she did tell was about her and my father when they were first married and living in Liverpool in a flat above another relative's restaurant. A man had burst in on them one night wielding a hammer.

People round the table nodded, knowing what was coming. Everywhere you went there were men for whom getting a hammer and Doing a Chinky was as uncomplicated a source of cash as collecting the deposit on Coke bottles was for me.

'Where's all your money?' this man with this hammer said.

And my father said, 'Barclay's Bank.'

The man hesitated, raised the hammer higher.

'Don't get cute.'

My father, during the telling of this, looked a little bashful to have been called – even by a man, even in the course of an attempted robbery – cute.

'I'm not being cute,' he said.

'I was saving up to come here, buy a house,' he said to us. 'I put every penny straight into the bank.'

'The robber's face . . .' my mother said and couldn't go on for laughing, couldn't have been heard, had she been able to go on, for the laughter of others.

When it finally died down I tried asking what happened with the man and his hammer, but my father waved the question away, caught my uncle's eye, tapped his glass with the flat of his index finger.

My father on these nights allowed himself a couple of lagers. Maybe more than a couple. I occasionally moved a glass from beside him and replaced it with one less full. My sisters were avid viewers of public-information films. They were learning through them the wicked ways of our world. It was my sisters who had impressed upon me the perils of drink-driving, though what scared me most was not that my father would get us killed, but that he would get himself sent to jail. You didn't need to be a brain surgeon to know that prison here was not a smart place to be Chinese in.

Unless maybe you were Tommy Yoo.

Tommy Yoo I had never met – he always seemed to have left the restaurant five minutes before we arrived – but he was a living legend in the Far East. He drank in bars where para-militaries hung out. He sold cheap cigarettes, cheap watches, cheap whatever else you wanted. He was so well known, my uncle joked, that people all over the east of the city called out when he passed, 'Hey, Yoo there!'

Tommy Yoo was trouble, said my father, who would normally have gone to great lengths to avoid it.

When I reminded him of the drink-driving limit, however, he lifted the emptier glass I had left by his elbow and told me he was fine, the police here had too many other things to occupy them.

I was just glad that the roads on a Sunday night once the churches got out were so quiet there was nothing for him to hit.

Tit told me he fancied one of my cousins. She had been over staying with my sisters one night when he called. He stared past me through the open living-room door.

'You kept her quiet,' he said.

She was my kid cousin, she hadn't struck me as anything to shout about.

For days after, Tit never gave over, moaning and getting on. In the end I had to tell him to away and wise up.

'What do you think your ma and da would say?'

'You don't mean to tell me she's a Taig?' Tit said.

I laughed along with my friend, though in fact that's exactly what my cousin was: what I was, if I was anything. Not that it would have occurred to anyone to ask. People in this city seemed to think Chinese was a religion in its own right.

Still, I wasn't complaining.

I'd picked up something over the years of what went on in these streets in the Seventies, the families who moved out. 'Tension' was the word that was used. Like a letterbox forced to the full extent of its spring.

Mr Hideg down the street assured me that, really, a lot of what you heard said about those times was an exaggeration. It was not Cyprus, he said, not the Lebanon.

Mr Hideg walked to the bakery on the main road every Saturday morning to buy soda bread and potato bread for his lunchtime fry. The bakery was next door to the newsagent's where I was sent each Saturday to pay the weekly papers.

The clientele of the cluster of shops was very different from the one I saw on weekday afternoons when I was coming home from school. Saturday morning was the men's time. They stood talking outside the newsagent's, their papers folded open at the sports pages. They came and went from the barber's, like wasps in and out of a hole in the hedge. Many of them carried blue and white bags of soda and potato bread. No other kind of shopping. There was nothing sissy about a fry-up.

I tried not to leave the house at any set time, hoping in this way to avoid bumping into Mr Hideg every week. He was friendly enough, but it was a fifteen-minute walk from the shops and friendly or not he was still an adult and fifteen was a large number of minutes to fill with talking.

But it didn't seem to matter what time I left. More Saturday mornings than not, as I came out of the newsagent's, the receipt for that week's papers in my fist, there would be a knock from inside the bakery window and there would be Mr Hideg, gesturing to me to wait so that we could walk up the road together.

If something had happened the day before, an explosion or a shooting, he read out the report from the newspaper, shaking his head.

'Terrible, terrible,' he said. His English made me think of the way a rubber glove sometimes felt on your hand, almost too good a fit. 'But nothing to what your father and mother must have had to live through.'

Mr Hideg appeared to have got it into his head that my parents were some early version of boat people. This might have been why he had taken a shine to me. We were anti-Communist brothers under the skin.

Mr Hideg had his own business, 'plumbing merchandise', which Tit said was a polite way of saying he sold bogs. Tit reckoned he was worth a mint. I found this hard to believe. All right, he'd had a garage built and an extension connecting it to his kitchen, but apart from that – and the Wild West wooden shutters he'd put around all his windows – his house didn't look much different from the other semis on the street.

Maybe if he could have been bothered to open to the public on Saturday mornings . . .

'Work to live,' he told me, 'don't live to work.'

What it really was, Tit said, he was stashing his money away for when the Americans nuked the Russians and he was able to go back and buy himself an entire village in Hungary.

'Sure he is,' I said.

And he and Mrs Hideg used to have wife-swapping parties in their house. And Graham Robertson was a sex offender.

'Sure he is.'

The summer of the GCEs, Tit went off to Malta with his parents and I wound up in the Far East six days out of seven, lunch right through to mid evening, waiting tables and helping out when called on in the kitchen. By the end of the first fortnight I had sixty quid in my pocket, but no time to spend it and no one to spend it with even if I had. I was scalp to sole cooking smells and so browned off it just wasn't true.

Tit came home with his hair bleached by the Maltese sun and a great big grin plastered across his suntanned chops.

'OK, what's her name?' I asked him, half in jest.

'Maria,' he said and my heart sank.

She was two years older than him, worked behind the counter of a souvenir shop in Valletta. Tit had gone into the shop on his second day there and fancied her straight off, only there was some old doll who ran the place, Maria's great-aunt or something, watching her like a hawk.

'This isn't a park for strolling in,' the old doll said, shooing Tit with the tips of her fingers. 'Buy or bye-bye.'

('Like she thought that was fucking hilarious,' Tit said.)

Maria bit her lovely lip.

Tit went back every day hoping to find her on her own. He showed me the stuff he'd bought: pencils, biros, decks of playing cards, nail clippers, keyrings, all kinds of crap with the Maltese Cross stuck on.

'Must have left two-thirds of my holiday money in there.'

He bought so many postcards he was stuffing them down gratings, skimming them off the sea wall. Then just when he was beginning to despair, on his second-last day, Maria handed him a note folded small with his change. Written on it was the name of a café. Maria had drawn him a little map and a circle with hands pointing to eight o'clock.

They drank Pepsi out of glasses with Fanta on the sides. They walked together from the east harbour to the west, up and down the steep streets of Mount Sceberras. (Valletta developed for me frame by frame as Tit continued with his story.) When it was time for him to return to the apartment where his family was staying, Maria put her arms around his neck and spoke his name an inch from his ear. Roy. He got goosebumps again just telling me this. She lumbered him then for about twenty minutes straight, pressing up against him so hard he thought he was going to come right there in his pants.

And that was all. And it was because that was all that I believed him. And I suppose it was because I wanted to have something of my own to tell him that I invented the story I found myself coming out with about Graham Robertson trying to fruit me up.

'What? He actually touched you?'

Tit had flown into a rage. I was back-pedalling.

'No . . . it was just the way he was looking at me.'

'*Looking at you?*'

I worried that I had back-pedalled too far too fast, that Tit was beginning to suspect I was spoofing. Which I was, I knew, though I had seen Graham Robertson one day while Tit was away, when I was coming home from work. He sort of jerked his head as he passed on the other side of the street, did something with his face.

'He winked,' I said, watching for a change in Tit's sceptical expression. There was none. 'Winked and nodded at his house, you know, like, come on inside.'

Tit at last shook his head. 'The fruity bastard,' he whispered. 'Maybe he can't help himself. I mean maybe he's soft in the head.' I'd had all the reaction I needed. I thought this would be the right tack to take over the next few days until Tit got his first letter from Maria or something else happened and he let the subject drop. 'Sure, what about the football pennants and all that? He is, he's soft.'

The following night a piece of broken glass was scraped down the side of Mr Robertson's Mini Clubman, from head-light to tail light. One of the rear tyres was ripped right open.

Joyriders, people on the street were saying. There had been a couple of car thefts in and around the twelve streets in recent weeks. The joyriders were thought to be coming in from other areas. They had no respect. What they couldn't steal, they vandalized. Like Mr Robertson's difficult-to-steal, joyrider-must-have Mini Clubman, obviously.

My parents were agreed it was a disgrace. Indeed, for people who had once borne in silence shit shoved through their letterbox, they discussed the incident at great length.

Tit and I didn't say a word about it to each other.

I got eight GCEs out of eight and went into the sixth form. Tit got three GCEs and a one in his CSEs and signed on to do resits at the College of Knowledge in the centre of town. On his first day there him and half a dozen guys he knew from his old school piled into a bar near the college for a lunchtime drink. They turned up for afternoon classes bumping into doors, muxing ip their words, and nobody batted an eyelid.

He didn't come home at all after college on Friday after-noon. I saw him at teatime on Saturday. He was still hung-over. There was a disco on tonight he was thinking of going to, a private party in a hotel bar. He asked me did I want to come.

Yeah, right, me trying to get in the doors of a hotel bar. Who was the first person they were going to ask for i.d.?

I wouldn't say he was exactly broken-hearted when I turned down the offer.

He let me know about another party, almost as an afterthought it seemed to me, in the middle of the next week when we met up for a dander. Again I got the feeling he was relieved when I said I couldn't go. He didn't even bother to ask when he went out at the weekend. A couple of days later, when I bumped into him on the street, I told him I was too busy with homework to go for a dander after dinner.

'Suit yourself,' he said.

My sisters wanted to join a church youth club on the city side of the main-road shops. All their friends went. My mother was dead set against it. We were not members of this particular church, we were not even members of the Protestant faith. My sisters told her it didn't matter. It was a youth club, they didn't have theological bouncers on the door. (My sisters were in their second and third years at grammar school, they enjoyed parading their vocabularies.) Besides, Mr Newton, who had recently moved into number 19, helped to run the club and he said it was OK. Mr Newton looked incapable of speaking an untruth. My mother, though, was still uncertain. Saturday night was my father's late night in the stores. My sisters would have to walk there, even if not back. You never knew who was out on that main road at night. She didn't want anything said or done to upset her daughters. Her daughters went into a fearsome double huff until finally she said they could go, so long as I accompanied them the first week. This satisfied nobody, but my mother would not be swayed; either I went or my sisters did not.

'Maybe Roy will go too,' she said.

Dream on, mother.

It was not quite dark when we left the house, the sort of smoky early-autumn dusk that even at sixteen could make you feel nostalgic. My sisters and their three school friends, mini Madonnas in their leggings and charity-shop dresses, linked braceleted arms. I walked a good ten yards behind them, but the chain was so wayward, so inclined to collapse in fits of laughter, that in the end I overtook and strode out in front.

When I was a wee lad, the Low Road, where you turned on to it from our streets, was just a few big houses sitting in their massive gardens, the odd one with a brand-new wall around it, other houses built on the outside smaller and closer together. Then the road was widened and, a couple of years later, widened again and even the newer houses had lost ground. The older houses were mostly offices now and you got the feeling that someone somewhere had forgotten there were people living here at all. You had to really crane your neck to see to the tops of the lamp-posts. Their lights at this hour of the day were pink and sherbety-looking. Cars bombed up and down beneath them like they were doing time trials.

I passed the old doctor's surgery, now a chemist's, next to the new flat-roofed health centre, and passed the entrance to the industrial estate which had opened last year and which named among its tenants, listed on a blue and white display board, me and Tit. FTA.

As I turned right on to the main road I saw five guys – eighteen, nineteen, older than me anyway, bigger – come out of the off-licence across the way with bulging bags of drink. They were already swaggering drunk. They planted themselves in the middle of the footpath to light cigarettes, like they thought they owned the place.

There was a Tit and a Tan on the wall of the off-licence, another in a red and purple flag on the side of the waste-paper bin that they didn't even attempt to get their cigarette wrappers into.

I walked on. Let them think what they liked. Fuck them.

Then I remembered the girls. I looked over my shoulder. Higgledy-giggledy here they came, all unconcerned, strung out along the footpath. The guys across the street found a new focus. The girls at the last minute reined themselves in and choked back their laughter . . . nearly. One stray titter was all it took. The next thing the guys had hefted their bags of beer and were wading into the Saturday-night traffic.

'Come here, love, a minute, I want you.'

'Hi, you, blondie, he's talking to you.'

Up on to the other footpath now.

'She's a lezzie.'

'Cock-tease.'

'What about your mates, Madame Mao and Madame Mao the Second?'

Oh, boy. Madame Mao and Madame Mao the Second. That must have stretched their brains.

I was still walking forward, glancing back. I was telling myself that my getting involved was not going to make things better; quite the opposite, in fact. As long as it got no worse than taunting, I reasoned, I would keep my distance. At which point one of the guys shook a beer can and aimed it in the girls' direction as he tugged the ring-pull. A frothing jet broke into spray above their heads. Amid the shrieks another can was shaken and opened. My sisters and their friends were running, the guys behind them hardly even bothering to shake the cans any more, just launching them at the girls' backs. I was running too, faster than any of them, away from the shops and their lights towards the brown silhouette of the church, thinking I'd have to get help, but I didn't know when I got there which of the outlying buildings the youth club was in. I ran up one side of the church and down the other, looking for an open door. By the time I came round to the front again the girls were in the church grounds and the guys who had been chasing them were nowhere to be seen.

'We were too fast for them,' the elder sister said.

'They were too fat for us,' said the younger.

One of the friends was coiling strands of blonde hair from the back of her head and holding them under her nose.

'Eugh!' she said, letting go that handful and coiling another. 'Disgusting.'

I sat on the steps under the notice of the week's services to get my breath back.

My younger sister came over, put her arm around my shoulder. 'I won't tell if you won't,' she said.

I shrugged off her arm. 'Tell who what? I was only running to find help.'

And my sister nodded. 'There was nothing you could do,' she said. 'Absolutely nothing.'

Some time in the dead hours of the following morning the Robertsons lost a living-room window. All up and down the street people stirred but didn't come fully awake, or so they said when they gathered in the bone-white light of sunny autumn day to lend a hand cleaning up the mess or simply to gawk at the apple-sized lump of concrete that had landed on the Robertsons' carpet, thinking no doubt that these were some very pissed-off and vengeful joyriders.

I found Tit sitting on the kerb looking the worse for wear. I crouched down beside him, nervous.

'What were you up to last night?'

'Your guess is as good as mine.' Fuck, but he reeked. 'First I knew I was even home was when I woke there now.'

A glazier's van pulled up, a plate of glass lashed to the wooden frame on its left side. George Moore hopped down from the passenger's door in a navy boiler suit, strutted up the Robertsons' path like he was the cavalry. He took after his father in looks and build, his mother in height.

'What's he like,' I said out the corner of my mouth. 'The turn-ups on that boiler suit.'

Tit nodded absently.

George had kids of his own, which of course, though you'd never have thought it to look at her, made Mrs Moore a granny, which in turn made some of my window-blind projections particularly perverted. The eldest wee lad, Young George, was in primary school and was already only a couple of inches shorter than his da and his granny both.

'Look at him looking at you,' Tit said.

I looked to see who it was was looking. Graham Robertson stood on the doorstep of number 6 in his slippers. I turned my head. 'He's not looking over here at all,' I said, but he was looking all right. Looking right at me.

'Aye, well he better fucking watch it,' Tit said, 'or he'll get something more than a stone through his window.'

I told him to keep his voice down, to be careful what he was saying, but Tit wouldn't heed me.

'What do I want to be whispering for? I've done nothing. I'm only saying, there's worse things can happen.'

★

Oh, this was unbearable.

My father was wiping the tears from his cheeks. It was Tuesday night and Tuesday night was *Terry and June* night. Of all comedy programmes, my father liked sitcoms best, and of all sitcoms there was none he liked better than *Terry and June*. And when my father laughed enough, he cried. Tonight he had started chuckling at the theme tune and built from there. My mother smiled from time to time, trying to keep him company. My sisters competed with one another which could look the more bored. I was struggling to keep up with what was being said on-screen. I felt as though my ears were on back-to-front, so that the sound of the world beyond the window was louder than that inside, louder even than Terry and June and their tearful one-man fan club. My stomach gurgled. I hadn't eaten much at dinner. I hadn't eaten much the last couple of days.

'Stop that,' my mother said. She was speaking to me. For a split second I thought she meant the gurgling then realized I had my hand at my mouth, my fingertips between my teeth. I jerked the hand away in some surprise, leaving behind a sliver of nail. My father dabbed his eyes. My sisters turned theirs, bright with interest now, towards me.

'That's I don't know how many times,' said my mother. 'You will have no nails left. Is that what you want?'

I said nothing.

My mother shook her head. 'Such lovely hands you have. I don't know what's got into you.'

Behind tightly closed lips I gripped the nail in my teeth, pushing my tongue against one sharp point. It hurt. I pushed again. My father laughed and hiccuped, my mother was drawn back to the television. My sisters' attention remained riveted on me. I pretended to scratch my nose and gave them the fingers. They pulled their exaggerated 'I'm telling' faces in the hope that my parents would notice, but they didn't reckon on June driving off just then with Terry (a very sack-like Terry in long-shot) clinging to the car roof. Their faces relaxed, the credits rolled, my father when he was able to speak said one of these days he would buy us a video recorder so that we could watch our favourite programmes any time we wanted. Watch *Terry and June*, he meant.

The younger of my sisters was waiting for me later on the landing as I came out of the bathroom.

'We know what's got into you,' she said and backed through their bedroom door, as though afraid I was going to make a lunge for her.

'There's nothing to know, you're talking out your arse,' I told her, but she kept backing into the room and I kept walking towards her. When I was over the threshold my other sister, hidden till then, closed the door, pressing her full weight against it.

'What's this?' I asked. 'Charlie's Chinese Angels?'

Shite, I know, as bad as the beer boys, but I was still trying to decide whether it was better to pretend to my sisters I couldn't care less about their suspicions of me or to appease them.

Appease, maybe. I took a packet of Juicy Fruit from my pocket.

'Want some?' I asked. They did. I unwrapped a stick for myself and looked for a clear space to sit.

The room contained two single beds either side of the window below which was a long desk, rarely used for the purpose intended (my sisters did their homework sitting on the floor), and a fold-down metal-framed chair-cum-clothes-horse. Facing the door, the wardrobe had been disembowelled.

There were several species of undigested stuffed animal in the entrails. I sat in the end where I had been standing.

'You're on drugs,' said the sister at my back.

I was turning to her, aghast, when the sister in front said, 'We saw an information film.'

'At school.'

'We recognize the signs.'

'Nervous, distracted.'

'Biting your nails.'

'Neglecting hygiene.'

'Hey,' I said. It was a touchy subject. 'I wash every day. Where do you think I was there now?'

Sister-shrugs.

'But you have been biting your nails, you're not denying any of the rest of it.'

I covered my face with my hands. I didn't want to laugh, not yet. Who knew how useful this might be? The twin single beds gave separate sighs as one after the other sister sank down on them.

'What is it you're on?'

'Hash? Speed?'

I nodded twice.

'Acid? Coke?'

A nod, a not-quite shake. An intake of breath from the elder sister.

'Anything else?'

Don't push it.

'No,' I said, quietly, behind my hands.

In the near silence that followed I could hear a small wristwatch tick, like a bird's heart, trapped. I hoped I hadn't pushed it too far already.

'Dad will –' *kill* me would have been too obviously out of

character, 'have a fit if he finds out. Why do you think he wanted us to grow up here and not England or Hong Kong? It would wreck him.'

I had taken my hands away from my face now, persuaded by my own selflessness. I made a direct appeal to each of my sisters in turn.

'Promise me you won't say anything and I promise I will try to get . . . clean.'

Their mouths were open when they nodded their assent. I could see the chewing gum barely juiced on their tongues. I picked myself up, imagining aching limbs. I rubbed my arms as though chilled to the marrow.

I stopped with my hand on the door handle.

'Dead secret, right?'

Again they nodded.

'Yous are brilliant, do you know that?'

I listened for a few moments on the landing side of the door. Not one word did my sisters speak.

It had been decided to set up a neighbourhood-watch scheme, like they had across the water. This, so far as I could tell, involved getting a couple of plaques made with a picture on them of a giant eye and lashing them to telegraph poles at either end of the street. Mr Blake seemed to be the principal organizer, perhaps because he trailed Billy, his decrepit Jack Russell, between these two posts every night as it was. For a couple of weeks he trailed the dog from pole to pole with extra purpose, usually in the company of one or more male neighbour. My father took his turn out there with him.

(He came in and went straight up the stairs. I found him in my room studying the joins of the woodchip. 'What's the matter?' I asked. He tapped the wall, shrugged his shoulders, turned out the light.)

If there was a noise of any sort in the street after half past ten, twenty-three doors would open and a lone voice would call from somewhere.

'It's all right, only me! Knocked the milk bottles over.' Or, 'Forgot my key again.'

At least though for a couple of weeks my appetite returned to something like normal. My sisters gave me surreptitious looks of encouragement across the table. I made a show of steeling my jaw, struggled another mouthful . . . and another.

Then we had two days of high winds and hailstorms, during which the giant eyes were torn free from their moorings. When the storms had passed, Mr Blake went back to the nightly dog-trail on his own.

∞

Sirens. Eye-opening, heart-accelerating, nearer-drawing, nearer . . .

I knew before they arrived that they must stop in our street. The clock by my bed read a quarter to two. I fumbled a V-shaped gap in the blind, through which to see a fire engine spotlit by a three-quarter moon come to an untidy halt on the road before the Robertsons' front path. Smoke poured out of the alleyway between their house and number 4. Already there were neighbours on the street, overcoats thrown on every which way. I picked out the Blakes, Mr Moore. Billy the dog tucked what tail he had between his legs and shook his back end, shook himself over. My mother and father were moving around on the other side of the wall from me, pulling open cupboards and drawers. I swung my legs off the edge of the bed. They were trembling. I found shoes on the floor, but no socks. I slipped my feet in even so. The shoes felt as though they were made of glass, cold and sharp-edged, impossibly heavy. The trembling in my legs was getting worse, but my father in any case knocked on my door and my sisters' just then and told us we were not to leave our rooms until he and my mother got back.

I had to will myself to return to looking through the blind, certain that the Robertsons' house would by now be consumed by flames, the Robertsons themselves beating at the upstairs windows, wide-mouthing screams.

In fact, Graham Robertson, dressed head-to-toe in his council-issue waterproofs, was standing with his father at the front gate, chatting to the only fireman in a white hat. Something about the tilt of Mr Robertson's upper body led me to think that not only was Graham standing with him, he was helping him to stay upright. Mrs Robertson was in the Moores' doorway with Mrs Moore, who wore a long coat that even I knew couldn't really be made from snow leopard.

The smoke was already beginning to clear. Dark-helmeted firemen were emerging from the alleyway. My father, at the rear of the fire engine, looked back towards our house and motioned to me to let go of the blind. I let go.

In the morning he told us that Mr Robertson had started the blaze himself. He had got confused when he was closing up the fire ready for bed and instead of putting the hot ashes into the hot ashes bin had put them in the rubbish bin. The same bin into which Mrs Robertson had earlier dropped a big block of fat scooped from the chip pan and wrapped in newspapers.

Mr Robertson, my mother and father agreed, was great for his age, but he was definitely getting on a bit. They wondered at him still being left to take the ashes out.

I took the opportunity of this turn in the conversation to ask them was there something the matter with Graham. My parents passed up the opportunity to give me a straight answer. It was hard for a man especially, was all they would say, to care for elderly parents on his own.

I didn't press them on it. I didn't even know that I wanted to look at them all of a sudden. Out of nowhere a ton-weight of sadness had descended on me, at the top of it a vision of these particular parents of mine grown too old to tell the ashes from the garbage, to stand at all without my arm around them.

Mrs Moore called later to show my mother her new Kenneth Hom book. She said the back of the Robertsons' house was a real mess. The paint was all off the back door and there was a big, greasy scorch mark up as far as the bathroom window.

'Honestly,' she said, 'as if they haven't had enough to worry them.'

'Is it any wonder Graham's such a fucking retard, a da like that?' Tit said as our bus passed a steeply sloping street, which opened like a door into another dimension on a view of no buildings whatever, just flanks of purple mountain, sky.

It was midday of the Wednesday after the Big Bin Fire. I'd had the morning off school to go to the dentist. No fillings, but a lot of poking and scraping and yanking with the wee hook. Tit said he couldn't remember if he was supposed to have classes this morning, he was only going into college to see his mates.

I was sore. He was ranting – had been ranting for about twenty minutes solid – about Mr Robertson.

'I fucking hate old people like that.' He'd had a suede-head since last I saw him, DIY, all traces of summer blond shorn away. 'They should put them down as soon as they're seventy.'

'You'll not be saying that when you're sixty-nine,' I said.

'Want to bet? I'll be pushing up my sleeve, begging them for the fucking needle: Kill me! Kill me! Kill me!'

The man two seats in front placed a gnarly hand on the seat back and turned himself to look at us. Sixty-nine, seventy-ish. He took in Tit's cropped hair, my entire face, shook his head as though that kind of language was no more than could be expected of us.

'You have to feel a bit sorry for him,' I said. Tit tutted. The bus pulled in at a stop level with a lavender and pink neon sign. *Biggsy's Burgers*. The next stop was my school. I slipped my forearm through the straps of my duffel bag, hauled myself out into the aisle. 'He's harmless. The whole family is.'

I had made it halfway down the bus before Tit called out after me. 'Wanker!'

'Tosser,' I called back.

'I'll phone your principals,' called the man who was sitting two in front of us.

As the bus doors opened I heard Tit tell the man to go ahead and fucking phone, then. Out on the footpath I waited for the window Tit was at, to give him a sign that we had only been raking each other about, shouting like that, but he was still arguing with the old boy and he didn't give me so much as a glance.

Christmas, New Year, Chinese New Year. Crap, crapper, crappest. If I'd seen anything at all of Tit I could have asked him had we actually fallen out, but never mind streets, we might as well have been living in different countries these days. In mine nothing very much happened except school, homework, the monthly trip to the Far East, evenings in before the telly, my father as likely as not in floods of happy tears. On Saturday nights I walked my sisters and their friends down the main road to the church youth club. All pretence that I was protecting them was dropped between us, though my sisters kept it up with my mother. It got me out of the house, I suppose, which no doubt was their intention. Even so it was many weeks before I would let myself be persuaded to join them inside. My sisters were overjoyed, as if I had accepted the offer of a lifeline, and, though not in the way that they thought, perhaps I had, for I had been bored half to death without my mate.

The hall had a stage at one end, doors out to the toilets at the other, and was otherwise a school gym with chairs around the walls instead of wall bars. You entered via a corridor, on the opposite side of which were two smaller rooms, the first little more than a store, the second Mr Newton's tuck shop. (Tuck shop, jealous or what, Tit?) All were lit by electric strip lights and smelt troublingly of leaking gas.

At the foot of the stage stood a table with a music centre. My sisters and their friends made straight for the steps to the side of this. I stuck my hands in my pockets, attached myself to a group of lads watching a game of pool. I recognized a couple of them from when I was knocking about the streets with Tit.

'Right,' I said.

'Right,' they said back.

Someone told me it was winner stays on. One by one the lads I was standing with challenged the winner. After each game the loser's cue was handed on. As a matter of course it was handed to me.

'You playing?'

'Sure.'

The cue was split just above the grip. It appeared to have been tipped with a hardened disc of chewing gum. I didn't even bother asking about chalk. I broke, watched my opponent pot a spot, then foul the white, and I had to return to the table only twice to put away all seven stripes and the black. I shaded the next game after the guy I was playing missed an easy black, and the one after that, on stripes again, I won with two spots still on the table. By the start of my fourth game a crowd was beginning to gather. The fella I was up against pocketed one stripe off his break, another off his next shot, missed, and sat down. When he stood up again it was to pass on the cue to the next challenger. I'd cleared the table in eight consecutive shots.

Two games on, I was sensing as much resentment as admiration around me. I was playing a guy I had already beaten once before. He had his own cue he had brought along in a black vinyl bag and screwed together. He seemed, quite apart from the two-part cue (and if I wasn't mistaken a sneaky cube of chalk in his trouser pocket), to be taking this all particularly seriously. I could see how in the previous order of things he might have been the person everyone else had to beat. The girl he sat down beside between turns at the table was gnawing the pad of her thumb. I missed a straightforward pot. My concentration was wandering. I had only come in here tonight to kill a bit of time. It was entirely likely – I was on again, potting well – there would be time to kill other weeks. Why use up your entire store of goodwill in a single evening? Besides, after so long on my feet, I was busting for a leak. Besides *that*, I knew I could beat him if I wanted to.

'Shit,' I said. I had completely missed the last of my seven balls, leaving him with two free shots and his own last ball covering a centre pocket. He put it down and doubled the black into the top right-hand corner. It was a sweet shot.

He offered me his hand, too elated or relieved to affect nonchalance.

'Can't do much against potting like that,' I said and he told me I was unlucky to foul so close to a clearance. I got a few more *bad luck*s as I walked away from the table, all resentment dispelled by my defeat.

My younger sister had been watching from the top of the stage steps. She came down to find me.

'Where did you learn to play pool?' she asked, worried, I thought, that my prowess might be connected in some way to the drugs, which on occasion I had to remind myself did not – never did – exist.

'I didn't,' I answered truthfully, unless watching *Pot Black* and building a staircase into the roof space qualified as a pool education. I hadn't held a cue in my life before tonight, but I would never have been welcome in that youth club again if I had told anyone other than my sister that.

A couple of Saturday nights later, coming off the pool table after I don't know how many straight wins, in the excuse of a queue for the tuck shop, I turned suddenly and found myself eye to dark eye with a girl who told me I was standing on her toe. I stepped back, looked down at the depression in her blue leather Doc, up at her black hair, lobeless ears, plum-glossed lips, anywhere but her eyes.

'Sorry,' I said and she said, 'I know your sisters.'

'You call her Sian,' my elder sister told me. Our parents were on a rare night out alone together and we were walking home. 'She's half Chinese. Or, wait, is it her mum is?'

My other sister wondered what that would make our

children if Sian and I were to have them. Three-quarters, three-eights, depending.

'Shut up about children. I'm only asking who she is. I've never seen her around.'

'Oh, she's been around,' said the elder sister and the two of them and their friends laughed in that way that made me think that girls were born knowing more about these things than boys.

'Yeah, yeah, yeah,' I said.

'We'll give you her number,' the younger sister said then put on a voice I presumed was supposed to be mine. 'Uh, hello, uh, Sian? I was, uh, wondering, uh, if, uh . . .'

'Yeah, yeah, yeah,' I said again and walked on ahead.

In the middle of the next week, in the middle of some crap with the guy from *Man about the House*, the phone rang. My mother never answered the phone if the rest of us were there, my father never if there was a sitcom on. My sisters usually clambered over one another to get to it, but not tonight. Tonight they cast sidelong glances at me.

'Somebody answer that phone,' my mother said.

'Well, it's hardly going to be for me,' I said, but still my sisters refused to budge. 'OK, I'll go, but see if it's for one of you two . . .'

It wasn't. It was for me. It was Tit. In a phone box, judging by the noise. Singing.

'Tan the man, Tan the man, Tan the man. Tan the man, Tan the man, Tan the ma-an. Tan the man, Tan the man, Tan the man. Tan the ma-an, Tan the Man.'

I slipped in behind the curtain covering the front door to stop my voice carrying into the living room.

'Have you been drinking?'

'Fuck off, have I been drinking.'

He was plastered.

'So?' I said.

'So?' he said right back.

'What you up to?'

'What you up to?'

'Haven't seen you for a bit.'

'Haven't seen you for a bit.'

While I was thinking whether to ask him was he just going to repeat everything I said, he asked, 'Are you just going to repeat everything I say?'

'You're very funny,' I told him.

'You're very funny,' he told me.

I didn't know what else to say.

'You have been drinking.'

'Call the cops!' he said.

'I'm only saying.'

'Call the cops!'

'Tit . . .'

'Don't *Tit* me.'

His money was running out. I heard him trying to force another 5p into the slot. I was praying he wouldn't make it in time. There was a pause, I thought he was gone, then he was singing again, to the tune of 'London Bridge is Falling Down'.

'Tan the ma-an call the cops, call the cops, call the cops. Tan the ma-an call the cops, call the co-hops.'

I tried to interrupt as he started another round. 'I can't keep up with this.'

He sang louder.

'Look, I'm going to hang up, this is doing my head in.'

Now he stopped singing.

'Well, you should have thought about that, shouldn't you, before you started making allegations.'

'I haven't made any allegations. All I said was you sounded like you'd been drinking.'

'Don't,' Tit's tone was nasty, 'come the funny cunt with me, wee lad. You know what I'm talking about.'

I was scared I was going to lose control of my voice. Worse, that I might even start to cry. 'I don't, really, I don't.'

Not that it made any difference what I said.

'Fucking cops lifted me as I came dandering out of the college the day, in front of all my mates, chucked me in the wagon and drove me around for half an hour asking me questions about smashing windows and slashing tyres.'

'Oh, fuck,' I said on to the front door's frosted glass.

Across the road a vanilla slice of light appeared, where the Moores' living-room door had swung open; hovered, then was swallowed.

'Oh, fuck's right,' he said.

'Wait, you're not trying to say I had anything to do with it, are you?'

'I'm not trying to say anything.'

'That's OK, then.'

'That's OK, then.'

'Right.'

'Right.'

'See you around.'

'You better fucking believe it see you around,' Tit said.

I had to wipe my palms on my trouser legs before going back into the living room.

'Who was that?' asked my mother.

'Nobody,' I said. 'Roy.'

'Roy?' she said. Stretched out on the floor my sisters, heads together, sniggered. 'Why would Roy *ring*?'

I didn't answer, she didn't pursue it. No sooner had my

bum hit the settee than the phone was going again. I leaped up, ran to the hallway. I knew when I opened my mouth the sound that came out was unmistakably that of a frightened boy.

'Hello?'

'It's me,' said the girl's voice. 'I got fed up waiting for you to call.'

'Was that *Roy* ringing back?' asked my younger sister, turning to look over her shoulder as I came back in the living-room door.

'No, that was Sian,' I said, 'wanting to know would I go out with her.'

I flopped down on the settee. This had been a fuck of an evening. Even my father was looking at me, dry-eyed in astonishment.

'What?' I asked. '*What?*'

Sian dropped me after only two dates, that is after only twice meeting down at the youth club and then taking a walk together to a dark privety corner of the church grounds where we snogged, or rather didn't much.

'Is there something the matter with me?' she asked the second time. 'Or is there something the matter with you?'

No, no, there was not a thing the matter. Except that I was afraid my ex-best friend was going to do something completely fucking mental, quite possibly to me, and every time I closed my eyes to kiss her I saw scenes of suburban carnage.

'You're allowed to speak, you know.'

It was when I didn't that she said it was all off between us.

She rang me a few days later.

'I must be mad doing this,' she began, 'but I'm warning you, this is your last chance. Do you hear?'

'Yes,' I said. 'I hear.'

For the fact was I thought I might very well love Sian, if I could only get my head clear for five minutes of all this stuff with the Robertsons and Roy Stitt.

The easiest thing would have been to make good the original offence, to call at Tit's door and tell him that I had invented the story of Graham fruiting me up. I had meant it only as a bit of a joke – bad taste had never stopped us before – but it had all got out of hand.

(Out of hand . . . fruiting me up . . . Do you get it, Tit? Do you get it? Tit?)

Who was to say, though, even then that Tit wouldn't decide it was the retraction I was inventing because I hadn't the bottle to see this business through to the end?

It was at this point, every one of the hundreds of times I had turned it over in my mind, that I found myself wondering whether there wasn't some way I could bring the end on faster, get it all over and done with.

Of course I was horrified by such thoughts. Of course I banished them. Of course.

I took very particular care assembling the materials. The rule was use nothing that could be traced back to me or this house. I went to a second-hand book store in the centre of town that had a reputation in my school for its vast array of well-used mags and its utter lack of surveillance. The owner didn't look up from the book he was reading as I entered. He didn't even look at the cigarette he reached for in the ashtray next to his idle till as I walked out, ignoring the piles of *Men Only* and *Fiesta*, with a bodybuilding monthly in my duffel bag.

I scouted around on buses for abandoned tabloid news-papers, asked a boy in my Maths class to give me the loan of some paper out of his file block and took more than I actually needed for the lesson. I wouldn't even use the scissors we had at home, but borrowed them from the store cupboard at the youth club.

(I was going to put them back, and the Gloy. I was.)

I told my parents I was working on an important project for school. I really mustn't be disturbed. Next year was my A-level year. If I said no one was to come into my bedroom when I was working, no one would come into my bedroom.

Still, as an added precaution I eased back the bolt on the old cupboard door and crept up the stairs to the roof space where the newspapers, the magazine, the borrowed A4, scissors and glue were hidden behind the water tank. It seemed that no matter what the weather at the bottom of those stairs it was always raining by the time I reached the top. Exaggerated, effects-department rain. I had to leave off two, three times a minute, straining to hear through it had there been any change in the distribution of the voices on the floors below.

I wore gloves, for warmth and fingerprint anonymity. It was slow, slow going.

The bodybuilding magazine was a nice touch, if I said so myself, should anyone have wanted to go to the trouble of reconstructing the publications from the fragments I used. I took from it three whole words in solid, inch-high capitals, from two separate adverts: GET, YOUR and MAN. (The text on the back of MAN, all energy conversion rates, was a complete giveaway.) From one day's *Sun* I got the *S* and the *n* of the *Sun* itself, a big black O to go between them; from another day's an OUT, an OR, an IS and an A. I could have had a complete DEAD five or six times over, but I decided it looked better – scarier – all chopped up, with the 'd's in small letters.

I went back to the bodybuilding magazine for the uv (managing not to dwell for too long on thoughts of Mrs Moore) and I aligned it with the F of Freddie Mercury from a *Sun* pop page. It wasn't *such* an unlikely looking combination.

A week and more of evenings. I muddled through the days in between, lay awake long into the nights, wondering was I right in the head any more, picturing, only half in dread, old Mrs Robertson picking up the letter from the hall mat, working her finger under the gummed flap as she turned back into the living room . . . Sitting suddenly in an armchair, the page floating to the floor. Graham rushing in, asking what was the matter, reading the words upside-down.

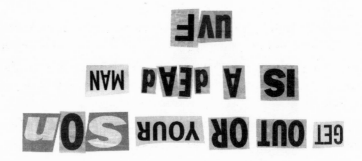

The only problem was getting it over there.

There was no question of me addressing the envelope by hand, right or left, even with gloves. It was the first thing a detective would check. I could just see the desk in the middle of the street, residents in a line stepping forward one at a time to pick up a pen and write.

The policeman's voice: 'And now the other hand, please.'

Me standing with my father, getting ever closer to the front, crapping myself.

Outside of school, where you had to ask to be let into the typing room and then had someone looking over your shoulder the entire time, the only typewriter I could think of was in the office above the Far East. The letter 'e' stuck. Sticky letter 'e's were what got blackmailers nicked in TV movies.

No, I would have to forget about the postal service altogether and take the envelope over there myself, which of course opened up a whole new set of difficulties. It was by my reckoning only a dozen yards or so door to door, but that didn't begin to express the distance I would have travel to hand-deliver this thing.

(Was there some sort of by-law that stated there must be someone on our street *every* minute of the day?)

I would just have to be prepared to act on the first opportunity, spur of the moment. I kept the sheet of paper with its threatening message in my room, moving it from between the leaves of one schoolbook to the leaves of another. Watching, waiting.

I tried to console myself with the thought that what I had here was an insurance policy. So long as I had the letter I had some control over what happened when.

All the same, I made good and sure I didn't run into Tit.

Sian and I made a date to meet in town, in daylight, away from the youth club with its time-slots practically for the cop-off corner by the big privet hedge. It was late on a Saturday morning, the first of spring. Outside the city hall daffodils were being sold from black plastic buckets. A few headers were risking shirtsleeves. Sian told me Miss Selfridge's and Top Shop were crap and took me into one after the other.

'What do you think?' she asked, coming out of a changing

room in something tight and pink, standing on tartan-sock tiptoes, holding her hair up, looking at her back – at her bum, in fact – in the mirror.

I thought I need air, looser trousers, stripped to the skin and dragged to the floor.

'Nice,' I said.

'Do you think?' She took a couple of steps away from the mirror, a couple of steps back, made a face. 'I think it's stinking.'

I knew from my own sisters this was normal. *I* felt normal. Any looks we got from guys on the street were because of Sian. This was normal too. We spent half the afternoon in the Wimpy with all the other normal teenagers.

Sian made an Olympic symbol out of the five-for-a-pound bracelets that were all she had bought.

'I'm glad you wanted to get back with me,' I told her.

'I'd heard how cut up you were.' She put two of the bracelets in front of her face, batted her eyelashes spectacularly. 'If you're lucky I'll let you take me for a night out somewhere too, get me drunk.'

'Anyone ever tell you you're full of yourself?'

She set the bracelets on the table, looked at me steadily a moment. 'Anyone ever tell you . . .' she started but didn't finish, never intended to finish.

'What?'

She bit her burger. 'Forget it.'

It was a tease, I knew. I could read as much as I liked into the gap she'd left. I might be miles out, I might be spot on.

'Tell me what?'

'*Forget it.*'

I would work out what to do about taking her drinking another day. Right now, as soon as she swallowed what she had in her mouth, I was going to lean across the table and kiss her.

It was already early evening when I got home; still I was surprised to see my father's car parked out the front of the house. Most Saturdays he didn't get finished till half-seven or eight.

He was waiting for me in the hallway.

'Go into the dining room,' he said and looked up the street before pressing his fingers between my shoulder blades. 'Go.'

I was apologizing, telling him my watch must be wrong, wondering where my sisters were, why the TV wasn't on, when I caught a familiar tobacco smell from the back of the house. My Far East uncle was sitting at the dining table, along with his cousin from up the coast and another man I didn't recognize or even look at much, for there in a space cleared on the table, between the teacups and the French-cigarette boxes and the half-full ashtrays, was my letter to the Robertsons.

The unknown man squashed a cigarette, picked the letter up by the top corner. Now I looked at him. Ponytail, narrow moustache, too many teeth, or too little mouth. He wore the collar of his jacket flipped up, its sleeves and the sleeves of his red silk shirt pushed to just below his elbows. His forearms were out of all proportion to the rest of his body, so that for a moment before I saw them flex I wondered whether his rolled sleeves hadn't cut off the circulation. If it hadn't been for his forearms, I'd have said he was about six and a half stone.

He was not quite what I had expected, but I was in no doubt who he was.

'How long have you had this?' he asked me as my father closed the door into the living room.

When he opened the door, an hour and a half later, I walked without a word or a backward glance to my room, where I stretched out on the bed and stared at the ceiling.

About one in the morning, a pale blue notelet was slipped under my door. I knew who it was from. I could guess what it said. I let it lie there till three, when at last I undressed to get under the covers.

My sisters were sorry for going through my things. My sisters had thought from the way I had been behaving lately that I was back on drugs. When they discovered the horrible letter, my sisters were scared – they were still scared – they didn't know what else to do.

But it was better this way, out in the open, they wrote. Wasn't it?

Let's see now. Our father, a man who for all his tears of laughter and horsing around, who for all his reticence on the matter, had toughed out some pretty unpleasant situations in his day, believing that for the first time one of his children was directly under threat, having somehow crossed or offended or simply come to the attention of the local paramilitaries ('How many times were you told about writing your name? Those are *their* walls for painting on!') had instantly, and overcoming all reservations, called on the services of Mr Tommy Yoo, had indeed in my presence handed over, don't ask me where he got them, three £50 notes on the understanding that Mr Yoo would take the matter up with his contacts and ask them to use their influence to get the threat lifted.

My own claims that this was all a misunderstanding had been taken as evidence of the sheer terror I had been living in while trying to keep the letter secret. Mind you, they hadn't sounded more than half true to me either.

'It's somebody messing around.'

Tommy Yoo, who had seen many such letters in the past, shook his head, slowly, sadly. This was the genuine article.

'Too much care has gone into making it for this to be someone playing a game.'

(A victim of my own application!)

It was suggested that I lie low for a while, maybe go away altogether, until things could be sorted out.

'But his school,' our father said. 'He has his A-levels next year.'

Tommy Yoo dragged on his cigarette, shrugged, like fat lot of use A-levels were to a dEAd man.

Oh, yes, Sisters, it was much, much better this way. Thanks.

Convincing the doctor that I was sick was a doddle compared to convincing Sian. I could almost hear her eyebrows knit at the other end of the line.

'What did he say it was again?'

Sian was doing Latin *and* Biology O-level.

'I can't get my tongue around it.'

She breathed down her nose. 'I don't know. This better not be just to avoid having to take me out.'

'Sian!'

I lowered my voice, coughed a couple of times.

'I'm not even able to go to school.'

And I wasn't well, really. I could hardly make myself get out of bed some mornings. What was the point? This was not a life any more, it was a lesson, a fable. I remembered, from childhood, hearing how the souls of the dead were held by the god of Walls and Ditches before being sent to have their deeds judged by Yen-Wang-Yeh, the Lord of Death. (I remembered Horse Face, Yen-Wang-Yeh's gofer, and thought of Tommy Yoo's overfull mouth.) I was the lie that spawned another lie that spawned another and another and another until now there was such a mass of lies it was impossible to wade through them, either forwards or back. Better not even to try, but simply wait for the moral of the story of me to be revealed.

The one thing that I hadn't counted on was Tommy Yoo turning out to be an even bigger liar than I was.

I had been not trying for a week and a day when he paid his return visit. He wore a blue silk shirt instead of the red one he had on first time he called, but the jacket was the same, the collars and cuffs identically arranged. Without waiting to be asked or led, he walked into the dining room and sat down at the far end of the table. My father and mother followed him through the kitchen door. I trailed in last. We adopted our poses, the accused and his counsel, opposite Tommy Yoo. He looked at us each in turn then grinned. 'All sorted,' he said. 'No more worries.'

My mother clapped her hands. 'Oh, thank you.' She threw her arms around me. 'Isn't that fantastic?'

Managing to get a threat lifted that never existed? Fantastic wasn't the word.

Tommy Yoo's smile narrowed to next to nothing. He glanced down at the table. Only thing was, he said, it was going to cost my father and mother another £100. My father nodded, closed his eyes lightly. I imagined him bidding a silent farewell to VCRs, to dreams of *Terry and June* on demand.

I didn't know whether to spit or cry. I hauled deeply through the back of my nose to keep from doing either.

Before he left, Tommy told my parents he wanted a word with me on my own.

'Sit,' he said, when he had tracked their footsteps to the top of the stairs.

I stayed standing.

'I don't know what you're looking at me like that for. Your parents feel safer having paid out that money,' he told me. He took out a cigarette, tapped one end then the other on the table. 'I was sure you would understand. I even said to myself, a person who would plan on sending this sort of a letter could have a very good future working with me.'

He lit the cigarette, turning in his chair side on to the table, crossing his legs at the ankles.

'Think about it,' he said.

I focused on his maroon moccasins, his less-than-clean white sports socks. I was thinking all right, thinking like mad.

Graham Robertson was not, had never been, the problem. Here was the problem:

T'n'T – T = ?

T?

T'n'T*n't*?

How to be me without being me-without-him.

That was the problem.

'So?' said Sian.

'So, I'm better.'

'So?'

'So, I was thinking we should go out for a drink this Friday night.'

'A *drink* drink?'

'In a bar bar, yes.'

'Wow. Are you sure you're not still sick?'

★

My sisters insisted: black T-shirt, oldest jeans. I showed them my new second-hand cord jacket.

The younger sister squinted. 'Is that *pink*?'

'The label said rose. Weathered rose.'

'Oh, well then.'

'Don't listen,' said the older sister. 'You'll look fine.'

Sian looked deadly. She got on the bus the stop after me in a black PVC raincoat, a little leather cap.

'Good jacket,' she said and kissed me before I could say anything back.

The bus set us down not far from the College of Knowledge.

'Where were you thinking of?' Sian asked and I pointed to a bar on the opposite side of the street, with a long line of people waiting to be frisked and bag-checked.

'That place?' she said.

'Do you not fancy it?'

We were already halfway across the road.

'It's *spidey*.'

'It's not.'

'It is. Look at the queue.' She recited to me out the corner of her mouth as we walked along it, 'Spiderman, spiderman, spiderman, spider*woman*, spiderman . . .'

The term had obviously outgrown its skinhead roots. The queue seemed to me pretty representative of the city's current youth styles.

'Here's the trick,' said Sian, behind her hand. 'When you look at them, can you imagine them in a *band* uniform? Spide.'

We made it to the end of the queue – just – without me staring at anyone too closely.

'Everywhere's spidey, if you put it like that,' I said and every half-minute or so from then until we reached the bar door,

Sian would break into crazed hummed snatches of the *Spider-man* theme tune.

'You'll get us barred, you, before we even get in.'

The doormen, though, looked us up, down, up (one of them smiled at Sian's primly buttoned lip), and with a pat of our pockets nodded us through. So long I had put the moment off and in the end it was so, so simple.

We were in a room about the size of the downstairs at home with upwards of two hundred other people. The ceiling had elaborate plaster mouldings, left over from another life. The walls, or what I could see of them, were painted dark brown and glistened. I couldn't locate an actual bar, just pints being hoisted up and over the heads in one corner of the room then passed down into the throng. I didn't know either where the music was coming from precisely, only that it was all around us. ZZ Top. I could feel it in the pit of my stomach, on the soles of my feet.

'It's all right,' I said into Sian's ear.

She nodded. 'Not bad.'

We were borne for a minute this way and that then navigated our way to an anchorage against a pillar bearing an out-of-date Rag Week poster.

'Do you reckon a lot of these are students?' Sian asked at the very moment I spied the one person I knew for sure was, pushing towards the beer collection point.

I yelled. He didn't hear. I yelled louder.

'*Tit!*'

Several dozen people looked my way, but he alone flinched before glancing round.

'Tan?' He looked like he was about to smile, but the next instant his expression turned sour. 'You've a fucking neck, coming in here.'

'Your bar, is it?'

Tit swivelled his head to see who had spoken and I told him, 'This is Sian.'

Someone was tapping his shoulder. One after the other, three pints were reached out of the crowd into his hands and through them into a pair of hands that appeared from behind me. He turned again to face us, licking the condensation from between his forefinger and thumb. My stomach churned with the guitar intro of 'How Soon is Now?' *I am the son*, sang Morrissey, *and the heir* . . . Tit licked between the forefinger and thumb of his other hand . . . *of a shyness that is criminally vulgar. I am the son and heir of nothing in particular.*

'I don't know. You boys, it's just chat, chat, chat,' Sian said, and whether it was this that did it, the next thing the two of us boys were trying to talk at once, stopping, asking each other what, starting again together, carrying on regardless. I was telling him that I was spoofing about Graham Robertson, all right, but I never did go near the police, honest.

Honest, as it happened, was almost the only word I got of what he was saying, the moment I had finished, but what was I going to do, ask him to start again?

'I believe you,' I said.

I thought I heard him say the same thing back.

There was another tap on his shoulder, more pints coming through. This was some enormous round he was in and I wondered how many of them had been bought since college ended this afternoon.

The Smiths ground on. Sian had her arms folded waiting for the rest of the night to begin.

I stuck out my hand.

'Mates?'

Tit considered a moment then catching hold of the hand

dragged me to him. I had a fleeting vision of my dinner outside me instead of in.

'Mates. Only, Tan,' he said, 'never you call me that fucking name again.'

And Sian at my other shoulder shouted in at him, 'Who do you think you're calling *Tan*?'

Sian asked to know what that was all about.

'I can't tell you.'

'I think you'd better.'

'You'll hate me.'

'I'll hate you if you don't.'

I got us a drink, she somehow got us a seat, a pocket of something like quiet, below the belts, buttons, braces, elasticated waistbands and, even now, occasional safety pins of two hundred or so of our fellow Friday-night teenage drinkers.

I went right back to last summer, told Sian the whole story. When I reached the end her arms were folded again across her chest.

'Told you you'd hate me,' I said.

She had already drunk the last of her lager, now she drank the last of mine.

'Should we get another drink?' I asked.

She shook her head.

'What should we do? Go some place else? Go home?'

She shook her head again. I saw a chance to lighten us up.

'No we shouldn't go some place else or no we shouldn't go home?'

Sian thumbed the first of her raincoat's broad black buttons into its hole. Stood up to do the rest.

'No we shouldn't do anything,' she said. 'You do what you like. You're on your own.'

I went to get up.

'Don't,' she said and was lost to me in the crowd.

Eliot

YOU DON'T NEED A KING'S RANSOM TO PURCHASE . . . THE 'IDEAL HOME' FOR THE GROWING FAMILY

ACCOMMODATION COMPRISES:
Entrance hall: single-panel radiator
Lounge: 11′4″ × 10′10″ Tiled fireplace. Rayburn glass-fronted fire. Double-panel radiator.
Kitchen: 11′2″ × 6′0″ Single-drainer sink unit with mixer taps. Access to understair storage.
Dinette: 11′2″ × 9′10″. Double-panel radiator.

FIRST FLOOR:
Landing: Hot press, copper cylinder, immersion heater.
Bedroom 1: 11′2″ × 11′0″. Double-panel radiator.
Bedroom 2: 11′2″ × 9′10″ Range of built-in cupboards. Single-panel radiator.
Bedroom 3: 7′10″ × 7′8″ Single-panel radiator. Permanent staircase to partially floored roof space.
Bathroom: Bath, pedestal sink, low-flush WC. Single-panel radiator.

OUTSIDE:
Well laid-out gardens front and rear.

The property has been beautifully maintained, but requires the minimum modernization and is priced accordingly.

Two nights before we were due to move in, the phone rang.

'Catriona?'

I reached for the remote, killed the volume on *Blind Date*.

'Artie.'

I called Steve's aunt, as I called his mother, Mrs Eliot, but his uncle was only ever Artie. Even the kids called him that.

'Have you been looking in the paper?' he asked.

'Some,' I said. I was sitting in an armchair with a Royal Doulton dairymaid in my lap. I found the top corner of the torn sheet of newspaper in my hand and saw that it was in fact tonight's. Shit. 'Why?'

'That funeral. It's Monday morning. You're going to have to put off moving.'

This was Saturday night. The van-hire place was closed Sunday. We had our pretty hefty and non-refundable deposit paid.

'Artie, there's no way we can put off moving. We've the van booked. Steve's cancelled all his jobs. I've had to rearrange a schools group.'

Artie sighed. Artie was emphysemic, a sigh could sound like the passing of life itself.

'Well, it's not going to look very good, now, is it? You lugging your three-piece suite in at one end of the street while they're shouldering a coffin out the other.'

Artie had phoned us on Friday ten seconds after the story had been on the evening news.

'He says that man lived on our street,' Steve told me when he'd put the phone down, though there had been no mention of an address in the report. 'Artie sold him the house.'

'Artie seems to have sold half the houses in this city.' Artie was forty-five years in the business before he retired. 'How can be possibly remember which one he sold to who?'

Steve shrugged. 'Maybe some of them just stick in your mind. And, like, that name . . .'

The phone rang again. It was a colleague of Steve's from the Electronic Shop who had been watching the news on the other side. They had given out the home address. Artie was right, it was the street we were moving to OK.

'I'm sorry for how it's going to look,' I said to him now, wrapping my dairymaid in the newspaper, leaning over the arm to lay her in the box at the side of the chair, 'but there's not an awful lot I can do about it at this stage, is there?'

I took down another figurine from the mantelpiece to my left, pulled another double sheet of newspaper from the drift at my feet. The *Star* this time. Boobs one side, bingo the other. Artie hadn't answered.

It was my turn to sigh. 'I'll talk to Steve.' Steve had gone out for a farewell drink with a couple of the ones from the lower landings. 'I'll get him to call you.'

Artie was saying, 'I'm only thinking how it would look' again at the same time as I was repeating, 'But we've the deposit and all paid, I've the day booked off work.'

We each stopped to let the other proceed and for a moment neither did.

'Goodnight, Artie,' I said at length.

Artie wheezed. 'Goodnight, Catriona.'

Old so and so.

Using the toe of my slipper, I separated the newspapers on the floor until I found the photograph which last night accompanied the front-page headline and tonight had already slipped to page six. I looked again at the handsome, quizzical eyes, the slightly parted lips (almost as if he had seen in the photo-booth's flash a premonition of how the picture would

come to be used), and attempted to match Artie's pronunci-
ation with the printed name of the man who was so nearly
my neighbour. András Hideg. Courageous Magyar, the cap-
tion called him.

I read a couple of paragraphs. Born some place with a zed.
Studying in Budapest. Russian tanks. Daring escape. Met and
married local girl. Two children. Successful business.

His successful business in fact might have been the motive
for his murder. Plumbing supplies. It had the contract for
fitting out all the city's police stations with urinals. He had
been working in his office at the back of his new showroom
on an industrial estate less than a mile from his home (and
only a little more, looking another way, from where I was
sitting at work at that moment on Friday morning) when two
men pushed their way past staff and shot him in the head at
point-blank range.

Paul Blake, neighbour and employee, said he didn't stand a
chance.

It was, the police said, a cowardly and despicable attack on
a man who had already overcome great hardship in his life.

His wife Jill (53) said simply that her heart was broken.

My own heart lurched at the thought of a husband walking
out of the house and never coming back. How on earth could
you carry on living there? And yet how could you bear to
begin to pack away the life you had shared?

I sat a few moments looking around the flat, at the carpet
rolled to the side of the room under the window, at the
cardboard boxes with their contents marked on them in numbered code, listening to the adrenaline-thump of Martin's
music through the two walls separating me from his bedroom,
while Cilla gave the word and the *Blind Date* screen drew back
to reveal to skinny, blonde Geordie Denise lardy Dave from

Fulham. On the left side horror, on the right delight. Boobs. Bingo.

Patricia came through from the hallway doing up her coat.

'You'd better not be long,' I said. I hadn't been going to let her out at all, she'd hardly made a start on her room, but Steve said it was her last Saturday night with her wee friends, how could you keep her in? An argument which had nothing whatever to do with the fact that Steve himself was itching to go for a couple of pints.

Patricia's arms were about my neck.

'What's up, Mum, *Blind Date* getting to you?'

She kissed my cheek, down which, I now realized, a tear had run. I pulled her to me and told the top of her coconut-smelling head that she wasn't to be in too much of a hurry to go on dates, blind or otherwise. She was laughing, trying to wriggle from my grasp.

'What do you think I am, mad?'

I thought, you're almost thirteen, you'll soon slip away from me altogether.

'Mum!' She straightened up, finger-combed her hair. 'I'm going to be late.'

I shouted after her as she went back out into the hallway to tell Martin to turn the music down. She pounded on his door as she passed.

'Mum says you're to turn that down.'

'No she never.'

'Yes she did.'

The front door banged shut. Martin's music blasted as loud as ever. I took down the last figurine and started to wrap it in the page I had just been reading, with the face of the Courageous Magyar and the words of his heartbroken wife, then decided this was not appropriate at all and balled the paper in my hand, launching it towards the bin bag squatting slack-mouthed in the centre of the floor. Which was worse, of course, much, much worse. I was out of the chair as soon as I was able to get the figurine back on the mantelpiece, almost before the ball of paper had skidded to a halt in the corner beyond the bag. I smoothed it flat, folded it, and spent the next half-hour looking for a place to lay it decently to rest.

We put off starting to move until after lunch on Monday, a good two and a half hours after the morning news said the funeral was to depart from number 18. The street was still deserted when we steered the van in, every blind lowered, every curtain drawn. Our own windows in contrast resembled irreverently open eyes. The first thing I did, before we went back to the flat to reload, was ask Steve to help me tack up sheets, telling myself all the while that whatever Artie might think at least by moving in today we were taking the bad look off the place.

Even allowing for his disapproving of our timing, I was surprised we hadn't had him on the phone this morning offering to come and lend us a hand. Unless he was worried we would actually take him up on it this time. Artie had arthritis as well as emphysema. He was all talk nowadays, Steve said. I had my suspicions that talk was what he had mostly always been.

Steve and I were on our third run before we met a neighbour. Or rather, were met by. Youngish, long thin face, Reactolite glasses, dark suit, black tie, of course. Number 19, Joss Newton, he said, short for Joseph, not Jocelyn. He told us Mrs Hideg was in no state to have a whole lot of people back to the house so his church had laid on tea and sandwiches for the mourners.

That's what he called it. Not the, not her, not their: *his* church.

Steve had left a supermarket bag filled with sand by way of a parking cone on the road before number 5. This Joss Newton asked, very politely, how much longer we reckoned we would be. Another two runs should do it, Steve said, and Joss Newton said we weren't to think he was being unwelcoming – 'Not at all,' we both said – but just with the size of the van, and the funeral car bringing Mrs Hideg home . . .

Our last run slowed to a crawl through the early-evening rush hour. We actually sat for five minutes outside the arts centre. I could just see, over the top of the hedge, Lorraine at my desk on the ground floor, acting up. The lights were on in the upstairs gallery, which Nick had been having painted.

We got the van back to the hire place with less than two minutes to spare before we incurred a penalty of the next day's hire charge. It had been dark for over an hour when Steve and I returned to the house in our own car. The street was end to end cars. The bag of sand had been lifted from the roadside and placed next to our gate. We had to drive out the bottom of the street and round the corner to park.

'Never worry,' I told Steve.

Martin and Patricia had got as far with the unpacking as plugging in the TV and connecting it up to the outside aerial, which Steve had been round last week erecting.

'Look at this,' Martin said.

The funeral was on the news. Solemn-faced people, three-, four-deep on the footpaths, some even standing in gardens, all focused on an end-terrace with ranch-style shutters, a hearse backed, tail slightly raised, into its driveway.

For a few seconds, as the first of the pallbearers appeared at the front door, I thought that the volume had been turned down then the silence was broken by the squawk of a bird (though no bird I had ever before heard) and I realized that what I had been witnessing was the sound of the world without human speech.

The coffin emerged fully, draped in a tricoloured flag, and the news reporter began to speak, his voice lost under Patricia's.

'Is that . . . ?'

'Hungary,' I said.

'Oh.'

A woman, her features contorted by grief, clutching to her breast a single rose, followed the coffin out the front door and after two steps had to be helped back in. I recognized, by his Reactolite glasses, Joss Newton among the helpers. The coffin continued down the drive without her. The pallbearers paused uncertainly. The wind caught a corner of the Hungarian flag, turning it back on itself.

Four more men came forward to take a lift. They walked with the coffin a few paces behind the hearse, drawing in their wake mourners from the footpaths and gardens, down the street and – all of us registered the strangeness of this, judging by the renewed hush in the room – right past our front door. Our front door two and a half hours before we began properly to live here. And even though it was now close to eight hours since the cortège I was viewing had passed, I was half afraid that if I was to yank the sheet away from the window the kids would yell they had seen me on the TV, looking out.

'Magic,' Martin said. 'Our house is famous.'

Patricia gave her brother a clip. 'That man's dead, you.'

The thing was, though, death – even sudden, violent death – was not unusual to Martin. More than one person we knew from the flats had been killed in the course of our son's eleven years. The difference was that you couldn't pick out your balcony on the TV the way you could a front door.

We dined on a family bucket from the KFC down on the main road, amid the numbered cardboard boxes, the bin bags patched with masking tape, the displaced bedding and bath towels. We heard cars depart, more arrive, we heard many murmured conversations in the street. We watched *Family Fortunes* (I'm not thick, I know what irony is) and as per usual would have won ourselves a brand-new Ford Fiesta if only we had bothered to ring the number they give out at the end of every programme if you want to appear on the show yourself.

It was gone nine before I could face making a start on the unpacking. Mrs Tan had left the whole house immaculate. (Mrs? Maybe she was lucky. Maybe she had help with the cleaning.) I had seen it in this state for all of half an hour about a month ago before Steve went in and ripped out the old wiring. Hadn't been touched since these houses were built, he said. Plugs on skirting boards and everything. Steve could get quite worked up about wiring. A mate of his who owed him a favour did the damp-proofing and got another mate to come in afterwards and replaster downstairs. Between the three of them they finished off the attic, cutting a window into the eaves at the back to avoid having to apply for planning permission. They piped a radiator up there then took away the old solid-fuel fire from the living room and replaced it with a flame-effect electric one and an oil tank at the bottom of the back garden.

Even after all this work, though, I was still finding notes here and there in a careful, unfamiliar hand. 'Drawer sticks – lift as you pull.' '40 mins immersion = 1 full tank nice hot water.'

The fire had been lit in the living room since the early

afternoon, the heating was set to high, but I switched on the immersion for half an hour anyway. Just to be sure. Once the kids were in bed I ran a bath so hot it was ten minutes before I could lower myself all the way in. Gorgeous, gorgeous, gorgeous. I had been soaking for less than ten minutes more when Steve slipped in the door.

'We'll need to put a lock on that,' I said as I watched him start to unbutton his shirt.

And I know I should be ashamed to say it, but I went to bed happy that night, to be living here, to be alive.

I was happier still to be able to walk to the arts centre the next morning, even if I did underestimate the distance on foot and arrive seven minutes late. Nick was looking at his watch.

'I thought one of the bonuses of you moving house was that you'd be closer to work. What were you doing, arranging your ornaments?'

Ornaments was not a word Nick liked the taste of. He practically spat it out. A pity even the tiniest fraction of the people who collected Royal Doulton figurines hadn't the stomach for his own 'found object' sculptures, he mightn't have had to manage an arts centre for a living and Lorraine and I could have got on quite happily with actually running the place.

I cupped a hand to my ear. 'I don't hear anyone hollering to be let in.'

There were no classes for another hour and none till the afternoon that needed my particular supervision.

Lucy looked in the door. 'Nick? A word?'

Nick smiled, as well he might. Without the goodwill of artists like Lucy, captive – the official term was resident – in the studios of the old timber yard, there would have been no classes of any sort in the centre. They left the room together.

Nick stuck his head back in. 'Tea?' he said to Lorraine. It wasn't an offer.

Martin and Patricia were still in their school uniforms watching TV when I got home.

'I thought you two were doing your rooms?'

'There's too much crap up there,' said Patricia, who had won the toss for the roof space, eventually. Best of seven.

'I don't suppose it crossed your mind to sort some of it out?'

'It's not my stuff,' she said.

'Not mine either,' said Martin.

'Nobody said it was,' I said, going through to the kitchen. There was an unopened drum of salt on the countertop. I had unpacked all the kitchen boxes myself, I didn't remember an unopened salt.

'What's this doing here?' I shouted.

'What?'

'Where?'

'This.'

I walked back into the living room with the salt in my hand. Patricia managed to indicate her ignorance and lack of interest using only her nose. Martin cocked an eye as though it was the third or fourth drum of salt he'd been asked to account for today and he wanted to be sure before he answered that he had the right one.

'Woman over the road,' he said, turning again to the TV.

'What would a woman over the road be doing giving us salt?'

'Don't ask me. All she said was she was sorry she didn't get it over to us yesterday.'

'It's meant to be for luck,' Steve said when he got in. 'Did you never hear of it?'

'Listen to Brain of Britain here,' I said, for the kids' benefit mainly, because it never ceased to amaze me the curious bits and pieces my husband carried around in his head. I gave him a big hug. God, but he was still strong.

Steve had been home on leave from the army when I met him, all biceps and Belize-bronzed, full to the gills on the dance floor, doing the bump like a wee lad in a dodgem car. Not my cup of tea at all. I'd always gone for long hair on a fella, something, we used to say, to hold on to. Steve, though, was too drunk to take a telling. I let him give me his number and then to shut him up declaring undying love in front of all my friends I let him walk me home. I heard later he'd got a kicking as he tried to find his way back to his own part of town. Fractured his cheekbone. He was a soldier, he was lucky not to get a whole lot worse. Naturally I rang him to see how he was and before I knew it I was seeing him every night.

Seeing? We were all over each other.

He told me he was going to buy himself out of the army and come back and marry me. I told him he needed his head looking at. Hadn't he already got himself one kicking, for dear sake? Besides, I was far too young to be thinking of marrying anybody.

I said to him, I know what will happen, you'll go back to Belize and write me horny letters every night and then every week and then just every now and again and then you'll stop.

'I won't,' he said.

And I said, 'You say you won't, but you will.'

So off he went and as I had expected after a couple of months the horny letters stopped. What I hadn't been expecting, though, was to find him on our front doorstep a fortnight later with his hair already beginning to grow out and a ring in his pocket.

'Told you,' he said, and I threw my arms around as much of him as they could take in.

Problem was his hair didn't grow out fast enough. For weeks after he got back he still looked like a soldier in civvies. A couple of times I was out for the night with him I heard comments passed.

'Come on,' I would always say, 'let's just leave.'

I didn't know until the police called, one night he was out on the town with his mates, and told me he was arrested, that he had started carrying a knife.

The judge at his trial said if the knife had gone in a quarter of an inch to the left he would have been standing before him on a murder charge.

The prosecution had tried to make out the motive was sectarian. One or two of his mates were known to the police. Steve denied the allegation. He had his back to me the whole time he was in the box. I knew I could tell by looking at his face if he was telling the truth. I asked him outright when they let me talk to him before he was sentenced: Was it, Steve?

'I'm an idiot,' he said and held my eye, 'but I'm not a bigot.'

Idiocy we could work on. I told him we would still be engaged when he got out.

The kids knew the whole story. We had sat them down as soon as they were old enough to understand. Better they heard it from us than from some wee skitter at school who had been listening to his parents gossip. Besides, looked at another way, Steve was a good example to them, proof that it was possible to triumph over your mistakes. At the Electronic Shop they didn't say we'll send out our engineer, they said we'll send out our *expert*.

Whatever their father had he had worked for.

Perhaps I had overstated this a bit. The last time Steve and

I had tried to talk to Martin about his schoolwork he had told us there was plenty of time for him yet. Anyway, he was going to do what his daddy had done and join the army. I waited till Steve was out of the room.

'Over my dead body you will,' I said.

Martin didn't seem to be all that bothered to be away from the flats, but Patricia took longer to settle. There was no one really for her round here. Ivy, who had brought us the salt when we moved in, said the street used to be teeming with kids out playing, which was nice to know but not a lot of help. Patricia asked to be let out to see her old friends four or five nights a week. We rationed her to Fridays and Saturdays and one Sunday a fortnight. Nine other nights a fortnight she pouted, she moaned, she lost all muscle power and fell face-down on her bed.

I ran through all the arguments. You must have homework. You must think your daddy and I have nothing to do but run up and down in the car after you. You're not walking back from that bus stop on your own. It'll be dark. It's pouring. There's thunder outside and lightning. *I'm not having you wandering in here with another dirty neck.*

We had let her out on her thirteenth birthday, a Wednesday, not long after we moved, and she'd come home sporting a big purple love bite. Every time I brought it up she swore blind again her mates had done it for a laugh, using their fingers. I was half beginning to believe her, though I teased her that I didn't. At least while she was arguing the point with me she was not going to ask why her neck was at greater risk of soiling in the middle of the week than it was at the week's end.

*

195

We hadn't been in the house six months when there was another funeral. Eric Robertson, who had lived for years next door to Ivy. I had never seen the man. He was in the hospital all the time we'd been here. Cancer. No cameras for this funeral, but a big crowd all the same. Mr and Mrs Tan were there with their youngest, a girl of about eighteen. The other girl was over the water now, like the son, at university. I invited the three of them in, but they were rushing to beat the traffic out of town.

You'd have thought maybe even five minutes, but then it isn't everyone who wants to see what you've done with their place.

After dinner, Steve and I walked across to Alma Robertson's. I was a little surprised that it was Alma herself met us at the door, even more surprised to be pulled down into a bony hug by her. She smelt of dental fixative and hair-setting lotion. The words 'holding it together' formed in my head.

'Isn't this great,' she said, meaning – I hoped – that we had taken the trouble to call, leading me by the hand into the living room.

Several elderly men, not from this street, nor long one or two of them for this life, sat clutching glasses on dining-room chairs in a line in front of the hearth. Behind them the mantelpiece was crowded with cards. Facing them, on the sofa, Jill Hideg was sitting with Joss Newton on one side and on the other a red-headed woman who I had never been introduced to but had a fair idea was Michele, Joss's wife. These three left together soon after Steve and I arrived.

'Dear help that girl,' Alma said, coming back from seeing them out and as though the reason for our gathering there had gone with Jill.

She asked one of the elderly men at the hearth to reach

down a large card from the mantelpiece and passed it to me where I sat on the cushion warmed by Joss Newton's cheeks.

'There,' she said.

What do you think of that? I heard.

I thought it was clearly home-made (black satin bow on white card, verse cut from a magazine), and wondered was I being asked my opinion out of some confused notion of what it was I did in the arts centre. And then I saw the signature. Holy Moly. The card was from our Patricia.

'There's not many would do that, now,' said Alma. 'The way the young ones are, off running.'

Steve had taken the card from me and was squinting at the signature as if to confirm that it wasn't a forgery. I pressed my thigh against his.

'Oh, she can be very thoughtful like that,' I said.

'Very,' said Steve.

There was another knock at the door. Alma wouldn't hear of anyone else getting it.

'Sit where you are. Boys, make sure people are all right for drinks.'

The 'boys' went out to the kitchen and returned carrying bottles. There was a son, Bobby, over from the States must have been getting on for sixty himself. The image of his father, the old men at the hearth agreed, from which I concluded that Eric Robertson had spent the last quarter of his life looking like a heart attack, not cancer, would do for him at any moment.

He had got no further than the sofa when Alma came back into the room with Annette Blake, who had brought a shortbread tin lined with greaseproof paper.

'A few wee buns,' she was saying as she passed through to the kitchen.

Bobby sat down beside me with a Bacardi bottle between his feet. Up close his florid complexion separated into a thousand broken veins and blood vessels, an intricate map of all the wrong roads he had taken.

He told me I was lucky to have my daughter. (And son, I said. And son, he said.) He told me his children all went with his first wife in 1965. He hadn't seen any of the three of them in years, wouldn't even have known now where to begin looking to tell them their grandpa was dead.

The other son, Graham, took the bottle from him eventually and carried on refilling glasses. He mightn't have said a lot, but in comparison to his brother he was a ray of sunshine. What little I had seen of Graham up to now had been on his way to and from work in one of the council yards, most of the time with a knitted bobble hat on him, the sort fellas wear to football matches, or used to wear about twenty years ago. To be honest it would have made you wish he'd had someone, a wife or a friend or a lippy teenage child of his own, who could have told him how ridiculous that hat made him look – how, I don't know, *arrested*. Such a contrast at the funeral this afternoon, in his double-breasted grey suit, raincoat over his arm. You couldn't have told him apart from any of the other middle-aged men on the street.

Before Steve and I left, Alma gave us a packet of fruit gums for Patricia and Martin. She patted my hand. 'Tell them I'm sorry I've nothing more,' she said and looked it, who had buried her husband today.

After the fruit gums came jelly beans, American style. Every Saturday Graham would drive Alma to one or other of the out-of-town shopping centres. (Not even Ivy could remember him learning to drive.) Alma brought the kids back the jelly beans the way we used to bring our friends sticks of rock from day trips to the seaside. There was a chart you could get with all the different flavours. Patricia compared taste notes with Martin and reported them back across the road.

I told Alma she shouldn't be bothering herself – I'd seen the beans in Woolworth's and they weren't cheap – but she said she was eighty-two, she had no grandchildren that she ever saw, she had to rack her brains thinking of things she could possibly need when Graham took her out. What else was she going to spend her money on?

When Steve put the word around that he was starting a sideline in satellite dishes, Alma was the first person on the street to enquire.

'It'd be good for Graham,' she said. 'I'm no company for him at all.'

And then, like that, Alma too was gone.

I feared the worst from the moment I heard the terrible roaring as I knelt on the back step getting ready to pour bleach down the drain.

Patricia met me rushing into the kitchen from the opposite direction.

'It's coming from over the road,' she said, all the colour gone from her face. Five minutes before she was jumping around like a two-year-old, delighted to be finished school for the Easter holiday.

'It's OK,' I said, though I knew she knew it was anything but.

I still had the bleach bottle in my hand when I pushed the Robertsons' open door and found Denis Moore in the hall-way talking on the phone. A red plastic ironing basket with the price tag on the bottom lay upturned on the floor behind him. Clothes littered the stairs, at the top of which Ivy crouched and Graham sat, in his donkey jacket and bobble hat, the roar reduced to silent sobbing into the heels of his hands.

Her heart just gave out, the doctor said. Ivy assured me that no matter how well she had appeared to be coping, Alma never did get over Eric's death. I thought of all the nights before we were married, before we had actually *slept* together, when Steve was in prison, and couldn't imagine how I would ever face a single night without him now. I thought of Jill Hideg's heart, broken at the age of fifty-three. Who could have sworn that in her place they would have spurned the consolations that Joss Newton and his church offered?

A week after the funeral Steve told me he had asked Graham Robertson did he still want the satellite dish.

'Steve!'

'What?'

'His mother's not cold in the grave.'

'That's what I was thinking, it would take his mind off it a bit.'

Patricia, who had walked in on the middle of this and who had taken Alma's death very hard, turned and ran from the room.

'Now look what you've done.'

Steve's face said *me?*

I shouted up the stairs. 'Patricia?'

Steve shouted from beside me. 'I'll put the thing up for nothing. Would that help?'

'Steve's probably right, you know,' Lorraine said when I told them next day in work.

Nick said we were not to get him started on satellite dishes. He said Rupert bloody Murdoch, Margaret bloody Thatcher.

He asked did Steve want to throw his wife on to the dole, Lorraine and Lucy and all the other artists on to the dole, Nick himself on to the dole? Because that was what would happen the way things were going.

'Is that you started, then?' Lorraine asked. 'Or do you still want us to stop you?'

Steve thought he could do a deal with the Electronic Shop where he went self-employed and they hired him back in for the work he was doing now. They saved themselves on National Insurance, holiday pay and the rest and Steve was free to develop the satellite sideline.

He reckoned we would be the big winners, even if the transition was a bit bumpy. I let Nick know I was on the lookout for a few extra hours. He told me there was a guaranteed two evenings a week going when the classes started up again in the autumn.

'If you can trust yourself being here with me after dark.'

Lorraine laughed her leg off when I reported this back to her.

'He has to be joking, right? I mean, he's seen Steve?'

Steve had wired up the centre's security camera. Lorraine said he made her want to go home and give her own husband a slap.

Wednesday night was Never Too Late For Pottery (Level 2) night. I would hate to have seen Level 1. I was supposed to get away by eight-thirty, but we were still picking gunk off the walls most nights at nine.

I was letting myself into the house this Wednesday in late October when I heard it. Nothing. In particular I heard nothing from Martin's room, even though his door (I could see the light fall across the darkened landing) was ajar. I eased my key from the Yale lock and called out as I pushed open the living-room door, 'Hello?'

Behind me a floorboard creaked under Martin's weight.

In the mirror above the fireplace I saw Steve and Patricia sitting at opposite ends of the sofa. His face was stern, hers shaped a weak smile.

'Everything all right?' I asked, without optimism.

'Tell your mother what you told me,' said Steve. Mother. Very bad sign. I sat without removing my raincoat.

Patricia blew out her cheeks. I couldn't decide whether she was trying not to laugh or trying not to cry.

'I'm saved,' she said, and I was so prepared for 'pregnant' that it was a moment or two before I took it in. I looked from her to Steve, whose face was sterner than ever. Maybe 'saved' was slang for something else.

'Saved like Jesus saved?' I asked.

'Yes,' her voice cheerier. 'Since yesterday.'

I widened an eye, the one Steve could see and Patricia couldn't. *Since yesterday*. It was far too soon yet to be certain.

God, I was still thinking pregnancy.

'Well that's –' one last attempt to fathom the reason for Steve's mood, a shy away from the word good – 'a big step, isn't it?'

'You don't have a choice,' Patricia said and I gave my attention over to her. She had the most gorgeous hazel eyes, my daughter. Her daddy's eyes. I didn't know when I had last seen them so bright. 'It just happens. You just feel God enter you.'

I was saved myself at that moment by a heavy footfall on the middle stair. Martin never could tiptoe. Steve shouted at him to get back up to his room.

Patricia appealed to me, as it appeared she had already

appealed to her daddy. 'Anybody would think I'd done something wrong.'

This was too much for Steve. 'You're fourteen and a half, for crying out loud.'

I wasn't quite sure I saw his argument. What was he saying – go out and get drunk, take drugs, have some sex and then decide?

Clearly Patricia didn't see it either. 'It's not like voting or driving a car, there isn't a legal age,' she said, and after Steve had blundered on about her not coming to talk it through with us first, 'Have you never heard of individual conscience?'

The only word to describe her tone was martyred. She raised her hands to her eyes and I gestured to Steve, chasing him from the room. He closed the kitchen door. I waited till I heard him at the sink filling the kettle.

'You know what it is, don't you? Your daddy's worried that you've gone and joined the Moonies.' Her head wobbled behind her hands. 'He has a very vivid imagination. We've got to wean him off that *Daily Star*.'

The hands fell to her lap. She pulled a far-from-new twist of peach toilet paper from her sleeve and held it under her nose as she shook her head, laughing noiselessly.

'Do you want to tell me how it happened?' I said when the toilet paper had been tucked away again. Her shrug suggested not casualness, but the sudden overwhelming of a crush.

'This girl in my class, Helen, was saved at a meeting on her holidays,' she said. 'Everyone's been keeping her going, telling dirty jokes and all around her. I just felt sorry for her. I started sitting beside her the odd time. That was all – like, I mean we weren't best friends or anything, but then some of the ones in our class started picking on me as well, calling me a Bible-basher, and in the end I just said to them, So what if I am?

And then I thought, well, so what if I was, what would it be like? So I went looking for her yesterday lunchtime and I asked her how you did it and she just looked at me and said, You don't have to do anything, only want God to love you and love him back. And as I was walking down the corridor away from her it happened. I wanted it and it happened.'

I crossed the room and sat next to her on the sofa. She angled her body into mine, head on my shoulder. Coconut hair. I rocked with her. From the kitchen came the sound of mugs clacking as they were lifted from the tree.

'Are you happy?' I asked her.

'Oh, Mummy,' she said, 'I am.'

When she went to bed I reassured Steve she would get over it in a week or two.

'Good,' he said, and rubbed his cheekbone. 'She was giving me the creeps.'

∽

Patricia was asking to be let stay out late on New Year's Eve. She and Helen wanted to join a minibus going around the city looking for derelicts to feed soup to. Helen was the only school friend she seemed to bother with now. She never went near the girls from the flats any more. If she went out at all these days it was to the Christian Endeavour or her Bible-study group.

I told her she had better ask her dad about New Year.

She came back in from talking to him, smiling. 'Thanks, Mum,' she said and went off to phone Helen, give her the new good news.

Steve came in smiling too, letting on he was getting no pleasure from it. 'What was it you told me? A couple of weeks at the most?'

'And how many minutes ago was it you last said that to me?'

He bent as though to kiss me. 'I love it when you admit you're wrong,' he said and ran before I could thump him.

Of course, Patricia hadn't turned into a perfect teenager overnight. We still had rows about the state of her room, her help around the house. She still got into wrestling matches with Martin over the remote control, over nothing sometimes you could actually identify, as though they were acting out a need they both felt to get to grips with their changed relationship now that Helen and Jesus had entered into Patricia's life.

She had asked me early on if she could say grace at meals. I had to explain to her that I didn't think this would be fair. Neither her daddy nor I, nor Martin for that matter, were believers (she looked at me, shocked) *in the strictest sense*. So, while we respected her beliefs, we would only be making hypocrites of ourselves, which would be a worse sin than not saying grace. Wouldn't it?

She had taken this on board. That was what my converted daughter did, took things on board. She came to me later that day and asked would it be OK then if we had a Quiet Moment before starting to eat. I couldn't really object to a Quiet Moment – as long as it was only a moment – though I said I would have to talk to her daddy all the same.

Steve was less than thrilled, but couldn't think of a good argument against it either. 'As long . . .' he said and I said, 'I know, I know.'

Steve told Martin and told him he wasn't to laugh or carry on and I told Patricia it was all right and when dinnertime arrived she came into the dinette looking pious, if maybe just a little proud, and seated herself at the table where Steve and Martin already sat with their hands out of sight on their laps.

I served the dinner – chops, spuds, carrot and parsnip, peas – on to plates lined up on the countertop. No carrot and parsnip for Martin, less potato for Patricia, an extra bit of chop for Steve. I called out the names as I passed them over and carried my own plate to the table.

We all looked at Patricia, then at our dinner, then at Patricia again. She had let her eyes close. Steve's brow had half a frown formed when she opened them again and asked for the brown sauce. Martin reached for the bottle, the lines cleared from Steve's forehead. It really wasn't the most painful thing you'd ever be asked to do.

In fact as the Quiet Moment became part of our mealtime routine I found myself sort of looking forward to it. Out all day working, racing home to get a dinner on, clearing dishes, out again sometimes to work, or standing half the night making sandwiches for the next day's lunches, it was rare otherwise that I got even half a moment's peace and quiet. After only a few meals I had stopped watching Patricia and let my own eyes close, let my mind – not empty, exactly – *breathe*, until I heard the rest of the family shifting in their seats, asking for the salt or pepper.

Steve confided in me that he had started seeing random numbers in the Quiet Moment. He had tried matching them to the numbers on pools coupons, even to the daily racing cards at the back of the *Star*, but had felt uncomfortable and soon stopped. A god who gave you racing tips was still a god. Start giving credence to that and who knows what you would end up believing.

Martin was the next to go.

Steve and I had sent him and Patricia to stay the weekend with Steve's parents to let us get away down south for our wedding anniversary. Patricia was *appalled* that we didn't trust her to look after herself and Martin. Look, I told her, you were only born again a year and a half ago, they'd arrest me leaving someone that age in charge.

Apparently I was hilarious. Apparently I should have been on the stage. Yes, and when I was off on my world tour we would have round-the-clock security on the house. Meantime she and Martin were staying with their granny and granddad.

As soon as we picked them up on the Sunday night I sensed the altered atmosphere in the car and since Patricia was the same as ever, that is the same as she had been since she ceased to be the Patricia of old, that could only mean that Martin had changed. Not that I had a hope of getting anything out of him. He was a teenage boy, I was told it came with the territory. I resolved to keep an eye on him for a while, which wasn't all that hard. Martin was far from friendless, his report cards suggested he had a few too many friends for the good of his schoolwork, but he was still a home-bird. He was too comfortable, according to Steve. If I'd been an unkind mother I would have said he was storing up fat for when he finally had to leave the nest.

No one, I think, was more flabbergasted than Martin when a couple of Saturdays later he was picked as reserve for the under-fifteen school football team. Steve offered to drive him to the game. Patricia had stayed the night at Helen's. I waited for five minutes after the car had left the street, to allow for forgotten shorts or boots, then I went and searched Martin's room.

I was a parent, I'd done worse.

Nothing on the surface appeared to be different. Same pictures on the wall, torn from magazines and inexpertly trimmed: men on their knees, heads thrown back, guitars upright between their legs. Larger, shop-bought posters of groups whose tousled hair and smiles, held it seemed a fraction too long, always reminded me ludicrously of girls' netball teams. There was the usual confusion of cassettes with and without cassette boxes beside the bed, a contrast to the neat stack of magazines yet to be plundered for pictures and the row of books arranged in order of height on the chest of drawers. At one end of the row and as holy as it would normally have got in that room was the *Child's Treasury of Bible Stories*, which my parents had bought when Martin started school and which had, I supposed, as much to do with serious religion as a bag of crisps did with a potato.

I found the tract under the pillow. 'Make My Life a Living Prayer', it said on the cover above a pair of crudely drawn hands, laid palm on palm and severed at the wrists. I sat on the edge of Martin's bed. Beyond the garden and its mirror image, in the bathroom of the house that backed on to ours, an indistinct man made careful passes with a comb across his head. There was a six-foot-high fence between our gardens. I had never spoken to this man, wouldn't have been 100 per cent sure I would recognize him if I saw him on the street, without the filter of frosted glass.

I blinked away a brief feeling of bleakness, opened the tract.

I tried to imagine, reading it, how the words sounded in Martin's head and why they appealed to him more now, when words like these had been a part of our daily lives for so long already.

Patricia was first home, which helped make up my mind for me to talk to her before I said anything to Martin. I wanted to be clear that she had put no pressure on her brother, hadn't given him any of that burning for ever in hellfire stuff that would have been so vivid to the heavy metal fan in him.

But, no, Patricia said. 'He came to me, Mum, weeks and weeks ago. I sent him away the first time. I told him he had to be sure he knew what he was committing himself to. Then the other week at granny and granddad's he came to me again. He said he'd thought about it and he was ready, so we said a prayer together and he gave me a hug and away he went.'

There were voices at that moment in the alleyway.

'Martin did well,' said Steve, coming in the back door. 'Played for nearly all the second half, had a shot just over the bar.'

'I gave away a penalty,' Martin said.

'The goalie saved it.'

'They scored from the corner. We lost three-two.'

Martin went to his room.

'He's a tube and he knows it,' Steve said to me under his breath.

I left it till after lunch to take Martin aside. He sighed when I told him I had guessed something had happened in his life. (I thought of escaped convicts giving themselves up, tired of being on the run.) I let him know that I was pleased for him, but that no one, not even Patricia, would think any the less of him if he changed his mind. He asked me would I tell his daddy. It was through worrying about Steve disapproving that he had put off saying anything himself.

Steve, when I did tell him, couldn't get to disapproval for despair. Even so I made him go and have a chat with Martin. Martin at least appeared cheered by it.

In the course of our next Quiet Moment, however, I broke my habit and glanced towards Steve. His gaze was moving from our son's intent face to our daughter's in a long, slow shake. He raised his eyes to mine. Where did we go wrong? they asked.

★

Graham Robertson's Mini Clubman hadn't moved from the kerbside since his mother's funeral. There was rust on the chrome, moss on the windscreen wipers, two and a half years of crisp packets and cigarette-box wrappers trapped in the hubcaps.

'Why doesn't he get rid of it if he's never going to use it?' Steve said.

I asked him who it was had talked Graham into a satellite dish.

Steve humphed. 'Sitting there, taking up space.'

Steve had just had to make a one-hundred-yard dash through heavy rain from our car. The problems we had had the day we moved in were only a taster, this street was a nightmare for parking. Steve complained that it took him as long finding a space some days as it did driving home from work. Not a week went by without someone rapping on your door asking you to move your car to let them in or out. I'd heard stand-up rows in the street. Grown men and women: *I was parking on this spot before you were . . . No you weren't . . . Yes I was*. One of these days punches would be thrown. I had told Steve time and again he was not to go getting involved in anything. (Anyone would have thought I didn't trust my husband.) I'd told him he was to park streets away if need be, I'd get him a collapsible bike for the boot to cycle from wherever he managed to squeeze in.

Steve, though, had other ideas. Specifically he had an idea involving the front garden. He shared it with me while we were having lunch one Saturday in a place we liked to slip away to when we could down the east coast.

I nearly choked on my scampi. *'Tarmac?'* All I could think of was the forecourt of the flats. 'Are you sure you wouldn't want to add a bay for the bin lorry to back into?'

Steve let this go. 'We can put a couple of planters out there under the window,' he said. 'I'll get you lovely black and gold gates.'

I wondered what it was exactly he saw in me that looked like it was longing for black and gold gates.

'No, Steve.' I set down my knife and fork. It wasn't the garden itself I minded losing, for all there was of it anyway, but the link with the street, a reason other than getting into the car for being out the front of the house. 'Just no.'

We passed the entire journey home in stony silence and of course at the end of it we couldn't find a place to park. Saturday afternoon, an extra-special nightmare. Still neither of us spoke. On our third lap of the block a gap had opened up outside Newton's. I made no move to open the door when the engine had been switched off.

'The neighbours are going to hate us,' I said. 'It'll spoil the whole look of the street.'

Actually, the black and gold gates weren't so bad after all.

'If there was a world record for changing your tune,' Nick said, 'you'd hold it.'

'Don't listen to him, I think it looks really well,' said Lorraine.

I had brought the photos in to show her of the work we'd had done.

'Ivy over the road's talking of getting a set of the gates for her driveway.'

Nick lifted one of the pictures, curled his lip. I'd seen him practising it when he thought there was no one around. 'Could you get the car any closer to the house?'

I carried on talking to Lorraine.

'And the people next door to us are going to see about getting the loan to do theirs. I've said to them, you won't regret it. After the first couple of days you can hardly remember ever having it any other way.'

'I hope you told them to tell everyone they work with they're going to have to live every riveting minute of it with them,' said Nick.

The phone rang. I was closest.

'Nick,' I said. 'Serge.'

Serge had been a short-term captive in the timber yard late last year. The old woman who had bequeathed the house to the city had stipulated that there should always be room for international artists at the centre. On the odd days he was let out Serge wandered the district none too inconspicuously (he was very tall, very bald, he dressed all in black), taking pictures, which he had been 'working up' back home in Brussels and which he wanted Nick to exhibit.

'Serge?' Nick said into the phone. 'I'm taking you upstairs.'

I listened for the click of the receiver being lifted and hung up.

'Did you see any of his stuff when he was here?' Lorraine asked me.

'No. Why?'

She made a creeped-out face.

'That bad?'

'Probably just not my kind of thing,' she said.

You rarely did get to see Lorraine's kind of thing, or mine, at the O'Neill Memorial Arts Centre.

'I like the planters,' Lorraine said, handing me back my pictures.

The DOE sent out an inspector, who checked that the slip on to the street met the specifications and signed the authorization for the release of the deposit we had had to lodge with the roads department. It was our own money, but after half a year without it it still felt like a windfall. Steve suggested that we use part of it to go for dinner, just the two of us, make up for the lunch we spoiled that time by arguing.

There was a new pizza and pasta place, *Bellissima!*, opened down on the main road, where Watt's the butcher's used to be. Patricia had an application in for a part-time job, but the waiting list for them was as long as the one for tables on Friday and Saturday nights. Steve and I booked for a quarter to seven Monday. He was late getting in from work and wouldn't dream of going out without a shave.

'We'll phone a taxi,' I said. I wanted us to take a bit of time over our meal, have a bottle of wine. But Steve came downstairs with the car keys in his hand.

'Come on, we're not phoning a taxi to take us less than a mile.'

The pips went for seven before we were out of the street. We picked up an R driver going about five miles an hour while we waited to turn on to the Low Road. Steve's thumbs beat the lost time on the steering wheel.

'Relax, we're going out to enjoy ourselves,' I said as the radio news reported a stabbing in the city centre. Steve parped the horn at the R driver in front.

We ate again in silence. When we had finished, Steve took my hand over our wiped-clean stone-base plates. 'I don't deserve you,' he said.

'Oh, I don't know about that.'

I pushed my knees against his under the table then let mine part. Steve shook his head. Unlike me, he had been drinking nothing stronger than Coke. His eyes were glistening. This was not the response I had been hoping for. I let up with the knees, massaged his hand.

'Hey.'

Then out of the blue he said, 'I wonder what happened to That Fella.'

'What fella?' I asked, as though I didn't have a pretty good idea from the capital T, capital F I heard.

Steve was looking down at his plate and the knife that lay crossed there with his fork.

'Probably sitting somewhere having a pizza wondering what happened to you,' I said.

Steve's chest rose and fell. 'A quarter of an inch to the left and he'd have been dead and we wouldn't be here. Patricia and Martin wouldn't have been born.'

I caught the waiter's eye, shaped the word bill.

'Really, when you think about it, it's a miracle.'

I woke at five past three in the morning to find the other half of the bed empty and cooling. When a quarter of an hour later there was still no sign of Steve I got up and put on my dressing gown. I found him in the dinette, a chair pulled up to the open Venetian blinds. I stood behind him, trying to see through the slats what it was he was peering at out there. I could just about separate the fence from the oil tank.

'Couldn't sleep?'

I felt his jaw touch my hand, detach itself, touch again: No.

'It's very close,' I said. He nodded. After a few minutes I knelt on the floor in front of him, chin supported on hands crossed on his lap. He had hurt his ring finger at work a while back and had taken to sleeping with it in a stall. He held it inflexibly apart from its pals. The fly of his pyjamas gaped, revealing tufts of his coppery hair. I imagined working my head between his thighs. It had been a wee while since I'd done that outside of the bedroom. He carried on looking out the dinette window.

'That fella again?'

Steve made no reply.

'Is it *anything* you want to talk about?'

'You're right, it's close,' was all he said.

I turned my head so that my cheek rested on the back of my hand. When next I opened my eyes I was in bed again, Steve breathing behind me, deep in sleep. He had discarded his pyjamas and whatever it was he was dreaming about, or however it is a man's body works, his penis was bone hard against my upper thigh. I adjusted myself, it slid, thwacked the inside of my other thigh, I moved again, relocating the pressure – not there, *there* – returning it a little, a little more, a little more . . . a little . . . Steve sprang up from the pillow, up from sleep, making me gasp so loudly I'd to jam a fist in my mouth. I felt about fifteen again, slipping the hand on a guy for the first time, astonished by the instant and unbelievable force of the reaction. Steve had managed to catch a hold of his thrashing penis, though there was nothing he could do now except choose his direction. I could *hear* the spunk squirt from him. I wanted it in me, on me, my hands on him. I felt I was about to laugh out of a surfeit of love, but my eyes were prickly with tears. I got the lamp on as Steve flopped back on the bed, a great big tear of his own falling – plop! – to the left of his navel.

'Sweet Jesus.'

Stephen Eliot, husband of Catriona, father of Patricia and Martin, was born again on Tuesday 4 August 1993, three days into the forty-second year of his unbelieving life. I couldn't say it was altogether a surprise. The nights spent sitting before the dinette window had been growing more frequent as the summer progressed and there had been a curious otherworld-liness to much of his conversation of late, especially after the evening news, so that I was tempted more than once to break into a rendition of that 'What's it all about?' song from *Alfie*, though speaking of films, watching him circle ever closer to the moment of decision ('Things don't happen without a purpose,' he had pronounced after some new climatic catastrophe), I began to appreciate how it must have felt to have been the last normal wife in Stepford.

Andy Capp was the clincher. I was standing peeling potatoes on to him one Sunday, thinking how unfunny I had always found him, when I realized Steve had gone back to the *Mirror*. Reading the *Star* had long been a badge of perverse pride for my husband. The more jokes were made about his paper, the more brain-rotting were said to be its effects, the more determinedly Steve . . . well, *read* was perhaps too joined-up a word for it. All those practically nude and more often than not teenage girls. Who knew what Patricia – and lately Martin, teenage boy though he was – had made of that paper, those pictures, lying around the house?

'I just got fed up with the other one,' Steve had said when I asked him about the switch.

'After ten years?'

'Why not? It's never too late to change your mind.'

Which was just close enough to being a line from an ad campaign to give me brief cause for hope.

Lorraine at work said it all sounded to her like a mid-life stock take, a hedging of bets, and despite the evidence from our son and daughter that there might be some family trait of stickability, I did find it hard at first to take my husband's conversion too seriously. He really had been such an un-believer before. *I* had more religion and I had none.

Steve brought this up himself the day after he confirmed what I had long suspected.

'Why don't you give it a try too?' he said. (Give it a try – I mean, they were hardly the words of the irretrievably saved.) 'If someone as far from God as I was can find their way to him, think how much easier it would be for you.'

'If it's all the same to you, I'll wait and see how the two of you get on before I make up my mind,' I said, and then before he could say anything of his own, 'Sorry. Blasphemy, I know.'

God and Steve got on like a house on fire. They talked regularly in the evenings when the plates had been cleared away from the dinner table. Martin usually joined in (Martin's Bible had a sticker on the slip sleeve: This Machine Slays Atheists), Patricia too, as often as she was able once she had had the call from *Bellissima!* To begin with if I wasn't working myself I brought the ironing board through to the living room, watched the television with the sound on low. Or I dusted my Royal Doulton, tidied upstairs, washed the bath, buffed the taps. Our toilet was worthy of a rosette. After a while I took to just lying on the bed with a P.D. James out of the library. Half the time I would wind up drifting off.

I was awoken one night by a knocking at the front door. I looked down the bed at my big toe looking back at me from a hole in my tights. Between us were hills of pilly pink blanket, a little tent of a paperback pitched round about the midpoint. It was twenty-five to eight. I felt like I'd been asleep for a week. I unravelled myself with difficulty from the blanket, trying to remember what I had done with my slippers. I was still hunting under the bed when the front door was opened and Patricia said 'Hiya,' like it was someone she was expecting. I crossed the carpet on all fours, paused on the threshold of the landing, ear cocked to pick up a woman's voice mingling greetings with Steve and Martin in the dinette. It took me a moment squeezing my eyes shut to place the owner of the voice. Jill Hideg. I spied the heel of one slipper under the chest of drawers, found the second eventually on the window side of the bed. The wardrobe's mirrored door offered an unsympathetic portrait of me as flushed fluff-magnet. I banished the image, throwing open the door looking for something fresh to put on.

The dinette was as quiet as prayer.

I could have kicked myself for a chump. Jill couldn't care less what I wore or even if I made an appearance. It wasn't the Eliot *family* she had called to see. I picked up the book, swung my legs back on to the bed, leafing through the pages till I had found my place.

At least this was one mystery that was guaranteed a quick solution.

After Jill came Andrea, her married daughter, and a friend of Andrea's, Maura, who had lost a brother in a bomb, and Maura's husband, Noel. Word did what word was supposed to do in these circumstances – spread. After twenty-odd years of people being blown up and shot in this city you hardly needed a divining rod to pick up on the pain. It seemed not to matter that Steve had caused his own share of suffering once upon a time. If anything the others looked up to him as the greater sinner repented.

For as far back as I could remember, wherever I lived, I could point out the houses where 'wee meetings' were held. Round my parents' way it was the house belonging to a bandy ex-teacher who was sacked for getting her P2 class on their knees ready for the end of the world during the Cuban missile crisis. When Steve and I married we lived for a time close to a couple who went around with a go-kart collecting newspapers and magazines for the soldiers in the military hospital. I didn't recall once seeing them apart, or in the company of anyone else. Maybe nobody did attend the wee meetings they never failed to remind you about when they called at your door. Maybe they sat together in the living room every night praying for the bell to be rung. They lived in a queer-shaped end-terrace, its door cut into the angle of two walls meeting, its windows like lizards' eyes looking both ways at once.

The truth of it was, though, that all such houses had an odd look about them, as if something of what went on inside had leaked, the way I'd read radiation did, into the very bricks and mortar.

I took to examining my own house as I walked down the street towards it. I asked myself whether a stranger, thirsting, as they said in the dinette, would have spotted it straight away for a holy house, a religious shebeen. But all I saw was what I had helped make, a none-too-shabby, going-on-thirty-five-year-old inside-terrace with off-street parking.

No, there was one thing. The more I looked at it – and my eye seemed always to be drawn back there – the more puzzled I became about the door number itself. What on earth was a 5, after all? In weathered Bakelite it had the air of a sign more ancient and mysterious than four plus one, an air almost of pre-existence. (Another big dinette word.) On the wall beside the door to the right of us was a varnished cross-section of tree trunk with the word three in white-painted italics. To our left was a no-nonsense brass 7, to the left of that no number at all, but a name, Dalriada. In fact, out of twenty-four houses, ours was one of only two with the original 1950s numeral on the original 1950s door.

I couldn't explain why it irked me so much.

There was no point saying anything to Steve. Between scaling the outside of other people's houses, aligning their dishes with outer space, and sitting in the dinette contemplating the infinite, Steve's waking hours were already taken up with things far higher than door numbers.

In the end I decided to have a go at it myself. Lucy from the timber yard had promised to make me a nice ceramic plaque, cut-price.

I picked a night when Steve had Martin out at a rare away meeting. He must have had the power screwdriver in the boot of the car. I normally preferred the manual anyway, but after half an hour's twisting, changing the head from thin to thick and back, I had burn marks on the palm of my hand, sweat running from the underside of my breasts. The grooves in the tops of the screws were worn away to nothing.

'Has he you out working again?' Ivy called from the far side of the street.

Ivy had a voice you imagined would sound no different if it was coming to you from the far side of a table or the far side of a valley.

'Just pottering,' I said. There was sweat too in the small of my back.

'Ours came loose on us as well,' Ivy said, for Ivy's indeed was the other house with its original door and fittings. 'I said to Denis we'll superglue it if needs be. You can't get them any more.'

I put the screwdriver back in the toolbox, spat on my hands to take the heat out of them, out of me. It was only a number.

The bastard thing.

After two hundred faxes, half as many phone calls again, after applications to funders here, there, everywhere in the EU, and what felt like more than fifteen months of everyone's lives, Serge's exhibition arrived at the arts centre. Nick had had the gallery painted again in preparation. White ceilings white walls white floorboards. Serge arrived himself, all in black, taller-, balder-, somehow more Belgian-looking even than before. He spent the best part of three days up in the gallery with Nick. I caught glimpses of the two of them, leaning against the window frame at the top of the stairs, smoking, dashing from the front door, jumping into Nick's car, returning half an hour later, dashing inside. Serge by the third day was wearing an un-Serge-like baseball cap to hide the stubble he hadn't had time to shave from his normally polished head.

Lorraine and I spent the three days making another few score calls to people we had sent invitations to who hadn't yet RSVPed.

We took ourselves up for a sneak preview while Nick and Serge were off on one of their mad dashes. The gallery ran the entire length of the front of the house then dog-legged right, into what was once the dressing room of one of the two bedrooms that were formerly here. There were sheets on the floor to keep the boards clean for the opening night. Starting on the left of the door and continuing round the walls for as far as I could see were deep box-frames, about eight inches by ten and about four inches apart. The photographs, common or garden Polaroids, were pinned to the backs of the frames like specimens in a museum. I peered in at a few. A flute band, a fruit and veg stall, a tattoo-parlour window, what looked like a dog tangled in reeds and carry-out bags at the edge of a pond.

'Frig me,' Lorraine said. She had wandered round the corner. 'You have to see this.'

'This' was a black and white image, easily three feet square, of a man's buttocks and a man's hand in a tight-fitting leather glove. Clearly from the way they were arranged, the hand and the buttocks could not belong to the same man. There was a faint mark on the left buttock that might have been the shadow of the hand or might have been the imprint of a recently administered smack. Below this and only just in frame was the waistband of what looked like army trousers, pushed down far enough to give a definite suggestion of bum hair and three-foot-by-three-foot-scale scrotum.

Frig was putting it mildly.

A councillor walked out of the opening in protest, stopping on the landing just long enough to supply one of the journalists with all the copy she needed for her next day's story: filth, fury, calls for ban. Serge flew home in a fury of his own. It was left to Nick to talk to the camera crews who in due course arrived.

Well, yes, the work was provoking, he said. *Thought*-provoking. As an artist himself he could never condone the censoring of the imagination. The people who were backing the councillor's call for the exhibition to be closed down hadn't even been in to look at the piece in question, to judge it in its context.

(Of flute bands, fruit and veg stalls, dogs gone belly-up.)

I was watching him from the sidelines. He was in his element, nodding in apparent agreement through the interviewer's questions, taking up the opposite position the instant he opened his mouth to speak. He went on to talk about ambivalence, about tension and tenderness and a lot of other things that *he as an artist himself* saw in Serge's photographs. He even managed to work in a reference to the rumours doing the rounds of talks to end the violence here. (Maybe that was

what a found-objects sculptor was, a scavenger for meaning.)
It was hard, just occasionally, not to admire the fella, or at the
very least his gall.

He asked the interviewer as the crew was packing up if
there was any chance of a tape in case he wasn't home in time
to set his own video. 'For our archive.'

Nick wouldn't have had the first idea which drawer I kept
'our archive' in.

It was hot in the gallery from the news crew's lights. I gave
Nick a hand, when they had gone, opening the stiff sash
windows. We wound up back at the buttocks.

Nick asked me if the image offended me.

'Offend? No. Why should it?'

'Oh, I don't know, with Steve and everything, and then the
way you used to rant about the page-three girls.'

Given his spiel for the cameras especially, it seemed an odd
sort of equation for him to make, though I wasn't about to
start arguing art criticism with him.

'I never *ranted*.'

'No need to be defensive, it was very entertaining.'

He had leaned against the wall between me and the main
body of the gallery. If it had been anyone other than Nick I
would have suspected him of trying to flirt. Maybe the lights
and the attention had gone to his head. Maybe – and this was
a truly appalling thought – the scrotum and bum hair on
display behind me weren't just any old scrotum and bum hair.

'I'm glad to hear I'm of some use around here. But you
know,' I said, guessing correctly that if I delivered this inches
from his face he would stand up straight enough for me to
pass, 'you've got it badly wrong about Christians and sex.'

Well, Christian Steve and sex anyway. Because I had to say
this for my husband, no matter where in the universe his mind

had been before he closed the bedroom door, he had never once forgotten what it was first brought the two of us together. He might not have talked me through in quite the same graphic way precisely what he was doing and was going to do next, but that did not stop him, three, four times a week, drawing me closer to him in bed, kissing my throat, the back of my neck, depending, hands caressing, where he knew I liked it, the curving in of my thighs. After so many years I could not even have said whether he was in comparison big or not, but he was right for me, which is to say just a fraction more at particular moments than I thought, pushing down on him, I was able to take.

'Oh, Catriona,' he said then into my skin. 'Oh, I love you.'

Now, really, who was going to argue with a religion like that?

Joss Newton was smiling at me from the front step when I answered the door. The clocks did not go forward for another month, so either he had been sitting staring into a light bulb or his glasses were stuck on last year's summer time, because I could see nothing of his eyes.

For a moment before he spoke he tilted his head like I was the one had come knocking on his door, like mine was the question, his the answer.

'Steve in?' he said at last.

'Not yet.'

I was just on my way back out myself. Nick was expecting the crowds after the feature on the evening news. I had no wish to get into conversation with Joss Newton.

'He can be a hard man to get, your husband.'

'Well, he has to work when the work's there, he's out on his own.'

'Oh, I know,' said Joss, the smile twitching, as though he thought I was completely cloth-eared, or there was a studio audience somewhere yak-yakking at his wit.

He had already, at least once that I knew of, made a comment to Martin about his daddy not going to an actual church. I had no doubt that whatever anyone else thought of Steve's past, Joss Newton had him marked down permanently as a bad lot.

'I'll let him know you called,' I said and crossed my fingers I'd forget.

I took an extra hour on Thursday morning to make up for working late the night before. Lorraine rang while I was still running around getting on me.

'Thought I'd better warn you since you're walking, there's a picket at the end of our driveway.'

'Bloody hell.'

'I know. Mad, isn't it? Maybe you'd be better off in a taxi. Hang on to the receipt, tell Nick you're claiming it back.'

I ignored my friend's advice and walked. Had to keep in trim somehow. It was a raw, raw morning. By the time I reached the gates of the arts centre the picket was buffeted and distracted-looking, half a dozen strangers in search of a windbreak. I was past before most of them noticed me. One woman with a toddler in a pushchair did give chase, yelling *pornographer* after me, then the child started crying that it had dropped its bottle of orange and she wheeled the chair around, cooing to quiet it.

Nick was bent over in the entrance lobby loading a roll of film into a camera the size of a small bazooka. I must have taken him by surprise. He dropped the film carton he had been holding between his knees.

'Souvenirs for Serge,' he explained.

I picked the carton up, popped it in his jacket pocket.

He smiled. 'I owe you one.'

Nick, it's a cardboard box.

'Right,' I said. 'I'll remember that.'

Lorraine and I watched him on the security-camera monitor, trying to act nonchalant as he set off down the drive, a dirty great zoom lens sticking out behind him.

'What on earth is he like?' I said.

'Odder than ever this morning,' said Lorraine. 'But who isn't?'

Lorraine had just taken her third call in twenty minutes from someone playing hymns down the line.

'They must have the tapes and all sitting by the phone waiting for something like this,' I said. 'Really when you think about it we're doing the public a service keeping them occupied.'

All the same, I was starting to wonder if the fuss was just going to blow over as we had been telling ourselves up to now.

A couple of schools rang in to postpone visits to the artists' workshops, 'for the time being', but this was offset a little by the arrival late in the morning of what must have been an entire year's art students, who lined up on the stairs to write their names in the comments book and stayed to wander about the house and grounds long into the afternoon.

Possibly pricked by the students' presence, the picket picked up after lunch and really took off once the local primary school let out. Someone arrived with a megaphone, through which they barked about bewaring sodomy for the benefit of passing cars, playing tapes of hymns betweentimes. Come to think of it, it could have been the person who phoned the centre earlier. Maybe the hymns were his normal form of communication, the barked comments the interlude.

An American TV station rang saying it wanted to come and do a feature – a sign, Lorraine suggested, that we were starting to have more news crews here than news – but they couldn't make it until mid evening. Could we guarantee there would still be a protest outside? I passed the phone to Nick.

'Well, we don't actually welcome the protest, of course,' he said before turning his back on Lorraine and me.

Later he asked could one of the two of us come in after tea, keep an eye on things for him for an hour. No need to ask what he would be doing.

'Sorry,' Lorraine said. 'Plans made.'

I had no plans.

'Sorry, Nick, no can do.'

He caught me up in the hallway when I was on my way home.

'Are you sure you couldn't manage even one hour, double time?'

'Not even an hour, not even quadruple time. I need a night at home.'

'It's just,' he dropped his voice, 'you're usually the one I can depend on.'

I preferred it when he was being a prick to me and Lorraine both.

'No, Nick, not tonight.'

He held the door for me to pass through.

'We're OK, aren't we?' he said.

'What's this "we" business, Pale Face?'

He half-laughed. I left at a trot. Seriously, I was thinking, what does he mean, 'we', what does he mean, 'OK'?

I brushed by the man with the megaphone. He turned to

me, said in what must have passed with him for a whisper, 'Do you know where you will be for eternity?'

Wherever it was, I hoped it was soundproof.

The dishes were washed and put away, Patricia was at *Bellissima!*, Martin upstairs doing his homework. (Diligence, if not yet excellence, had been the one welcome side-effect of Martin's rebirth.) I was psyching myself up for a week's worth of ironing. Steve sat at the table, hands folded on his Bible.

'Who are you expecting tonight?' I said.

Thursday was usually a popular night in the dinette.

'No one,' Steve said.

I set up the board in the living room, walked back through to the kitchen to fill the jug for the iron. In the seconds I had been gone Steve had opened his Bible and was frowning down at the contents. Well, I supposed, anywhere you opened it you wouldn't have been long finding something to frown about. I had the yoke of the first shirt done when I placed the iron on its end and peeked through the crack in the kitchen door. Steve was still frowning. I waited to see would he turn a page, and waited, and then pushed the door with my fingertips.

'Why are they not coming?'

Steve kept his eyes lowered.

'Look, it doesn't matter,' he said, at which point of course it started to matter to me a great deal. I remembered what I had been pushing to the back of my mind since last evening.

'That fella Newton's been here,' I said, with as much ask in it as tell.

Steve closed his Bible, folded his hands again.

'He said Jill has decided that coming here is no longer compatible with her attendance at his church.'

Jill decided my foot. Even through Steve's reporting of it it was pure Joss-speak. I stopped myself asking had Jill no mind of her own. He mightn't have looked a minute over thirty, but Joss Newton was already an elder in his church. His word had weight. I could just imagine how hard it would be for Jill's will to resist it, after everything (as I was sure she was reminded) the church had done for her when her husband was murdered.

'You know what that's about, don't you?' I said.

I really did think until I saw Steve's eyes at last raised to mine that what it was about was Steve's having been inside.

'Don't tell me it's to do with those photographs.'

He didn't tell me it wasn't.

'Well, I hope you told him where to go.'

He didn't tell me that he had.

Surely he couldn't agree with Joss?

'Steve, the things are hanging in an art gallery, nobody has to go and see them if they don't want to.'

I couldn't quite credit that we were having this conversation, if you could call me talking and him sitting there not answering a conversation.

'Will you say something?'

He sighed.

I exploded. 'Well . . . *balls* to the whole damned lot of you.'

Steve gawped like he was no more familiar with the word than he was with a spanked arse. I turned on my heel, snatched up the car keys from where Steve had left them – *where you know rightly you shouldn't have, Steve!* – on the mantelpiece next to 'Maid of the Meadow', came back in from the hall to unplug the iron, cursed myself as I made it out the door at the second attempt. The car lurched backwards on to the street, to the evident surprise of Ivy, who had come out to close her own black and gold gates.

I waved my apology. As I was about to turn out of the street, I saw her in the rear-view mirror, still looking after me.

The picket had moved from the driveway to the bottom of the front steps, possibly for the benefit of the American TV station, whose crew car was parked next to where I parked, in the beam of one of the spotlights dotted around the garden, throwing a shadow the size of a double-decker up the side of the house. The wind was really up now. Perished-looking kids had been pushed into the front line holding placards asking that they be protected. (Try taking them home, warming them in front of the fire.) They watched me stomp towards the steps, ready, by the looks of them, to throw down their placards and run if I opened my mouth to say boo. One wee thing, though, gave me a smile from beneath her hood, showing off her underpopulated gums.

'Hello,' I said then recognized her as a little Newton. She hid behind her placard, suddenly shy. Michele Newton swooped and snatched her up, with a face on her I hoped the child would never catch.

'Oh, come off it, Michele,' I said as the picket united in 'Rock of Ages'.

I went into the office, locking the door behind me, and perched on the old accordion radiator. I didn't bother with the light. I had all I needed already from the spots in the garden, the headlights sweeping by on the main road, the pale glimmer of the security monitor on which the protesters mimed greyly to the words of the hymn seeping in under the doors and through the hair's-breadth gaps around the window frames. I could read without difficulty the entry in my own hand in the bookings diary on a desk six feet away: Advanced Watercolour 7–9.

It was coming up to seven-thirty. I had a little over an hour and a half to decide what to do when the centre closed for the night.

Go home, of course, but to what reception and on what terms? The way I felt, if Steve so much as looked at me in the expectation of an apology I would be straight out the door again.

There was movement overhead and, after a few minutes, loud laughter on the staircase. An American woman said that something or other was totally *bizarre*. Nick agreed, totally. An American man said he wanted to double-check that Nick had signed the form. Nick had. There followed a short thanking competition.

'Thank you.'

'Thank *you*.'

'Oh, glad to, any time.'

'Well, thanks.'

'Yes, thanks.'

'Thanks.'

The volume went up on the picket as the main door was opened, went down again as it was shut. On the monitor a woman and man were engaged in conversation by Michele and now Joss Newton. A fifth person stood by with a camera on his shoulder.

On the other side of the office door a key found the lock at the third time of asking. I slipped down off the radiator, went and sat behind my desk. Nick came in and walked straight to the window, leaning in close to the glass, fingertips splayed on the sill, levering himself up.

(Seemed I was doomed to have to contemplate those buttocks.)

I thought if I didn't say something and he turned and saw me he'd have heart failure. I stood slowly, hoping I could inch towards the door, make it look like I'd only this moment come in. I didn't even manage the first six inches. He spun – leaped, practically – staggered back, hands groping for the bottom edge of the window frame.

'What in the *fuck*? Catriona?'

'Sorry. I was just . . .' What? Think. 'Sitting here.' Brilliant.

I sat back down. Nick folded and unfolded his arms, crossed his legs at the ankles, uncrossed them, did everything but scratch his head.

I could almost see the thought bubble forming: She came after all.

'Anyone ever tell you you're a very strange woman?' he said.

I was not so old or out of practice that I couldn't recognize a line when I heard it. The lousy ones always did stand out more. And yet I did feel a bit peculiar all of a sudden, unlike myself. 'It's gone a bit bonkers, hasn't it?' I said.

He tried folding his arms again then pulled the typing chair out from under Lorraine's desk and sat with his chest to its back. He smiled. I looked down and, out the corner of my eye, thought I saw a face looking directly into the room from the monitor between us. Who would have known where the security camera was better than the man who installed it? I glanced left and sure enough there was Steve, turned the wrong way, at the heart of the picket.

My first instinct was to shrink from his gaze. My next, which was equally ridiculous, I knew, since he could not see me, was to give him something to really protest about.

'What do you think Lorraine would make of this?' said Nick.

I turned my eyes from Steve's to his. I didn't know about Lorraine, but I could just imagine what Cilla would say. *'Oo's it gonna be, luv?*

The night bell rang. I looked at the screen. Steve was not where I left him. He wasn't *in* the picket, he had been pushing through. I nearly knocked over my chair running to the hallway to let him in.

∾

The first night we viewed this house, Steve turned to me as we got into the car to go back to the flat and said, 'Seven years.' Like he judged that to be the appropriate tariff for a family our size in a three-bedroom inside-terrace on this side of town. Today when I came off the phone with the estate agent and wrote *Sale Agreed!* on the calendar, I worked out that we had been living here for seven years, three months and four days. Time on for our occasional bad behaviour.

Of course I wouldn't have said a word of this sort, even in jest, to Rory and Antonia. Nobody wanted to be starting out in a place with someone else's thoughts about it hanging over their heads. Not that the two of them were short of ideas of their own. Rory, when they had come back for their second viewing, said the roof space would make a great mini gym.

'A gym?' said Antonia.

'Why not?'

'If it'd make you happy.'

'It'd make me happy.'

I asked Steve afterwards whether we should have explained that it wasn't a room as such, that the joists had never been reinforced.

'It's all there in the estate agent's description,' Steve said.

Steve was not quite the fan of Rory and Antonia that I was.

'They're very cagey about what it is they do.'

'They said they're in entertainments.'

'Exactly. What does that mean? I'm in entertainments, you might as well say.'

Steve, in fact, had been knee-deep in entertainments this past lot of months. We were moving up in the world thanks to him moving down into the cable trenches that were criss-crossing the city. He missed being his own boss, but it had been too good a package to refuse.

'Look,' I said, 'the estate agent's satisfied, their mortgage lender's satisfied. Why should we be bothered?'

'I'm thinking of the neighbours.'

'Somehow I think our neighbours will be OK.'

Patricia had already volunteered to stay behind if Steve was so worried and keep an eye on things. I knew what it was she wanted to keep an eye on, the same wee girl.

'I'll move my bed into the teensiest-weensiest corner of the roof space, make sure he has enough room for his weights. I wouldn't be any trouble.'

He was something to look at all right, Rory, and not, I got the feeling, unused to being looked at. Patricia asked me whether the reason for her daddy's frostiness wasn't that he was a wee bit jealous. Steve might still have been in great shape, but Rory did have twenty years on him.

'I think to be honest what's really bothering your daddy is that the two of them aren't married.'

'Oh, for heaven's sake! In this day and age?' said Patricia, with all the vehemence of the de-converted.

I didn't know to this day what had assailed my daughter's faith more, the hoo-ha that time over Serge's photos ('I mean, if they'd been protesting on the grounds of bad art . . .') or, since it followed hard on the heels of that, simply turning eighteen. It was tempting enough when doors were opened that up to now had been closed to you, and then there were just so many more – and more interesting – doors in this city all of a sudden. The Peace Dividend, as we'd all learned to call it.

Patricia had walked out the school gates and in the Habitat door. It was just like an ad: complete transformation.

Martin's faith had been lost as quietly as it was found. He had not yet come right out and told me, but the atheist-slaying machine (I had seen Rory and Antonia exchange looks, try not to smile) had been sitting on his dressing table unread for the last nine or so months. I knew, I was the one had to lift it to dust.

Which left Steve still believing.

There had been no wee meetings this long time, but he soldiered on alone.

I had opened my eyes tonight during the Quiet Moment. Martin's were pressed down on by a frown, Patricia's turned pointedly towards the dinette window. Steve's moved behind their lids. Dot, dash, dash, dot. Outgoing message to HQ. No complaints here below.

Or maybe not. I did worry sometimes that I no longer knew what was going through his head. And then just occasionally, if I tried really hard, I was certain I still knew how to crack the code.

Like now.

Concentrate, concentrate.

Yes. I had him. He was folding his *Daily Mirror* and looking at the clock, thinking it was ten minutes since the taps stopped running, the water would have cooled and I would have warmed up just enough and we never did get round to putting a lock on that bathroom door.

Butler/Baker

JUST ON THE MARKET!

From the outside you will undoubtedly say 'It's the same as the one down the street' – Well, you're wrong. Once inside this home your only wish will be that it was yours.

ACCOMMODATION COMPRISES:
Entrance hall into:
Lounge: 11'4" × 10'10" Feature fire-surround/Flame-effect inset.
Dining Area: 11'2" × 9'10"
Kitchen: 11'2" × 6'0" Fitted light-oak units with double oven and hob. Understair storage.

FIRST FLOOR:
Landing: Hot press, insulated cylinder.
Bedroom 1: 11'2" × 11'0"
Bedroom 2: 11'2" × 9'10" Built-in robes.
Bedroom 3: 7'10" × 7'8" Staircase to floored roof space. Velux window.
Bathroom: Avocado suite. Telephone shower attachment.

OUTSIDE:
Parking area to fore. South-facing rear garden, fenced, in lawn and mature flowerbeds.

Oil-fired central heating. Rewired. Damp and timber guarantees. uPVC double-glazing. Bright, tastefully decorated rooms.

The attraction of this ever-popular development will be further enhanced by the Little Lake shopping centre (with Tesco superstore) opening June 1997. Properties in this area rarely stay on the market long, so early viewing is recommended.

I was lying in the bath this Saturday morning, end of May, towel wound tight over the taps to make a headrest, when Toni walked in and handed me the Property Guide.

'Look at that.'

'What?'

'Bottom left.'

I looked, letting my lip dip in the water, I raised myself, I spoke. 'Fuck me.'

'Told you,' Toni said and left.

Number 12 across the road had just gone on the market at eighty-seven and a half thousand. Toni bought this less than five years ago for forty-six. I had always maintained it was overpriced.

'That's fucking unbelievable,' I shouted. Number 12 was Blakes'. I don't know if you could call people who seemed never to have worked retired. From the look of the house, though, their earnings and their interest in life had peaked together some time in the 1970s.

Toni came back in, sat down on the far side of the sink from me for a piss.

'I mean,' I said, 'you compare that to this one.'

'What you reckon, then?' Toni said. 'Ninety-five?'

'Fuck ninety-five.'

'Starting, I mean.'

'I reckon you'd have to be talking a hundred plus.'

Toni whistled, wound a yard of paper, wiped. I dropped the Property Guide on to the floor at the side of the bath. I drew my arms together below the surface of the water, parted them, brought them together again. The turbulence spread, buffeted my bollocks.

'You getting in here?'

Toni flicked water from her fingertips, hair falling forward as she looked down at me over the edge of the sink. 'You should be so bloody lucky.'

'Wrong,' I said, and Toni at the door said, 'Don't tell me, *I* should?'

I pressed my head against the muffled taps. Smiled at the touch of the sun through the window, at my own boldness. Toni returned a second later, threw something, and was off again before the something – a pair of her fucking whips – landed on the side of the bath three inches from my chin.

'Have one on me, Melly Boy.'

I flung the knickers at the closing door and followed them up with a volley of insults, which chased her down the stairs.

'Slutty fucker! Dirt bird!'

I heard the rattle of bottles in the fridge door, the French windows being opened, a chair being dragged from where the sun was hitting the deck at eight o'clock last night to where it was falling now.

Toni's knickers lay in an insubstantial heap at the foot of the door. I watched the idea of trying to hook them run through my mind. I watched me wanking right enough – double or treble bluff – and then thought, nah, Saturday morning, things to do. Besides they were *Toni's* knickers.

Toni's knickers and I went way, way back, further even than Toni and me. I had first encountered them looped over the banister at the top of the stairs in the house I shared with Rory in our final year of college. Their colour was a new one on me. Champagne. Satin. For the life of me I couldn't decide whether it was more polite to take them down and fold them or leave them hanging. It was three days before they were retrieved, another couple of weeks before I caught more than a fleeting glimpse of Toni, darting to the bathroom, or backing through Rory's door with the mugs of coffee and digestives on which they were apparently surviving.

I don't think we spoke more than half a dozen times the whole of that first term and then we were wary, Rory being our sole connection. Rory being Rory.

Rory had been a schoolboy hurler. He was fit, fanciable, my female friends said without exception. My other male friends all wanted to go on the razz with him. By that final year at college he had already started doing the kiss-a-grams. Tarzan, caveman, anything that called for him taking off most of his clothes and slathering himself in baby oil. About six months after we graduated he called at my flat to tell me he was moving back home and setting up a telegrams company of his own. Some mad idea involving balaclavas. I wondered had he fallen off the speed wagon again.

'What about Toni?' I asked and he told me she was going too.

I'll give her a month, I thought.

'All *right*,' I said.

'Why don't you come with us?' he asked. 'This is really going to take off.'

'No bloody chance.'

I hadn't spent all that fucking time educating myself out of the dump just to go back because a mate asked me. Besides I had a job, of sorts, writing reviews for the local listings mag. It paid pennies, but it got me into places and it got me noticed. I was adamant. 'Absolutely no bloody chance.'

In two years I received two birthday cards, two Christmas cards, and one letter on headed notepaper, all written by Rory. Then my phone rang in the middle of the night. I nearly broke my neck falling out of bed.

'Hello?'

Ghastly sounds of grief, wordless, mucusy.

'*Hello?*'

A sob that finally yielded a voice. 'Oh, Mel,' it said.

'Toni?'

'He's gone,' she said. 'Aa-ahaha-huh,' she said.

'What do you mean,' I said, because I was in no doubt who she meant, 'gone?'

'Aa-ahaha-huh,' she said, which was enough.

'Oh, Toni, I'm sorry.'

She sniffed noisily. 'The fucker,' she said. She'd picked up the accent.

I had wrapped my robe around me, taken the cigarettes from the pocket. I couldn't find an ashtray so I tore the lid off the cigarette box and used that.

'What happened?' I asked, though I thought I'd a pretty good idea.

'No,' Toni said, 'I shouldn't be disturbing you, it's too late.'

I resisted stating the obvious. 'Toni, it's OK. I want to know.'

So she started. I smoked three cigarettes one after the other and after the third decided to pace myself. I still got through most of the packet. I almost fell asleep once, she was talking so low; another time she was talking so very low I was sure she was asleep.

'Toni!'

'What?'

'Nothing,' I said and she picked up again, miles from where she had last been.

The story was much as I had imagined, albeit with a few local peculiarities. Rory had set up the company and for the first year everything went well, so well that Toni was having to dress up and perform instead of just taking bookings and driving Rory. The balaclava-grams in particular were a big hit.

They bought a house together, this house, number 5. Then suddenly there was this other woman. Rory brought her in to cover the weekends. The weekends were mad, twenty bookings a night some nights. The weekends were mad and starting earlier, ending later. Twenty bookings a night Thursday to Sunday was no joke. Toni didn't know whether it had been going on before the other woman started working with them, but within a few weeks it became clear that the woman and Rory were fucking. This was pretty bad, morale-wise, but Toni was a businesswoman now with responsibilities to clients. Then there was the money, that wasn't to be sniffed at, and now that she was here, in a house of her own, this wasn't such a terrible city to live in. So she let Rory get away with fucking this other woman – who was, Toni noted, exactly the sort of pert-arsed, pert-titted, tow-headed woman she always imagined men dreamed about fucking – while she concentrated on building the business and readying the house for the twenty-first century. The snag was that the woman (it occurred to me that what Toni was actually saying was *Ramona*), Ramona, who after all was in her twenties too and was hardly likely to have travelled this far into her life and now into theirs without baggage, turned out to have a boyfriend of her own, and this boyfriend had mates and the mates had connections and, well, basically weren't the kind you'd want to get mixed up with, let alone annoy. (It wasn't just the accent Toni had picked up, it was a whole way of thinking and talking.) Rory managed to keep all of this from Toni for several more months. If she had found out sooner she might have been able to do something. Instead, Rory had headed out in his car the lunchtime before the late night she phoned me and hadn't returned. Toni had six balaclava-grams alone that evening. She booked a taxi for the entire night, arrived home knackered and not a lot better off than she had been when she left, and found two messages on the machine. The first was Rory, ringing from a service station south of Carlisle, saying he was sorry it had worked out this way. The second was from Ramona, saying she owned the telegrams company now. At which point Toni got seriously beat into the vodka and then remembered me.

It was daylight when she finally stopped talking.

'What'll you do?' I asked her.

'What can I do?'

I lit my second-last cigarette.

'I don't suppose,' Toni said and then checked herself. 'No.'

'What?'

'No, it is, it's stupid.'

The magazine I had been reviewing for had folded three months before. I'd been sending out CVs all over, but so far I'd got nothing back. My lease would soon be up for renewal, I wasn't certain I could hang on to my flat. I knew what she was going to say. I didn't stop her. I helped her along.

'What's stupid?'

'You coming over here.'

Her voice was so deep and breathy. I wondered for the first time was she dressed.

'It's not stupid at all.'

'No?'

'No.'

For the first few months we fucked. Not like her and Rory, not night and day, but we fucked all the same, because we were a young man and a young woman in the same house, because we were neither of us too bad-looking, because there was no one here to tell us not to, fucked until we discovered that wasn't what it was between us at all. One night we just got into separate beds and that was where we had stayed. Maybe three times since, I had been woken in the small hours by Toni climbing in beside me, as she on a like number of occasions had been woken by me. I was cold, is what we tended to say. I didn't know about Toni, but the word I meant was lonely. The loneliness of one person unsleeping in the dark hugeness of the world.

Somehow Rory got to hear I was living in number 5. 'Somehow', because when he at last phoned again it was from Cyprus. We didn't talk long. He offered to sell me his share of the house. He had some formula worked out for how much that came to. I told him it wasn't really up to me. I gave the phone to Toni.

'OK, out with it,' she said into the receiver.

I went and got us both a drink.

'I have no objection,' she told me when she'd hung up. 'Except there's no way you're giving him that fucking much.'

I was still finding my feet, there was no way I was giving him fucking anything for a while yet. Toni paid him off out of her savings, half of their original deposit (Rory didn't complain, Toni was probably right he was in need of whatever money we would pay him), which brought us to where we were that Saturday, sharing the house and the mortgage, me in debt to Toni to the tune of two and a half grand.

I got a coffee and a banana on my way through the downstairs and stepped out the back. Toni, sunglasses, Cream T-shirt, sarong, was hunched over the low cherry-wood table, reading the international news, twisting her hair into a French plait. I sat astride the sun lounger, the Saturday magazine spread out before me. I ate the banana, flinging the spent star of its skin into the bird of paradise pot.

Toni's head flicked up. The lenses of her sunglasses were big and square, rose-tinted.

'Compost,' I said. Like Toni was really the Tidy Fairy all of a sudden. She turned her head slowly from the plant pot to me. Her mouth was not altogether shut. She went back to the international news and French plaiting. I looked to the sky and instead of sun I saw a bright hole where the sun might have fallen through. I blinked to clear the no-sun spots. Someone, two, maybe three gardens away, sneezed.

'You wouldn't seriously think about selling this house?' I asked and this time Toni glanced at me over the top of her glasses without raising her head.

'What do you think?' she said.

Down the street a radio came on in the middle of a song which I knew and couldn't place and which disappeared as the radio was re-tuned, through Radio 3 or Classic FM, to Dolly Parton and Kenny Rogers.

Toni and I looked up at each other, delighted, and sang.

'From one lover to another, aw-haw.'

In the early afternoon we got in the Citroën and drove out to the Little Lake centre with a scrap of paper saying olive oil and basil. There was a sale on in HMV, two CDs for fifteen pounds or six for thirty. I could only find three I wanted and rather than put one back I picked up another three more or less at random. Well, if you think about it, two of them were effectively free. Toni tried on a pair of indigo cinch-back jeans. I told her I wasn't mad about the colour. She left them on the rack by the changing-room door, but when we were halfway down the concourse to Tesco's she touched my arm and ran back to the shop.

Our two-item list turned into half a dozen bags of shopping. We stopped for milkshakes on the way back to the car and sat at a table next to the café's floor-to-ceiling window. It was always a spectacle, the first shorts Saturday of summer. Horror, hilarity, heartbreak. Toni nudged my foot. I glanced at her. She was sucking on her straw, jerking her head at the floor. I looked down, looked up, nodded.

The carpet was bogging.

Carpets were what Toni and I did. Nightclub carpets, strictly speaking, though there was no reason why we couldn't have done a café in the Little Lake shopping centre, no reason except that we were flat out Monday to Thursday as it was (there was no time for anything other than running repairs once the weekend began in earnest) and up to our eyeballs in paperwork all day Friday.

I'm fairly sure I speak for both of us when I say that the words Host Dry Extraction Cleaning System had not figured largely in our adolescent career plans, but the day I moved back across the water Toni already had the machine laid out on a sheet on the living-room floor. From what I could gather its presence there related in some way to the transfer of ownership of the telegrams business. I had a feeling it might have been intended as a joke, but if it had been the joke was on Ramona and her man. The whole balaclava thing had unravelled yonks ago. Telegrams were a fad, telegrams were fucking eight-track, but people were never going to stop wanting to go out and dance.

Toni's gag last year to our friends who had businesses: 'I don't know how you did at the Millennium, but me and Mel cleaned up.'

★

'What's the betting on Ivy?' I said going round and opening the boot to get the shopping.

'I wouldn't be too sure,' said Toni, 'she has a dinner dance tonight.'

I threw Toni the car keys, took two bags inside in each hand.

'I'll put enough coffee in the pot for her anyway.'

Nothing drew Ivy out like a shopping bag. It was not unusual for her to sit in our kitchen watching us unpack. She blamed the Chinese family who used to live here for getting her so interested in food.

'What are these?' she would want to know. 'How do you cook that?'

She had even gone out and bought the odd thing on the recommendation of its appearance on our countertop, though it was hard to believe looking at her that she ate anything much at all, and as for Denis . . .

'He was up half the night with that sweet potato,' she would say, or, 'Those courgette flowers were hardly in him.'

Ivy talked about her husband's bathroom habits with all the candour with which Toni and I talked to our friends about the bedroom. Perhaps it was an older person's fetish. Perhaps your bowels were what was left to interest you when everything else had started to go. Perhaps that was all Ivy's generation, born to rationing, ever did talk about.

Toni was wrong about the distraction of the dinner dance. She and Ivy were standing by the Citroën talking when I returned for the last of the groceries.

'Tell Mel,' Toni said.

'Tell Mel what?' I leaned into the boot for the basil pot.

'A woman,' Toni and Ivy said together, though with differing intonation.

'While you were at the shops,' Ivy went on alone, 'she was out here looking at your house.'

'Anyone we know?' I said to Toni.

'Well, it's no good asking me,' she said.

So I asked Ivy. 'What was she like?'

But Ivy had been putting a colour in her hair. (Her hair was indeed spectacularly plum coloured. GM-, *irradiated*-plum coloured.) She couldn't come out to the front door like that, couldn't even get her glasses on for a proper look.

'She was probably here to see Blakes',' I said, 'having a bit of a nosy about the street.'

The basil was particularly strong. I wanted to get it into the house and out from under my nose.

'She was knocking on the door,' Toni said, as though there weren't people in and out our door all the time, 'looking in the window.'

'I thought for a minute she was going to go up your alleyway,' said Ivy.

This was pointless. I closed the car door with my hip and started back into the house.

'Thanks, Mrs M. I'm guessing if it was anything important she'll call back again, whoever she is.'

Whoever she was, she called again at half-eleven the next morning. I was still in bed. I had no idea how long the knocking had been going on already when I woke. I made it to the door half-dressed just in time to see the back of a woman's head in the rear of a taxi as it pulled away. There was no one else about, not even Ivy. Church time. Ivy went, as they said here, religiously.

I called up to Toni, but there was no reply, no indication anywhere downstairs that she had been home. We had been out together round the clubs until gone three. We got free entry most places, we tended to flit. About half an hour after we arrived in the last club, the Man Who Invented Cocaine came in with a clatter of fellow actors and cocaine acolytes. He talked about all the cocaine he'd been doing since last Saturday when he came in at the same time talking about all the cocaine he'd just done, then asked Toni and me did we want to go with him into the manager's office to do a few humongous lines.

Toni looked at me.

'You go ahead if you want,' I said. Like courgette flowers with Ivy's Denis, coke did not agree with me. 'I'll hang on here for you.'

She came out a quarter of an hour later, glittery.

'I think I'll stick around a while longer,' she said, which was when I said I'd see her in the morning.

I spent the remaining minutes of it going over the possibilities in my head.

I owed no one money, apart from Toni, that is. I couldn't remember how long it had been since Toni and I had anything in the house that would bring a person to our door in a taxi at eleven-thirty on a Sunday morning in search of it. Nor could I think of any relationship I had had where there had been unfinished business. In fact, apart from with Toni again, I had had a grand total of two relationships since coming home. Three months and six weeks, the last more than a year ago now. I couldn't imagine that either had left such a smouldering residue of emotion as could be sparked into life again after all this time.

No, the longer I thought about it, the clearer it seemed that this woman had to be connected to Toni in some way.

If only Toni would come home for me to ask her.

As much for something to do as to clean, I swept the floors downstairs. Ours was a two-car, no-vacuum household; at least, no domestic vacuum. Vacuums scored floorboards, vacuums bollocksed stone, and every floor in this house was either one or the other. (Ivy never walked through here but her head seemed, almost imperceptibly, to shake in contemplation of the floors, the exposed staircase, walls taken back to brick: 'What are you, *un*building the place?') I harried our dust and debris over the permeable border into the kitchen area, where I considered leaving it in a single long line as a chastisement to Toni, before boredom overtook me and I simply binned the lot.

One o'clock and still no sign of her. I took a sandwich up to the boxroom and sat against the near wall to eat and search the Rodney map for defunct countries.

We used to have a list somewhere of all the disappearances and reappearances and reconfigurations in the quarter-century since, according to the legend in red crayon, the map was completed. Armenia through to Zimbabwe.

Most of the friends who we'd had stay in the guest bed in the attic actually spent half the night down here, list on their laps, chewing their pen lids to flitters.

New Zealand wasn't on the list, though it wasn't on the wall either when Rory and Toni were done steaming and scraping – in places finger-picking – away the overlaying decades of paper. (They found the South Island on the back of one particularly stubborn strip.) Toni said they had thought about drawing it in themselves, but then thought they would wait to see how many people missed it. Precious few did.

Further up the wall lengths of coloured wool, emanating from all points in the Atlantic, from the Mediterranean and the Barents Sea, converged on our own little off-cut of continent, our own little corner of off-cut, obliterating it with fixing pins. The seaward ends of these strands used to terminate in Post-its with the names of hotels and bars that Toni and Rory were to hit in their balaclavas, a toying with perspective that clearly amused them as much as the expunging of New Zealand, though one by one the Post-its dried, curled and fell.

Toni arrived a little after six, looking completely wiped. She kissed my cheek inside the door, trailed herself straight up the stairs.

'Jesus, Toni,' I said, watching her go. Toni waved a hand, like, I know, I *know*.

I woke her a couple of hours later. She had been sleeping face-down on the pillow clad only in a pair of bright pink knickers. (They must have been new, I'd never seen them in the laundry.) A matching bra was stretched, cups up, across the duvet beside her. Her right cheek, when she raised her head, was tracked with welts from the folds of the pillowcase. She pushed herself up, hands flat on the mattress. Her breasts depended into taupe points between her arms.

'Do you want a T-shirt?' I asked and handed her the Bloody Mary I had brought.

The window was open and the muslin curtains were running gold in the evening sun. I hunkered down in the pools spreading out from them, searching the boxes beneath Toni's clothes rail for the T-shirt I had in mind. It was an ancient thing, red with a black trim and, in the centre of the chest, a felt star in triple-image, pale blue, then scarlet, then black at the core.

I tossed it to her with only a glance to ensure I didn't hit the glass. I picked up a few of her bits and pieces from the floor and stuffed them into the cream cloth-bag she kept for her dirty washing. When I turned around, Toni had the T-shirt on and sat on the bed, legs out straight before her, arms open and raised to me.

We hugged, chins on one another's shoulders.

'You're so sweet,' she said past my ear. She loved that star T-shirt.

I made small circles on her spine with the tips of my fingers. She lifted the hand that held her Bloody Mary and stretched her neck out over my shoulder for a sip.

'Mmm.'

'Did it get really mad after I left?' I asked.

She stretched her neck still further, slurped. 'I'll tell you in the next life,' she said.

Downstairs again, I heated up crab cakes and crispy seaweed and made a quick dipping sauce. We ate on the floor in front of the TV, a repeat cable cookery programme. Like fucking while watching a porno, said Toni. Not, I said, that she'd know anything about that, and she gave me her Saint Antonia face then gave me the chopstick finger.

'Fuck away off, you,' she said, in that acquired accent of hers.

I changed channels (what good was a five-year-old early-drinking wine recommendation?) and only then remembered the morning's caller. I moved on to the chaise, watched five minutes of a Sunday-night jazz-loving-home-counties-detective thing before I asked her.

'Toni, there isn't anything weird going on that you haven't told me about?'

I saw her shoulders flinch. She laid the chopsticks neatly on her plate and started telling me how things just got a bit out of hand in the club.

'Not last night,' I said. 'I mean, anything that would have

some woman coming knocking on our door two days running.'

In one movement, Toni was up off the floor and kneeling beside me. 'Was she back? Were you talking to her?'

'I was out for the count, I didn't make it to the door in time. She was in a taxi.'

'I wonder what it is she wants.'

'I'm fucked if I know. That's why I'm asking you. Think.'

Toni fell silent, her head by degrees turning towards the TV. She placed a cushion at the small of her back. The jazz-loving detective was watching police officers in plastic suits dig up a home-counties lawn. The shadow of a boom passed fleetingly across the azaleas.

I made more noise than I needed to gathering up the dirty plates and the dipping sauce.

'Fucked me too,' said Toni, without taking her eyes from the screen.

'Thanks for giving it your attention,' I said.

We said goodnight on the landing. I had kind of been thinking tonight might be one of those nights when we were too cold to sleep alone, but after only a few minutes Toni's breathing had modulated into a familiar rhythmic whistle. I had a smoke to help get me over. I dreamed that there was a back way into heaven through the bedroom's dangling light fitting, but it was only open a short time and I had to make up my mind: for ever in heaven, or uncertain life here. I spent restless hours before the alarm clock sounded in the sweat of that indecision.

The lights in my bedroom were halogen spots, flush with the ceiling. Nowhere in the house was there a bulb on a flex like I'd seen in my dream. I didn't know why I felt it hanging over me long into the following day.

★

Monday and Tuesday we put on upwards of six hundred and fifty miles in the Citroën. There were clubs these days in places I didn't know there were places when I was growing up. Clubs in hotels, clubs tacked on to bars, clubs behind doors which all but clubbers would have passed without a second glance, basement clubs, attic clubs, super-clubs and crap ones. If there was a carpeted area in it, it was ten-to-one on Toni and I had cleaned it.

Toni was a demon under pressure. As soon as the blue boiler suit was on, that was her, focused. (They were a really class blue, I have to say, our boiler suits. I mean, you sort of looked forward to getting up for work.) I did most of the driving both days and Toni did the talking on the phone. She would really rather have done the two together, which was how she came close to losing her licence the other year. Complete fluke, she insisted: unmarked police car. Couldn't happen today.

'What speed are you doing?' she asked me, time and again on Monday and Tuesday.

'Five more than I should be.'

'We were due there a quarter of an hour ago.'

'I'm already over the limit. What do you want me to do?'

Pit-pit-pit-pit went the thumb on the phone.

'Terry? Toni . . . I know . . . Yes, I know. Look, we'll be there in ten.'

'*Ten?*' I'd say.

She'd say nothing for a moment then crane her neck across the front of me. 'What speed *are* you doing?'

And so it went on.

We were on the road from a quarter to eight in the morning. It was half-seven before we were back on Monday evening, ten past nine on Tuesday. We barely spoke either night before falling exhausted into our respective beds.

My mum, with characteristic displacement, had told me at Easter that I had my dad worried sick. I would soon be thirty. What on earth was I playing at? Where on earth was I *going*? For they were fucked, as of course she would never say, if they knew sometimes.

To which I would, thankfully, never have to add, Fucked me too, Mum.

Wednesday's bookings were all in the city, so we were able to get home soon after finishing up at half past five. Toni went on into the house while I swapped over to the Seat and drove out to the fitness centre. I was no Rory, but I had been trying to make it along twice a week since my twenty-ninth birthday. This evening, though, I put in the briefest of appearances in the weights room before getting stripped for the pool. I did ten lengths then flipped over on to my back and floated, letting my thoughts float too, until I saw that frigging light bulb again, dangling in my mind's eye, and I swam to the side and pulled myself out.

I rang Toni and asked her did she want me to pick up anything for dinner.

'No,' she said. I thought she might already have had a drink.
'Sure?'
'Just get back here as quick as you can.'
'Quick as I can?' I said. 'A boy could get the wrong idea.'
'Yes,' said Toni, though whether this meant that a boy could indeed get the wrong idea, or that the idea a boy could get would not be entirely wrong, or that Toni was just not really listening to me, who could say?
'Are you all right?' I asked her.

'Fine. Come home.'

Before turning off the main road I pulled in at the off-licence for a couple of bottles of Cava. So what if it was only Thursday tomorrow? We'd had a good few days' work, we deserved something.

Ivy was waving to me from her window as I walked from the car, but I noticed her just late enough to let on that I hadn't. No time to talk tonight, Mrs M.

As soon as I was inside I saw, down through the house to the deck, Toni sitting, Bloody Mary in hand, facing a deeply tanned woman dressed all in aquamarine. I knew this could only be the woman who had been peering in our window on Saturday, who had taken a taxi to our door on Sunday, and the dread thought occurred that she was after all in some way connected to me.

'Hi,' I shouted, though I didn't go out to the deck right away, but took the Cava into the kitchen. There was a grainy pool of tomato juice on the countertop and a smell, whose source I couldn't pinpoint, of spilt alcohol. Toni's mixing, like all her kitchen efforts, was a little bit slap, a little bit dash. (On the wall next to the microwave hung a framed cover from a local lifestyle magazine with a picture of Toni in front of the boxroom map. 'Welcome to my world,' the headline said. Toni herself had inserted 'dirty' in whiteboard marker between the last two words.) While I was putting the bottles in the fridge, pouring myself a beer, I was able to observe the woman from another angle. Hair straight at the crown, wavy where it was tied back just below her nape: a grown-out perm; slight sharpness to her nose and chin; wide, attractive mouth. The aquamarine trousers and top looked to me like silk. I was pretty certain that, Sunday's brief glimpse excepted, I had never seen this woman before in my life. She said something

I couldn't make out in an accent distinctly southern hemisphere and Toni laughed her second-least-guarded laugh. I lifted my beer and headed out to join them.

'There you are,' Toni said and, turning to the woman, '*This* is Mel.'

I shook her hand and the first words she said to me were, 'I've just been trying to work out with Toni which of you sleeps in my old room.'

'This is Penny,' Toni completed the introduction. 'Penny used to live here.'

When I was a kid I used to think that people in TV plays stood on their marks all the while the adverts were on, holding their breath and their facial expressions. I stood now like an actor in that ad-time limbo, glass arrested halfway to my mouth.

'Wow,' I made myself say eventually.

'Years and years and years ago,' said Penny. Australian, the accent, definitely. 'I left before I was three.'

'House has changed a bit,' Toni said somewhat obviously and as though on Penny's behalf. If it hadn't changed before Toni got the hold of it, it had certainly changed since. I doubted whether the people who sold it to her and Rory would even recognize it now.

Penny sipped her drink and turned her face to the evening sun.

'I don't remember it ever being like this, that's for sure,' she said. A grey and white cat with a swinging undercarriage paused in its traverse of the garden fence to look at us and sniff our air then dropped down into the house behind. 'All the photos of me seem to have been taken in winter.'

A little chill note had entered her voice. She took a longer drink.

'Can I get you another of those?' Toni asked, springing to her feet.

Penny looked at her watch, which she wore with the face on the inside of her wrist.

'If I'm not keeping you back.'

'Oh, don't worry about us,' Toni said. 'Mel and I tend to make up our nights as we go along.'

Penny drained her glass. 'All right, then. A small one.'

Toni brought her a medium-to-large and when Penny eyed it doubtfully told her to leave what she couldn't drink. Penny, though, drank all of that one and, without checking what size they were, the two that followed. I had another three beers. On one of my trips to the fridge I remembered I hadn't eaten and brought some feta and tomatoes and olive bread back with me on to the deck. Even with my share of that lining my stomach I was starting to feel pretty drunk. I had to keep reminding myself not to stare at Penny. She had no bra on under her aquamarine silk top. I was trying to work out in my head what three plus years and years and years might add up to and was getting answers, depending on how her head was turned, her expression composed, a couple either side of forty.

Despite the reminders to myself, she caught me in the end, while Toni was talking, doing my sums, and sent the smallest of smiles my way before inclining towards Toni again.

I closed my eyes – *Wise the fuck up, Mel* – and when I reopened them Penny was feeling around under her chair for her bag.

'I should really be getting back to my hotel.'

She was staying in the Hilton in the centre of town. I had asked her earlier had she no family here any more and she'd shaken her head. 'None at all.'

That was as much as she said about herself, other than that

her mother had died last year. No mention of her father, no mention of a husband or boyfriend.

Toni had the phone at her ear and was scribbling the number of a cab company on the back of one of her cards. 'Use these guys while you're here. These guys are good.'

I intercepted the card and wrote another number on the back. 'This is a useful one too.'

Penny stopped in the middle of the downstairs and did a turn, shaking her head. 'You know,' she said, 'it's a total blank.'

'Well, right about where you're standing would have been the fireplace,' I said.

She took a quick step back as though burned.

'Really,' Toni said, 'these houses only make sense now for people without kids.'

The good guys arrived ten minutes later sounding their horn. We walked Penny to the front door. It seemed darker at the front of the house than at the back, a deep, deep, end-of-May blue. A teenage girl stood on a garden path down the street, smoking, picking petals from an overblown camellia.

Penny was offering me her hand. 'It was really nice meeting you.'

'You'll have to come back another night if you've time.'

'Yes, do,' said Toni.

'Why, thank you.' Penny gave her a hug. 'I'd like that. Maybe remember to bring my camera this time.'

The taxi driver had done a U-turn to be facing the right way for getting out of the street citywards. His hands were crossed on the top of the steering wheel and I could tell by the angle of his head that he had just clocked Creepy Graham's car. A condom-pink bin bag was taped over the windscreen, protection against long-gone frosts.

'That'll help those people sell their house, I'll bet,' the driver said with a backwards nod to the Blakes' For Sale sign, and opened the door for Penny.

Penny paused, looking across the street.

I felt moved to apologize on behalf of the rest of the residents. 'I'm sure you're wondering why your parents ever left,' I said.

She smiled, shook her head then ducked down into the back seat. 'Thanks again,' she said.

Toni and I stood on the doorstep until the taxi had left the street.

'What do you think she wanted?' Toni asked, closing the door behind us.

'What sort of question is that? She wanted to see the place where she was born. She only said it about fifty times.'

'Oh, *right*,' Toni said and smacked her forehead with the heel of her hand.

God, she could be so annoying to live with sometimes.

I was on the point of dropping off to sleep when it occurred to me that the light fitting I had seen in my dream the other night was just the kind of fitting the room would have had when this house was new.

Had something been trying to alert me to Penny's arrival?

No, too scary to think. Much, much too scary . . . and, of course, stupid.

∽

Ivy wept as Ivy had been weeping for most of the last half-hour, with her elbows on our stainless-steel breakfast bar and her hands over her eyes. So violent were some of the sobs, so small and frail did she suddenly seem (a rare species, I thought, bred for experiments with emotions and hair dyes), that I worried she would sob herself right off the stool on to the floor. I was at a loss for what to do beyond keeping her supplied with Kleenex and repeating that I was sorry, that it must have been quite a shock.

I had not handled this very well. I should have thought it through more before launching in. I should not have said anything at all until Toni was here to back me up.

Ivy gave a mighty, full-body sniff.

'Do you want me to go and get Mr M?' I asked, but Ivy shook her head. 'Do you want me to make you a cup of tea?'

'Cup of tea,' she said back, with an effort, and then the tears overtook her once more. 'Ach, Stella.'

Ivy Moore and Penny's mother were close friends. Hardly a surprise, given what I knew of Ivy's insistent neighbourliness. Like I said, I hadn't thought this out properly before I started into telling her about Penny. Telling her, mind you, under pressure of her prompting; to that extent at least Ivy was asking for it, though that was not much comfort to me and none whatsoever to her.

'So?' she had said, busying across to me as I got out of the car. I left the front door open for her to follow me inside. 'That was her, wasn't it, last night, the mystery woman?'

I was actually imagining that the revelation of Penny's identity would please her. I had actually strung it out a while longer.

'Mystery woman.' I drummed two fingers on my bottom lip. 'Mystery woman.'

Ivy had climbed on to the stool, where she still sat, half an hour later, crying her heart out. She had folded her arms on the breakfast bar, leaning forward. 'Stop it, you. You know rightly who I mean. I saw her coming in.'

I folded my own arms on the other side of the counter from her. 'Does the name Falloon mean anything to you?'

A look of what I took to be the confusion of forgetfulness began to spread over her face. I should have stopped then. I didn't.

'Penny Falloon?'

Ivy put a hand to her throat.

'Penny Falloon's in Australia.'

'Was,' I said. 'Will be again ten days from now.'

I went to see were there any messages on the answer machine, so had my back to Ivy when she asked had Penny said anything about her mother being with her.

'Oh, no.' (*Brain calling mouth, brain calling mouth: abort, abort!*) 'I think she said her mum died last year.'

And that was when the floodgates opened.

Toni didn't need me mouthing 'Penny's mother' at her to know what was wrong. The second she walked in the door and saw Ivy in bits she guessed. She set her bag down in the centre of the floor and took Ivy gently in her arms.

'It's just not fair,' Ivy said into Toni's chest.

I finally finished making the tea and Toni persuaded Ivy to come and sit on the chaise. Toni stroked her hand until the tears had dried and Ivy had stopped apologizing.

We couldn't imagine what it was like, she said, back when these houses were built. They didn't see it themselves at the time, but they were quite cut off, more like a village really than a suburb. She woke up one morning to find a herd of cows dandering up the middle of the street. People were coming out with brushes to stop them straying into the gardens, then shovelling up the pats for fertilizer. People burnt briquettes as well as coal on their fires, some people were still able to get actual turf. At night, she could walk off the end of her garden – there were no fences, because there was nothing behind the houses on that side to separate them from – and find herself in pitch darkness after twenty feet.

'Stella was so pretty then,' she said, as though everything that had gone before was scene-setting for her, 'but she hadn't enough confidence in herself. She'd never enough confidence.'

I thought she might be going to cry again. Toni slipped an arm around her shoulder. Ivy tried to force a smile, but it was beyond her. She drew in breath, held it, then slowly exhaled. I got the feeling she was weighing something up. Weighing Toni and me up, maybe.

A phone rang. My phone. I traced it to the pocket of my jacket and walked out on to the deck to answer.

'Thanks for the useful number.'

'Listen, I'm in the middle of something. Can I call you right back?' I said.

By the time I returned, however, Ivy had got sidetracked into talking about the Hungarian man who was murdered back in the Eighties. None of this was news to Toni or me. The man's wife was still living on the street when Toni arrived. Toni said she couldn't think of the woman without a mixture of shame and embarrassment at the nature of the business she and Rory were running. Balaclava-grams couldn't have been a big belly-laugh to a woman whose husband was gunned down in his showroom full of unplumbed porcelain by men in black hoods.

I suspected Toni of engineering the diversion. This was a more frequently travelled path, after all. The Hungarian man was in a sense everyone's history and Ivy's tone was as a consequence a little more detached, a little less rawly emotional. And then as well, Toni had never been known to pass up an opportunity to talk about Hungary. Budapest was, she said, the most beautiful city on earth. She'd only been the once, shortly after she and I realized it wasn't working out us living as lovers in the same house. She had gone into a travel agent's to book a week in Prague and came out with the tickets for Budapest instead. Budapest was the new Prague, they'd told her. Which clearly meant, from the stories Toni brought back, that they no longer had club nights in Prague Turkish baths (swimming pools for dance floors) or shagged the arses off complete strangers there in the neon-lit corridors of reclaimed Communist Party offices.

I excused myself and went to the bathroom, but once there opened the window and leaned my arms on the still to press redial on my phone.

Penny answered in her hotel room. She told me thanks for calling back. I told her I'd thought about calling her all day.

'This isn't too weird?' she asked me.

'Weird how?' I said.

We made our arrangements for meeting. I closed the window and pressed the flush. Toni watched me as I came down the stairs. 'What kept you?' her look said.

Ivy was getting up off the chaise. 'Denis'll be wondering what's happened to me.'

She apologized again for all the crying, I apologized again for my complete lack of tact.

'You weren't to know,' she said and, sucking her top lip behind the bottom one, walked to the door. I watched from the window until she was across the road. She was dabbing at her eyes once more.

From behind me Toni said, 'Ivy wants us to ask Penny to call over with her.'

'Right.'

'If we're talking to her again.'

'Well, obviously,' I said.

Later we were having a smoke, watching an old *Frasier* on a comedy channel. Toni said, 'Did I ever tell you about when I was in Budapest?'

'Yes, Toni,' I said, 'you told me about when you were in Budapest.'

She dunted my arm, handed me the spliff.

'No, this one night, I ended up in these people's flat. Big old high-ceilinged Habsburgy place, friends of this DJ guy I'd met the night before. One of them lights this tiddly wee joint he takes from his pocket and offers me a smoke. And I'm like . . . I mean, it's really, really minute . . . I'm giving loads sucking, thinking it'll not be coming back my way.' She took our joint from me, smoked, handed it back. 'And then the next thing I know, seconds I'm talking, I'm getting just like the worst paranoia ever. Oh, fuck, you've no idea, and I'm looking around and the room is full of people and I can't see the guy I came here with and I don't know where I am in the city and of course there's no fucking way anybody who wasn't born there can speak the language and the cops anyway if you were to stop them on the street and ask them directions are complete fuckers and rapists and extortionists and the room all the while is echoing to this music I can't quite catch though I think I know or should know the singer and I ask someone and they're going guess and I'm saying I can't guess in fact I haven't a fucking clue any more who it might be so everyone's looking at me saying listen listen and then I hear the words.'

I was looking at her, joint held perpendicular to keep from spilling the ash.

'You know what they were?'

'No. What?'

' "We are not your friends, we are going to eat you".' She clapped her hands and cackled. 'I near *shat*.'

I set the joint in the ashtray. I didn't think I fancied any more.

'Fucking nice timing, Toni,' I said and she laughed harder, kicking her feet in the air.

'I swear to God, "We are not your friends, we are going to eat you".'

A boat, a car, a train, a plane.

I had never been in the Hilton's riverside rooms before, though the summer before Toni and I had spent a lot of time in a bar, whose roof I could see from the window, out back of the hotel, right on the water's edge, drinking Pimm's, looking downriver to where it was crossed in parallel by a motorway and the railway line out past the City Airport, hoping against hope for a full set in one frame: a boat, a car, a train, a plane.

I wished I could have told Toni I had finally seen them.

The plane banked and passed over the hotel, the train wriggled blindside of the apartments across the river, the car, my car, the one the sun had picked out for me from the many crossing the bridge, evaded the light, became moving metal, so that seconds after the tableau came together only the boat remained, bobbing before the weir which had made all this – the apartments, the bar at the water's edge, the Hilton and its fifth-floor window where I stood next to Penny Falloon – possible.

Late Saturday afternoon, cusp of June. It had been a mad, mad seven days since Ivy came tearing across the road as we unloaded the shopping, saying she'd seen a woman looking in our window. Toni was doing the shopping on her own today. I had told her, practically the only thing that was guaranteed to make her not want to come with me, that I was going looking for some new in-car-entertainment equipment.

I did call into the ICE shop. I wouldn't have told an outright lie. Besides, one of the guys was a regular at a club Toni liked to look in on on Saturday nights.

'You two,' Penny had said to me at lunch. 'I don't know what to make of that set-up.'

'Old pals and business partners,' I said. 'Don't tell me Australia's homes are strictly nuclear?'

I was fishing, though admittedly with pretty useless bait. She had no trouble refusing it.

'"Strictly"? Is that a northern-hemisphere word?'

My store of knowledge now contained these items: she was forty-one, she worked in marketing, with a ballet company, and was offsetting the cost of her trip by walking the few hundred feet from the Hilton to the concert hall next door and talking to the marketing people there. She favoured her father rather than her mother in looks, Ivy thought, and then not a great deal, otherwise she would surely have recognized her straight off, even at a distance, even without her glasses. She had a lifelong loathing of the smell of malt vinegar, serious enough for her to ask at each restaurant we tried this lunchtime if they used or served it. (What surprised me wasn't so much that we found a place that didn't at only our fourth attempt, but that in this the former chips-with-your-potatoes capital of the world none of the staff in the other restaurants appeared to consider a vinegar aversion to be in any way remarkable.) Oh, and she used towels as opposed to tampons. I had seen them in the bathroom when we came up to her room after lunch. I had no idea if she was using a towel at lunch, or if she was using one this minute as we stood side by side, watching the boat before the weir – a tourist launch – turn towards and then away from us to point back upriver. I had no idea when or even if I was going to find out about the towel situation, because the truth was I was not picking up the signals I would have expected from our telephone conversation the other night to have been picking up by now.

Of course, it may have been that I was not giving out anything that she felt she could give back and amplify.

Squadrons of starlings had been making runs up the river all the while we were standing there, swooping in low to the water then veering up and away only to return a minute later regrouped and reinforced. As the numbers had grown, from scores to hundreds to thousands, possibly, so they had become more daring in their stunts, twisting and turning, standing skyline on its head, coming together now in an unstable concentration, before exploding to all corners of the sky.

Iron filings, is what I thought. The unseen hand of God, with magnet.

Penny was smiling.

'Mad-looking, aren't they?' I said. 'That's every day at this time.'

'I was just counting up,' she said. 'In Australia the government pays out a dollar a time for shooting those things. I could make a fortune.'

She popped at a few with her finger. My unseen hand went unsaid.

I turned from the window, from the roistering starlings, into the room. 'I should give Toni a call,' I said.

Toni and I did not always, or even that often these days, come home together on Saturday nights, but only very exceptionally did we not go out together. I was halfway through dialling her mobile when I changed my mind and rang the house. Answer machine. I uncrossed my fingers.

I said I was just going to stay on here in town, have a couple of drinks, maybe get something to eat. I made it all sound very casual, spur of the moment.

What I didn't make it sound was at all like me.

'I'll check in again later in the evening.' That was more Mel-ish. 'See if I can catch up with you somewhere.'

Penny came and sat on the bed.

'So what'll we do?' she said.

The taxi dropped me off at two. The alarm was on. Toni had not yet returned from wherever it was that I did not phone to find out she had gone. There were bags of shopping waiting to be unpacked on the countertop next to Toni's dinner dishes. I opened the washer but the stuff in there was dirty too. A single-shot grapefruit schnapps bottle sat, empty, atop the microwave, to the left of which Toni beamed at me from her magazine cover. I had the curious sensation of having been absent for a considerable time, of having inadvertently willed myself, like Jimmy Stewart in *It's A Wonderful Life*, into not-being. I chucked a powerball in the washer, the schnapps bottle in the bin, then wandered through the downstairs, turning out lights. Under the lamp by the hi-fi was an HMV bag with half a dozen CDs inside. I looked at them, couldn't believe it was me had bought them.

Maybe Penny was right, maybe it was time Toni and I took a long hard look at our set-up.

Monday evening we got back from work to find two more For Sale signs had gone up on the street. Numbers 16 and 23.

Toni told me that there was already an offer in excess of ninety on Blakes'. Ivy said they were hoping now for ninety-five.

'This is only the start,' Toni said. 'Watch and see. Six figures average by the end of the year.'

I still couldn't get over the figures we were already talking. I sat in the car looking across the road. 'What sort of dick would pay ninety-five for Blakes'?'

Toni turned to grab her bag from the back seat and put a hand on my shoulder. 'Dicks like us, honey.'

I put the steering lock on and caught her up inside. 'Are you sure you're not still annoyed about Saturday night?' I said.

'No, but I will be if you don't quit asking me.'

It was, to be fair to her, the tenth or twelfth time I'd asked her. She'd already answered once, at lunchtime, that I seemed almost to want her to be annoyed.

'Why would that be? What would that prove?' she'd teased. We were eating a sandwich in the car park of a club over-looking the sea. 'When are you going to come clean and ask me what it is you really want to ask?'

'Wise,' I said, through a mouthful of egg and anchovy, throwing a crust for a seagull, 'the fuck up.'

Yet here I was hours later returning to the question again. I didn't care what she said, though; lunchtime aside she had been distant and uncommunicative with me since yesterday morning. If only *she* would own up and have a row with me and get it off her chest.

My story was I'd run into Penny in a bar. She had been at a loose end, and it wouldn't have been polite just to get up and walk out, and then she wasn't really a club person. We both kept ordering, I didn't realize how much I'd drunk until I stood up to go. I got a taxi to drop her off at the hotel and came on home.

'I told you she wanted something,' Toni had said and before I could open my mouth added, 'Company.'

Among the things Penny did not want was to go to bed with me in the end on Saturday. We had rolled around a bit in her hotel room. But not that. Not yet, she said.

I said I understood. Period.

She gave me a look. 'Is that another northern-hemisphere thing?'

She told me I wasn't to get her wrong, this just wasn't quite what she had come here expecting.

I made as light of it as I was able in the circumstances. 'Just as long as you leave yourself enough time if you change your mind.'

I already knew she had plans to hire a car at the start of the week, leave the phone and the distraction of work calls with the bulk of her luggage, and head off for a few days to see Something of the Island. How long she stayed after that, she said, was still pretty much open.

'At the *Hilton*?' I said. With the exchange rate she was getting, wasn't it ever just a little expensive?

One, she said, work was paying part; two, the Hilton was not that much dearer than any of the other hotels (and a damned sight better placed for cars and boats and trains and planes), and three, where else was she going to stay if not in a hotel?

I didn't say a word. Honest.

'Oh, yeah,' she said. 'I'm sure Toni would be delighted to have me arrive on the doorstep with my bags.

'Anyway,' now she was the one hamming, 'where would I sleep?'

The way we had left it was that she was to call at number 5 on Thursday evening on her way back from seeing the island.

The house was only a short detour off the road into the city centre, she didn't need to go to the hotel first. Besides, she'd have her camera in the car, she could take those pictures she'd been hoping to get.

I told Toni, of course, on Monday night, about the calling round to take photos bit at least.

'Sure, why not,' she said, and then, 'You know we're up in the north-west on Thursday?'

No, shit, I'd forgotten. I tried ringing Penny throughout Tuesday, to tell her not to break her neck getting back, Toni and I might be home a little later than I'd imagined, but she had obviously done what she had said she was going to and left the phone behind.

I persuaded myself I was worrying about nothing. Thursdays were almost always early-finishing days and by the time we were coming back from the north-west, the traffic would all be headed in the opposite direction. All the same, I decided after some wrangling, on Wednesday night, to ask Ivy to keep an eye out – 'There's a slight chance,' is how I said it, 'that she might call' – in case Penny was to end her trip much earlier than anticipated.

Shortly after I'd been across to Ivy's, Toni and I had a huge bust-up. Twenty minutes in, I could hardly remember what the argument was about when we started, though what it was about by now was more or less everything to do with the two of us. Who was doing too little or too much of a, b and c. Why I/she wouldn't stand for any more d and e and f. There were a good few low blows landed. We pursued the argument all through the ground floor, up the stairs and into the box-room, right around the world and out again. We roared ourselves close to hoarse, slammed our bedroom doors, stood either side of the stud wall and croaked a few sexual slurs for good measure. It was almost midnight before I ventured downstairs again. Toni, on the chaise, in her star T-shirt and old grey trousers, hand curled around a Bloody Mary, did not look up. The vodka was open on the countertop. I would have replaced the lid if I'd been able to find it. Instead I made myself a camomile tea and leaned against the breakfast bar watching Toni watching television. One of those programmes where beautiful young things are left on an island in the Indian Ocean for a couple of weeks to forage and fight and fuck one another over on mini digicam.

'I can't go on living like this,' I told Toni, who answered, as though I was one to be complaining, 'Hah!'

'I can't,' I insisted. 'We can't. Look at us, it's doing our heads in.'

Toni flipped to a music channel. Prince, 'Sexy Motherfucker'. Flipped back again to the island.

'Nothing wrong with my head,' she said. 'You want to do something, do something. Quit work, move out.'

'Oh, yeah.' This was so typical of her, always make it somebody else's problem. 'You'd like that.'

Toni looked down the length of the chaise, down the length of herself at me. 'No,' she said, 'but I think you would.'

Toni slept in the passenger seat through the early-morning traffic, the stop-start of traffic lights and roundabouts that was our city's ring-road system.

I'd got up for a pee some time after four and had seen a light still on downstairs. Toni was dead to the world on the chaise. I went back upstairs for a blanket and when I came down for breakfast three hours later Toni and the blanket were gone.

She had thanked me as she was getting into the car, the last words she spoke before falling asleep. She stirred once, when I stopped for petrol and a coffee, but opened only one eye, and only a fraction, and only for a second.

Our first club was in a little graveyard town surrounded by roadworks. We came here twice a year, though by rights the carpet should have been cleaned quarterly. Well, I call it a carpet, though in places it was little more than threads held together with chewing gum. Not for nothing are nightclubs so called. By day they have all the magic and charm of a dismantled fairground. This place was particularly mean-looking. In a business notorious for scumbags, the owner was one of the very scummiest.

'Fuckers could be ankle deep in shite and they'd never know,' he said. 'Just give it a light skim.'

I pointed out to him that there was no such thing as a light skim – we either cleaned it or we didn't – not in the hope of making any lasting impression on him, but to make sure he didn't start any capers about the price.

Toni, who had in the past voiced her suspicion that the mirrors in the women's toilets were two-way and was usually on her mettle when we came here, appeared content to let all of this pass her by. I decided she wasn't up to much more this morning than dabbing the worst stains and sprinkling the wood flour for me and the clean-machine to work into the carpet. I packed the rest of the gear into the car myself, giving the chemicals time to do their stuff, then went over and over the carpet with the vacuum and packed it away too. Two hours twenty-five start to finish. The owner tried to batter us down to a hundred pounds below the quoted price.

'I could do that my fucking self, save myself three hundred quid,' he said, as he always did.

Toni did not, as she sometimes did, suggest other things he could do him fucking self. We got our three hundred and got in the car.

Watching the town recede in the rear-view mirror, I comforted myself with the thought that when the roadworks had gone and the bypass, which had been campaigned for for years, was completed we would never have to return there, because there would be no nightclub to return to, no town worthy of the name. The hole.

It was a forty-five-minute drive to the second club of the day. We arrived to find the place locked. I parked the car, as I had been told to, in the alley at the side and made a few calls, but no one anywhere was answering.

'It's lunchtime,' said Toni, closing her eyes again. 'There'll be somebody along in a while.'

I paced up and down out the front, looking right along the sloping street, then left, checking my watch, trying the blasted telephone, until someone, a woman dressed as though for a meeting with her solicitor or minister, did finally show at two-fifteen.

The woman, Valerie, told me her son had been taken bad at school. The school had phoned her and she phoned her mother, but her mother was at *her* mother's and they had just left for the market (Valerie hoped she was half as fit at half her grandmother's age), and so Valerie had to go herself and collect the wee fella and then wait for a neighbour coming in to keep an eye on him to let her away to open up the club for me. An excuse like that you couldn't make up, though that didn't stop me feeling ill-disposed to Valerie. She hung around while we were preparing the carpet, asking us interested questions. What's the stuff in the big white bucket? How much would you pay for one of them vacuums?

Toni had begun to perk up and was obliging the woman with detailed answers, though we were asked these sorts of things all the bloody time. I worked around the two of them, one eye on the clock.

The hands were pointing to twenty-seven minutes past four when the police arrived. A woman constable and a man, both in short-sleeved shirts.

'I'm going to have to ask you to vacate these premises immediately,' said the policewoman.

'Anyone else in the building?' asked the policeman, while the policewoman went on, 'There's been a bomb warning rung through to the local paper.'

'Oh, Janie,' said Valerie and held her stomach as though in pain. 'My mummy, my granny.'

Toni said, 'It'll be some kids mucking about, right? Or someone not able to face late-night opening.'

Bomb warnings on Thursday nights were once as common as fish on Fridays.

The policewoman shrugged. 'There was a code word.' A bona fide Troubles Re-creation Society then. 'We're clearing the whole street.'

I started to gather up the equipment. The policeman told me there was no time for that. Come on, I said, it'd only take me a minute.

'I said there's no time.'

Valerie was already at the door, anxious to lock it; the policewoman followed her out. Toni had hung back to help if the policeman relented.

'Look,' I said, 'we're finished here. All's I'm asking is a minute. We'll be in the car and on our way.'

There were dark stains in the creases where his shirt and underarms met.

'I'm not going to tell you again,' he said and his hand hovered about his hip and the notepad clipped to his belt.

'Come on, Mel,' Toni said and for almost the first time since yesterday evening's argument there was fellow-feeling in her voice. 'The sooner we get out, the sooner they can check the street and let us away.'

I had unbuttoned the shirt part of my overall, slipping it off my shoulders and tying the arms around my waist.

Toni placed a hand on the small of my back. 'Don't worry, we'll get you home in time.'

So damp was my T-shirt where she had pressed it against my skin that I was amazed, seeing her raise both hands to push open the nightclub door, to find that she had not been touching me all the while.

I squinted, adjusting to the outside light. To our right, where the road rose and a solitary car alarm sounded, like an auditory arrow pointing (*me-me-me-me-me*), the street was entirely deserted; to our left it was packed with people, their backs to us, their footsteps tripping into headlong flight, as though everything that was without foundations or brakes had been unable to resist the gravitational pull of the slope.

Toni and I turned left, went with the flow. The police-woman who had been in the nightclub just now was ushering staff out of a shop supplying hearing aids, looking back the way we were all coming.

'Keep moving it along,' she said as I imagined her being taught to say in police college, waving us past the giant ear in the hearing-aid shop window. 'Keep moving it along.'

The assembly point was on the far side of the next junction, where the street was crossed by another, populated in the main by estate agents. The evacuees had gathered on the kerbside and in the road, reluctant even at this distance from possible hazard to stand too near the windows. I spotted a red T for Tennents jutting out from a bar down a side street. I tapped Toni's shoulder, she nodded, smacked her lips.

At half past six, the street with the nightclub on it was live on the evening news. A bomb-disposal man (I'm guessing man, there was too much padding to be certain) was walking backwards out of a draper's store, uncoiling a spool of cable. The car alarm, a red herring as it had turned out, was still bleating, still trying to draw attention to itself. The bar was not as full as it had been at half past four. Most of the evacuees who lived locally had long since given up and walked home. A church hall a few streets away had opened its kitchen and volunteers were serving soup and sandwiches to those who lived further afield and whose cars or businesses were in the cordoned-off area.

I was on my third non-alcoholic beer, having already drunk a pint and a half of the alcoholic stuff.

The bomb-disposal blimp backed behind an army vehicle with what looked like a Roger the Rabbit head stencilled on the side.

'Ladies and Gentlemen,' Toni, beside me, slipped into her low-rent-game-show-host voice. 'It's time to play . . . *Hoax or Bomb.*'

'Bomb,' I said, thinking it would just be my luck.

There was a muffled thud from inside the draper's. Applause broke out in the bar, cheers and whistles carried in from the street.

'Uh-wrong,' said game-show Toni.

I was already out of my seat, leaving my half-drunk alkohol-frei beer on the bar. 'I didn't really think it was a bomb.'

'Too late to change your mind now, sir,' she said.

'Stop, you're killing me,' I said, holding my ache-frei sides.

Valerie, of course, was nowhere to be found when after a delay of another half an hour to allow the bomb-disposal team and the fire crews and the news crews to decamp, Toni and I got back to the club. I was all for kicking in the alley doors and grabbing our stuff when Keith came sauntering along. Keith was the assistant manager. Keith was OK, normally. Keith had clearly been in a bar somewhere else in town.

'Aw, fuck, sorry, they never told me yous were still here waiting.'

I'd fucking had it with being made to hang around. I didn't want apologies. I wanted the money and I wanted out of there.

'I think that's the elves you're thinking of, Keith, just disappear in a puff of green smoke when they're finished.'

'Didn't I say I was sorry?'

Keith pulled a big bunch of keys from the pocket of his hoody. Each door appeared to throw up the same twenty or thirty options.

'Oh, for fuck sake,' I said.

Keith, at the door to his office, turned to say something and kicked over a five-litre jug of disinfectant that we had had to leave, its lid not properly on, when the police evacuated us. Not our fault. And at this time on a Thursday night, not our problem, said Toni, coming through for me. We left Keith directing the bar staff, who had been arriving behind him, to clean up the mess.

Traffic was sluggish until we were beyond the retail-park fringes of the town, from where we had a clear run back to the city, a good half of it motorway. Toni gave me updates on the time as I drove.

'It's only twenty to ten,' she said as we turned from the main road on to the Low Road.

'If she's any sense she'll have gone home hours ago,' I said.

But just as I didn't really think there was a bomb in the draper's, I didn't really expect Penny not to be sitting outside number 5 in her hire car.

From the expression on Ivy's face as she came down her driveway to us, I knew that Penny wasn't in her house either. From the expression on Ivy's face, in fact, you would have been hard pressed not to conclude that Penny would never be back again.

Toni had got out to open the gates, but I couldn't wait and left the car with the engine still running. As I reached Ivy's side of the street I heard a crunching beneath my feet. I cast my eyes down. All around me were granules of glass, the scrapings of a larger breakage. I looked to the most obvious source, the car parked at the kerb, nose against my thigh. Graham Robertson's Mini Clubman. The offside headlight had been smashed.

'What's been going on?' I asked.

Ivy

A ONCE-IN-A-LIFETIME OPPORTUNITY

Superbly renovated 1950s terrace dwelling. As featured in Northern Woman magazine.

ACCOMMODATION COMPRISES:
Original 1950s front door into extended open-plan ground floor with spacious living area and high-spec fitted kitchen (slate work surfaces, tensile-steel shelf supports etc).
Wood and metal feature staircase to:

FIRST FLOOR:
Bathroom: White suite including power shower in glass-brick recess.
Landing: Hot press, copper cylinder.
Bedroom 1: 11′2″ (3.4 m) × 11′0″ (3.35 m)
Bedroom 2: 11′2″ (3.4 m) × 9′10″ (3 m)
Bedroom 3: 7′10″ (2.38 m) × 7′8″ (2.33 m) Unique 1970s mural.
Wood and metal feature staircase to:

SECOND FLOOR:
Bedroom 4/Study: 21′2″ (6.45 m) × 20′10″ (6.35 m) Velux window. Eaves storage, fitted floor-to-ceiling shelves at chimney breast and gable.

OUTSIDE:
Parking to fore. Extensive cedar-wood deck at rear, accessed by French windows and leading to mature garden in lawn and shrubs.

- OFCH
- Alarm system linked to 24-hr monitored network
- Mixture of polished limestone and natural wood floors throughout.
- All rooms with phone and cable TV point.

Stella would have been able to do the sums in her head. Sixty years equals so many days, so many hours, so many minutes and seconds. Zeros from here to the middle of next week, to the middle, I wouldn't wonder, of my sixty-first year.

Sixty, sixty-one. It's like saying five hundred in *Monopoly* money.

The longer I live the further away old age gets. It's official, watch any American chat show. I think when I was sixteen I imagined myself by now in one of those bath chairs they used to have in the comics, wearing a big black sack of a dress with lace collar and cuffs. I imagined that the memories would get more and more jumbled up, but they're all there in their proper order, like slides packed on to a carousel. Just, sometimes more than others, like tonight, the carousel jumps.

I don't know that in all the however many millions of minutes it is I have been on this earth I have had a shock to match the one I had when I first opened the door to find Penny stood by herself on our front step. I dropped to my knees and took her wee hands. They were blue with cold. It was the end of January. The wind whipped snow and grit across the footpaths. The road in between was slush: a great grubby sorbet. Aran-knit mitts dangled on elastic from either sleeve of Penny's cardigan. She must have pulled them off to rap the door harder. Dear knows how long she'd had to knock before I heard her, the size of her fists. The child wasn't yet three.

'Sweetheart, what is it?' I said. 'Does your mummy want me to mind you again?'

Harry was in the hospital. I'd looked after her a couple of days already that week.

Penny shook her head. Her lips were pressed tight, as if to

make sure she didn't lose a word of the message she had been sent across the treacherous street to deliver.

'You've to come,' she said.

'I haven't on me yet, lover.' George wasn't long left for school. A couple of the older kids on the street walked him and the other wee ones right up to their classroom doors. You wouldn't dream of letting them go off like that now, whatever the weather, any more than you would dream of staying at home once they were school age instead of going out to work. Some mornings I would still be in my housecoat at eleven o'clock. Some mornings I just went back to bed. 'Why don't you come in a while till I get dressed?'

Penny thought about it, but decided it wasn't in her instructions.

'You've to come,' she said again.

I looked over the road, over here, trying to read in the front of the house what her mummy was thinking of letting her out on her own a morning like that.

'All right,' I said and put the mitts back on her. 'Don't move. I'll not be a minute.'

I wedged the door open so that I could see her as I backed up the stairs. I tore into our room and grabbed a couple of things, girdle, slacks, a crewneck sweater.

'Are you OK down there?' I called and I heard the wee voice say yes.

I dressed at the head of the stairs.

'Coming now.' I stepped into the bathroom, looking for my hairbrush. There was a lipstick on the cistern. I smeared a little on, powder-puffed my cheeks. 'Coming now.'

Penny held out her hand again as soon as she saw me. I put the door on the snib and followed a step behind her down the path.

'Is something the matter at home?' I asked.

Bad news from the hospital, I was worried. Harry had come down with some bug or other while he was in having his tonsils out. Maybe it was more than just a bug. Penny didn't say a word, but held tight to my hand and pulled me through the slush. Her own front door had been left snibbed too. A touch of her free hand was all it took.

I stand now where I stood then, if here can really be there when there is no longer a hallway as such, when the staircase is different and the floor at the end of it is new. Only the silence is the same, beginning to be unsettling. I increase the pressure of my right index finger on the trigger of the plant sprayer just to hear the hiss, the delayed patter of the water on the leaves of the weeping fig between the door and the foot of the stairs.

Use green sprayer only, the instructions say. The green sprayer contains actual rainwater. And not from any old bucket either, but from a container bought specially, which stands outside the French windows. *Once a week should be plenty.*

'What are you thinking of, going over there tonight?' Denis asked me.

'I told them I'd keep an eye on their plants.'

'It's your sixtieth birthday.'

'And I've had a lovely day.'

And I have had, from the yellow roses on my breakfast tray on.

(*To the only girl for me*, he'd written. Now who's showing his age?)

'You've your good clothes on you.'

'I'm watering the plants, not scrubbing the floors.'

'The family's all here.'

The family at that moment were all watching *Charlie's*

Angels. The shop where George bought me my DVD was giving away a copy of the film with every new player. I wouldn't have minded seeing it, but what with the tricks you could do with the remote, and seven pairs of hands fighting to hold it, we'd been watching two hours and were still only a quarter the way into the film proper.

'Denis,' I said, 'it's my birthday, humour me. I'll only be ten minutes.'

I've been twelve already. I've done the orange jasmine (*Clear jug, water only if bone dry*) and the dwarf banana besides the fig. I turn the instructions over. <u>Upstairs</u>, they say, underlined. I bend to retrieve the clear jug and have just put a foot on the bottom step when the carousel jumps again.

'Stella?'

'I'm up here,' she said from the back bedroom and it was plain in the invitation behind her words that she was not herself, for there was normally no one more private about her person than Stella Falloon.

I hoisted Penny on to my hip. Her face was that cold it was throbbing. 'Do you want me to come up?'

I had already climbed a few more steps. I didn't hear her say stop.

'Stella, I'm coming up. Is everything all right?'

Worried and all as I was, I didn't want to be just barging in on top of her.

'I'm at the door.'

And my heart, all the while I was waiting on her answering, was in my mouth.

The phone rings.

I nearly tip the jug of water in my left hand over the landing floor. Down below, the answer machine switches on. Toni's voice says sorry there's no one here to take the call. The caller hangs up when she's in the middle of giving the mobile numbers.

Mobile probably wouldn't work anyway over there. Young George wasn't able to ring his girlfriend on his when he was down south last year for the rugby. Don't ask me why he didn't just go into a phone box like any normal person.

The girlfriend asked, and when he couldn't tell her, dumped him.

I don't know, you believe everything you hear, they're the solution to the whole world's problems, and really all they do is give you something else to fret about. Like Mel, that day in the summer, waving his phone about, telling me he had tried and tried and tried to ring Penny, as if saying it often enough could put things right, as if anyway talking to her, letting her know he was going to be late getting back, would have stopped what happened happening, when he didn't even know what it was he should have been trying to stop.

A misjudged attempt at reverse parking.

I heard the smash when I was out the back hanging washing. It was a warm June evening, I'd thrown the sheets in the machine before I would start to get the dinner on. She must have had the car window down because I heard her quite clearly in the silence that followed the smash say 'damn'. She put like an 'e' in it, which was how I knew it was her. I saw, over the back fence, Graham get up from the table where he'd been at his own dinner. I had been meaning all week to have a word, to prepare him, but it had been that long since I'd had a proper talk with him I hardly knew where to start.

I launched a duvet cover at the line. It landed half-on, half-off. I glanced back. Graham's head was just visible in the kitchen doorway. I scrabbled at the pegs, got the second half of the duvet up as the first half came down. I looked again and Graham was gone. I left the duvet trailing on the ground.

The hire car was stopped at an angle to the kerb. Penny had been hunkered down between it and the Mini Clubman. She was already straightening up when I opened my front door the second after Graham opened his.

'I'm terribly sorry,' she said, looking from one of us to the other. 'Is this your car? Yours?'

She had come to the edge of the footpath and the bit of a hedge between the two gates.

'I don't know how I did it. I was backing in and, next thing . . . I really am terribly sorry.'

I was wrong what I had said to Mel. She was Stella's daughter to a T. Graham, at his front door, gasped. Penny looked at him harder then at me. A change came over her face, brows furrowing then slowly starting to rise, rolling back the years with each line erased, and I saw her again as I had seen her that morning almost forty years before, leaning forward in my arms on the landing, helping me to give the bedroom door a push: so.

Yucca. Mel's room. Stella's then.

My legs nearly went from under me. A creature with Stella's face sat on the edge of the bed. There was hair all over the pillows and bedclothes, on the bedside table and the carpet, on the Stella-creature's lap and upturned hands, everywhere apart from where it should have been. It – she – Stella – was utterly bald.

('Lucky man, that Harry,' Artie Eliot had said the day before, though it might as well have been a lifetime.)

I turned to put Penny out of the room, then realized that she must already have seen her mummy and that leaving her on her own would only upset her more. I set her feet on the ground and drew her to my side.

'In the name of God, Stella, what did this to you?'

I didn't even want to think 'who'. I was sorry I'd allowed Artie to enter my head. But, no.

'She was fighting with Graham,' Penny said.

I looked from her to Stella in horror.

'Oh, no. Stella?'

'I seed them. Downstairs. On the floor.'

Stella closed her eyes.

'Stella, he didn't, did he?'

Her head moved from side to side, sprinkling hair to the left and right, and I knew she was about to be overcome by tears. I decided I had to get Penny out of this after all, take her downstairs, give her juice and a rusk for being a good girl coming to get me. Give myself time to work out what to do.

As I was leaving the bedroom I looked over my shoulder. It was harder if anything after that brief turning away to believe what I was seeing. Stella, girl, you were like something out of the camps.

I asked her did she need a doctor.

'I can't think,' she said and tossed the hair cupped in her hands a little into the air. 'I just can't think.'

Penny pointed to the carpet in front of the fire as we passed through the living room. 'There,' she said. Where Graham had been fighting her mummy, she meant.

I ushered her through to the kitchen. 'Chop, chop.'

'I don't like Graham,' she said.

★

Graham took a step towards her down the path. Penny began rubbing her temples, as though trying to bring the memory into better focus, or else wipe what was already there.

It was too late for avoidance, nothing to do now but make this as easy as possible on them both.

'Penny. Graham,' I said. 'Why don't yous come into our house a minute.'

'Oh, my God,' Penny said.

'Wee Penny,' said Graham, like they were words from a language he'd only just remembered he knew.

Wee Penny nibbled at her rusk in silence. There was a smell in the kitchen of vinegar, of clothes left standing too long in the sink. I opened the window, breathed in, an icy purging.

Penny tugged my sleeve. 'My mummy's ugly,' she said in a whisper.

'Now, that's not nice.'

She frowned into her beaker of juice. I'd swear I heard her mutter before she took another drink, 'It's true.'

Stella came down a few minutes later in housecoat and headscarf. The vinegar smell was coming from her too. She scratched one bare foot with the toes of the other, over and over. Chilblains. I opened the fire and made her sit by it while I put the kettle on. She held on to the teacup and saucer with her two hands, so tight it looked as though it was them keeping her from rattling and not the other way about. I had to fight against the fear in my throat when I spoke.

'What *has* happened to you?'

She was concentrating on the cup and saucer, trying to work out how to separate the two without them losing control of her.

'Stella, I've a good mind to call the police.'

'There's no need,' she said. She had given up on the tea. 'I made him.'

'Who? Graham? Do that to your hair?'

I knew that wasn't what she meant at all, but even at this late stage I was hoping not to have to hear.

'I made him do it with me.'

Anger rose up in me, driving fear and all before it. I wanted more than anything to race across the room and hit her a slap.

How could she? Behind her husband's back, under their own roof, with a neighbour's son who was, OK, not a child, but still, *Graham*, and while her own daughter . . . From where I sat I could see her in the kitchen playing with her empty beaker.

'Penny!' I hurled at Stella, the venom of a shout without the volume. 'You let her see all that?'

'She was asleep,' said Stella and moved a hand lightly over the headscarf as if in hope that it had somehow taken root. 'Or I thought she was. You know what a good sleeper she is. I said to Graham to be quiet.'

I could just imagine how likely in the circumstances that would be.

She paused, glanced at me, almost for a moment looked like smiling. 'He has a girlfriend, you know. At least he says he has.'

'Is that supposed to make it all right?'

The suspicion of a smile disappeared completely. She tightened her grip on the saucer, but it was too late. Before my eyes, from the inside out, she fell apart.

'It's all over,' she said. 'The second I heard the door open and saw my baby standing there, I knew it was all over. I shouted at her to get out, I shouted at Graham to get off, but neither of the two of them moved.'

For a minute, maybe more, neither of the two of us moved, or spoke, until I asked again, 'Your hair?'

She gulped a sob.

'I think,' she said, 'I think I felt it come loose that very first second. It was like my scalp all shrivelled, like it just couldn't hold on to it any more. Next thing it was coming out in handfuls. Oh, God help me, Ivy. Harry. What'll I say?'

'We'll think of something.'

I had no idea yet what that might be.

'I'm marked for life.'

'Nonsense. It'll all grow back.'

A tear fell into her tea.

'There's none left,' she said. 'Anywhere.'

And only then did it sink in, her eyebrows were gone.

Whatever could have connected Stella to the back bedroom went long ago. Even the built-in cupboard has been pulled out. In its place is a chrome clothes rail, the kind you see being trailed here and there about department stores. A table lamp stands on the floor on one side of the futon bed, the yucca and a wooden shoe rack on the other. And that's about it. These new furnishings too look as though they could be spirited away at a moment's notice. The yucca is the only thing, bar the clothes rail, above knee-height.

I consult the instructions: *Yucca will probably be OK*; I touch the earth through the hanging leaves. It's OK. If Denis knew how little actual watering I had to do he would really wonder at me coming over, tonight of all nights.

The things that Denis doesn't know. At sixteen I'd have said after forty-four years I could have filled a book with them, but in all truth I could probably fit them on the back of an envelope.

1. How I Once Spurned the Advances of Another Man.

A couple of years after we were married. Artie Eliot used to park his car in the street when he was on his rounds and have a chat with whoever was about.

'How are my girls the day?' he'd say.

I wouldn't let him away with it.

'Your girls? You'd have to do a lot more than stand there smoking a cigarette for us to be your girls.'

Stella, it's hard to credit it, used to be appalled.

Artie would narrow his eyes against his own smoke, smirking, every inch the man of the world.

The day he came rapping at my door he had a hat on him, the collar of his raincoat turned up, like a spy.

'Artie,' I said, looking past him. 'I didn't hear the car.'

'Never mind the car. Can I come in?'

He looked flushed under the hat, distracted. I was afraid if I shut the door he'd walk through it glass and all without noticing.

'Come on ahead,' I said, and had no sooner turned my back than he blurted out he was in love with me. I told him to away and scratch, trying to laugh it off, but he was deadly serious.

'I do, I love you,' he said. A flake of skin fell, like a dry tear, from the corner of his eye. 'I don't know what I'm going to do.'

This was a man in his late thirties, I was eighteen.

'I know what you're going to do,' I said. 'You're going to get into your car, wherever you've left it, and tootle on back to your work, and you're not coming round here again until you've learned to behave like a grown-up.'

'But what about all those times . . . the way you smile and get on?'

Smile and get on?

'Where were you brought up?' I said. 'Did they not have flirting there?'

He rubbed the bridge of his nose with the hat brim. 'Oh, I see.'

Poor Artie. I'm not sure that he ever did see properly. I would still run into him out on the street now and again. He even called at the door the odd time, though he was as good as gold after that. A perfect, perplexed gentleman.

I always had a soft spot for him. And his.

2. How I Saved Artie's Nephew's Marriage.

Maybe. The trouble had been brewing for days, though it seemed the only people couldn't see it were him and her. Neighbours were getting involved. Worse, religion was getting involved. Even the TV was involved in a roundabout way. It was turning into a Holy Soap right outside our front window. Denis said to me we weren't to go getting mixed up in it too.

'You mean me.'

'I mean we.'

He meant me.

He was right. I shouldn't have, wouldn't have either, if Catriona hadn't nearly knocked me down this night pulling away from in front of the house. I only caught a glimpse of her face as she straightened up the car, but I knew the look on it all too well. I didn't stop to wonder what Denis would say, if I told him.

Steve opened the door to me with the Bible still in his hand.

'I'm probably speaking out of turn,' I said, 'but if you're thinking of relying on that to get her back then God help you.'

It made perfect sense to me, and to him.

'I was just going,' he said. He was in his slippers.

'Go,' I said. 'Run.'

And he ran, showing me a pair of foam-backed heels, down to the arts centre, to O'Neill's timber yard.

Stella poured out to me the whole John O'Neill saga while we were sitting wondering what to tell Harry when he finally came home from the hospital. I had even less of an idea when she finished talking than I did when she began.

'Why didn't you say something to me sooner?' I asked her, over and over, like Mel with his mobile phone, like the right answer could magic her hair and eyebrows back.

The eyebrows, Penny said, never did grow back. In all her memories of those first years in Australia her mummy wears a headscarf or a sun hat. She had a vague recollection of connecting this in some childlike way to the baby, though as time went on she could have told you less and less about life before the baby's arrival, before the headscarves and sun hats, before Australia. When her mummy and daddy talked about the boat that brought them to Sydney *berthing* she imagined the four of them beginning all at once, together.

She couldn't say for certain when the hats and wraps came off, but there on her mummy's head was a grey pageboy cut, which kept its length, its shape and its colour without apparent trimming or tending right up until the day she died.

Brain haemorrhage.

Wouldn't have known a thing about it, the doctors said, which is something to be grateful for.

A lot of this was in the letter Penny sent me when she got back to Australia. She had started writing on the stopover in Singapore. (Singapore. Sixty, sixty-one. House on Mayfair, £200.) Pages and pages she filled. It had all been a bit much for her, she wrote, the past crashing in on her like that. Or her crashing into it. She hadn't been able to organize her thoughts, ask me what she wanted to ask, tell me all that she had to tell.

Her mummy and daddy separated when she was fifteen. This wasn't an unusual occurrence among the parents of the children she grew up with. Both remarried quickly. Kyle and Barbara. They stayed near neighbours, good friends. She wanted me to understand that her daddy, that Harry, had seemed to her when she was a girl to be very much in love with Stella.

That at least was not news. I'd seen him myself, in those awful final weeks here, transformed by love. Some people you don't know at all until you know them in adversity. Like I didn't know my own husband until he came to me in the hospital after George was born, looked at the drips surrounding me, saline solution, morphine, blood, at the oxygen on standby should I start to slip again, and said, him that had dreamed of having a whole squad of kids, he'd make sure and never put me through anything like that again. God love him.

Australia was not Harry's idea. Stella suggested it, he went along, for all their sakes.

He had tried to talk Penny out of her trip – he followed the news from home on that Internet, the place was a bigger madhouse than ever – but it was him gave her this address. Not that you're likely to find a whole lot, he said, a last attempt maybe at putting her off. The street was probably reduced to rubble donkey's years ago.

If only Penny had stayed around to take photos in here, he might have discovered he was closer to the truth than he knew.

Penny sent Graham a letter too. She apologized for how she had reacted that day on the street. She hadn't come into our house like I'd asked her, but instead had got straight back into the hire car. She drove once around the block and nearly hit the Mini a second time pulling up. Graham and I were still on the doorsteps.

'I'm only back to sort out the insurance,' she said. 'I don't want to be ending up in jail here.'

She included in Graham's letter a photograph of Peter with his wife, Abbie, and Patrick and Niamh, their children, Graham's grandchildren. She hadn't said anything to Peter, or to Harry yet, but she would understand if Graham wanted to get in touch. Graham had the photograph framed and put it by the bed with the photos Stella had sent for the first dozen or so years, until in fact, I worked it out from reading back over Penny's letter, she remarried. Kyle had kids and who knows what secrets of his own. Perhaps life just got a bit too complicated. It was all so far away to me, it was almost beyond imagining.

I asked Graham would he write.

'Maybe,' he said. 'Some day.'

Then he told me about the money. Alma had made him open a Post Office account. He put a bit into it every week in case he ever had to support the child. All these years, long after the last photo from Stella, he had kept adding to it. Even at a couple of pound a week it must have run into thousands now. I said to him he should take himself off somewhere, go for a cruise. He had lived two-thirds of his life and more on hold.

At the very least, I said, when they towed away the Mini Clubman, he should buy a new car.

He hasn't yet.

Sometimes I hear Eric Robertson saying to me that, long before they took him out of his old school and moved him over to this side of town, he could be a very contrary wee boy when he wanted.

Enough.

I pull the back bedroom door – click – closed on all of that.

I don't turn on the boxroom light, but nudge the muslin curtain aside seeking out the light of my own front room, behind whose blinds Denis and George and Angela and Young George and Yvonne and Alec and Brenda, the Family, sit – sprawl – slap one another's behinds – *Move, you* – stuffed with sixtieth-birthday cake, watching DVD.

I let my gaze drift to the bedroom window, remembering the times I was tempted to wave, out of sheer badness, to the wee fella Tan.

'Tell you what, why don't *I* give him a wave?' Denis said, though Denis deep down didn't blame him any more than I did.

When houses are as close together as ours it's an effort a lot of the time not to look, a heartache now and then what you do, without meaning to, see.

Our George and Sid Stitt, tiptoeing away from the Tans' front door late one night. George was seventeen, out at work, earning a wage, within a year he would be a parent himself. He came very near that night to getting his ear broke. I told him, drinking and carrying on was one thing (sorry, Denis: 3. How I Covered For Our Drunken Son . . . Dozens of Times), but it wouldn't cost me a second thought to pick up the phone to the police if ever I caught him skulking round there again. Here again.

Here again.

Jiggedy-jig.

I quick-step up the final flight of stairs. A free-standing

mirror, flanked by tea chests, faces the opening into the attic room. I rise to meet it a little over halfway in my kitten heels. The small package of me, wrapped in burgundy taffeta, finished off with a gold rosette at the right shoulder strap.

I turn side on, turn back. Not bad for sixty. A little off tum and bum. I lift my chin, raise my arms. Justice with jug and rainwater sprayer.

I like to think I would have phoned them too, the police, but though I kept an eye out I'm glad to say I was never put to the test again, not by George.

The bird of paradise is wintering between two more tea chests, beyond the computer desk, in a large pot directly below the Velux window for maximum light. *Water well*, the instructions say, at last. In the summer, out on the patio thing, this has the most gorgeous orange and blue flowers, like plumes sprouting from its beaky, swan-necked stems. You wouldn't be surprised if it was to blink open an eye, go cheep at you.

I stop watering, hear myself, what I'm humming:

'*Wydoo* birds suddenly appear . . .'

I can see Andy's face, as perfect as a picture projected on the wall, turn purple. 'Rodney, you're very funny.'

'Every time you are near . . .'

'The funniest man on the whole street, everybody!'

You could be as well sometimes, Rodney, funny ha-ha. And sometimes – walking into a room, in your railways blazer and tie, looking at us all like you owned the system rather than drove a train around it – Sometimes . . .

Well, which of us isn't funny peculiar sometimes in other people's eyes?

Not Andy himself, that's for sure. I would have run a mile when I was younger sooner than talk to him. That way he had of leaning in towards you when he listened, staring. X-ray without the specs. Never mind Magyar, he might as well have been from Mars he was that alien from anyone I'd ever met till then.

Of course as time went on I realized he hadn't a bad bone in him. There was no one more hospitable; or handy about the house, according to Jill, or helpful, or better with the kids . . . Whoa, whoa, *whoa*! We used to tease her. Was she not afraid, him being so good, she'd be made to give him back?

We never thought then, of course, not for a minute.

After he was murdered, she tormented herself. If it hadn't been for her catching his eye all those years ago he would have carried on, like he'd always planned, to the USA; if it hadn't been for her encouraging him to help Paul Blake out he wouldn't have had the compensation to start up his own showroom when Paul's shop was burnt. (And to think it was Paul, swamped by debt, we were all sorry for.) We tried telling her, Jill, it wasn't you was at fault, it wasn't Andy. This was not something that anyone could have imagined, at least not anyone sane.

Murdered for selling urinals.

Talk about another world.

Toni sent me a birthday postcard, arrived this morning from Budapest. Food good, weather wonderful. Short sunny days and deep cold nights. The picture on the front is of a suspension bridge across the river Danube. On the back she has written that this is where the depressed of Buda and Pest have traditionally come to end it all. She and Mel have been in the city four days and so far neither one has felt like jumping . . . or throwing the other off.

(It was *throwing* she wrote, wasn't it?)

Budapest is their test.

A month ago the house was on the market. Now it is withdrawn from sale. Temporarily. I don't know if the tea chests all around me in the attic are half packed or half unpacked. I don't know either what role in any of this Penny's blowing in and out of their lives played. All Toni said to me, when she came to tell me they were putting the sale on hold, was that four years was a hefty chunk out of anybody's life. (I didn't even blink.) Maybe what they needed was time away together, see what was there, what was not.

In my day they called it a holiday.

Good luck to them all the same. And to their plants.

I am just turning away from the bird of paradise when I catch sight of it. Spider's web, top left-hand corner of the Velux window. Way beyond me.

Leave it be, Ivy, I think, and never one to take my own advice go in for a closer look.

The tips of two legs stick out from the hide he has woven himself tight against the frame, holding crookedly to the thread that runs to the very heart of the web. I purse my lips and blow to make the thread vibrate. A third leg appears with the remainder of the first two. They're big enough nearly that I can count the hairs. I build him up from these three legs into a monster; spin out the web for another week, imagine Toni and Mel coming home to festoons of mummified flies.

I breathe in and out through my nose.

He'll have to go.

I could drown him with pure rainwater. And drown everything else in a two-foot radius probably, myself and my burgundy dress included.

A swat, that's what I need.

I glance at my watering instructions. The page is too small. I hunt around on the desk looking for a large envelope, or a blank sheet of foolscap, or – there! – the very thing: a sheet already so dog-eared it can stand a bit more mangling by me. I squint at it through half-closed eyes to make sure it's not something I shouldn't be reading, but all it is is columns of words – I open my eyes a little wider – *countries*, those that I recognize, with more added randomly about the page in other colours, other hands. Kiribati. Kampuchea. Nauru. Palau. Byelorussia/Belarus. Bosnia and Herzegovina. Djibouti. Turkmenistan . . .

I roll it into a cornet, stand on my tiptoes, head now clear above the sill, looking out on to the top storeys of the houses behind and the chimneys of the houses behind them, the sky beyond them all, salmon-streaked, blue fading into black, and before my toes would give out, I take aim, swipe.